ACCLAIM FOR *SE*

"Shelley Gray writes a well-paced story full of historical detail that will invite you into the romance, the glamour . . . and the mystery surrounding the Chicago World's Fair."

—COLLEEN COBLE, *USA TODAY*
BEST-SELLING AUTHOR OF *ROSEMARY
COTTAGE* AND THE HOPE BEACH SERIES

"*Downton Abbey* comes to Chicago in Shelley Gray's delightful romantic suspense, *Secrets of Sloane House*. Gray's novel is rich in description and historical detail while asking thought-provoking questions about faith and one's place in society."

—ELIZABETH MUSSER, NOVELIST,
THE SWAN HOUSE, *THE SWEETEST THING*,
THE SECRETS OF THE CROSS TRILOGY

Deception on

SABLE
HILL

Deception on

SABLE
HILL

SHELLEY GRAY

ZONDERVAN

Deception on Sable Hill

Copyright © 2015 by Shelley Gray

This title is also available as a Zondervan e-book. Visit www.zondervan.com.

This title is also available as a Zondervan audiobook. Visit www.zondervan.com.

Requests for information should be addressed to:

Zondervan, *Grand Rapids, Michigan 49546*

Library of Congress Cataloging-in-Publication Data

Gray, Shelley Shepard.
  Deception on Sable Hill / Shelley Gray.
    pages ; cm. -- (Chicago World's Fair mystery series)
  ISBN 978-0-310-33850-5 (softcover : acid-free paper) 1. Young women--Crimes
against--Fiction. 2. Young women--Illinois--Chicago--Fiction. 3. Chicago (Ill.)--
Social life and customs--19th century--Fiction. 4. World's Columbian Exposition
(1893 : Chicago, Ill.)--Fiction. I. Title.
  PS3607.R3966D43 2015
  813'.6--dc23
                                    2014040831

Cover design: Gearbox

Cover photography: Trevillion and Library of Congress

Interior design: Mallory Perkins

Printed in the United States of America

15 16 17 18 19 20 21 / RRD / 20 19 18 17 16 15 14 13 12 11 10 9 8 7 6 5 4 3 2 1

To Becky Philpot, my editor for this series. Becky, you are my own Eloisa Carstairs—you are truly as lovely on the inside as on the outside! Thank you for believing in the book and especially for believing in Eloisa.

Our greatest glory is not in never failing, but in rising up every time we fail.

—Ralph Waldo Emerson

Come back to me and live!

—Amos 5:4

CHAPTER 1

CHICAGO, SEPTEMBER 1893

Don't keep me in the dark for another second, Eloisa," Quentin Gardner teased as they waltzed across the gleaming parquet floor of his family's crowded ballroom. "Where have you been? No one has seen you in what seems like ages. You've missed quite a few of the events around the fair."

"I've been the same places you have," she replied, taking care to keep her voice light and steady. "Though to be honest, it would be a wonder if you were able to spy me among this year's debutantes clamoring for your attention."

He chuckled. "I've hardly been that in demand."

"*The Tribune* did just list you as one of society's most eligible bachelors." She raised an eyebrow, half expecting him to act surprised. Quentin enjoyed pretending he was above such things as the society pages.

He didn't deny the article. Instead, his cheeks flushed. "I was only on that list because of my family's money."

"And perhaps your good looks too." She tapped his shoulder lightly with her gloved hand. "I've been told that blue eyes and coal-black hair are an irresistible combination."

"You and I both know that article was mere gossip."

"One that has a shred of truth, though."

"Even if I was surrounded by a bevy of young ladies—which I most definitely was not—I would have noticed if you were in our midst. You have not been out, Miss Carstairs."

With effort she kept her expression impassive. "You sound so sure about that."

"That's because I am."

Just as she was formulating a reply, Quentin twirled her around. Then, as she chuckled at his exuberance, he eased her a bit closer. "I've missed your company, Eloisa. What made you decide to suddenly be so elusive?"

She had a very good reason. A very good reason that only a handful of people knew about. It was imperative that she keep it that way.

As she felt his warm breath brush against her neck, her unease returned. Pressing on his shoulder, she attempted to regain some space between them. "Quentin, there's no need to hold me so close."

Something flashed in his eyes before they filled with hurt. Anger? Frustration?

"I'm not doing anything inappropriate. I simply want to talk to you without having to raise my voice."

She tried to pull away again, but his arm around her waist was very strong. "The way you are holding me is rather improper."

"Hardly that. Besides, I can promise that no one is paying the slightest attention to us. It's a veritable crush here. I think my mother's guest list included every dignitary associated with the fair."

He was, of course, talking about the fair to commemorate the four hundredth anniversary of Columbus's discovery of America, the World's Columbian Exposition. Though some were still scratching their heads, wondering about the need to celebrate such a thing in such a grand fashion, no one could deny that the World's Fair of 1893 had certainly made Chicago feel as if it were the center of the universe.

The excitement surrounding the fair had been exhilarating, wondrous—and exhausting. Every dignitary and society matron had used the event as an excuse to hold a soiree, dinner party, gala, or ball. And because her mother was intent on Eloisa marrying well, she'd encouraged her daughter to attend as many events as she could.

The only excuse she would hear of for Eloisa to decline was a migraine headache. Therefore, Eloisa had made sure she'd had as many such headaches as possible.

When Quentin twirled her again, Eloisa tried to relax. Tried to remind herself he was doing nothing but dancing with her—in plain sight of everyone. "Soon all the visitors will go back to their homes and Chicago will seem almost empty."

"Yes, the fairgrounds will close on All Hallow's Eve, you know."

"I'll be glad when it's over."

Quentin nodded. "As will I. Our city feels filled to the brim with miscreants and vagabonds." Tilting his head back so their eyes met, he added, "I know how independent you are. I hope you are taking care when you go out. It's no longer safe for young ladies to go anywhere unescorted."

"It hasn't been for some time."

Regret filled his clear blue eyes. "Forgive me for frightening you. I imagine you're still reeling over the news about Douglass Sloane's death. It has been only two weeks."

She nearly stumbled. "Yes. His death has been something of a shock. I can still hardly believe the news is true."

"I'm still trying to figure out why he decided to go boating in September. It isn't quite the thing, you know. He was never one I would call a friend, but still . . . drowning in Lake Michigan? That's a terrible way to go."

Hardly able to even think about Douglass, she nodded and prayed for their dance to be over soon. Or, at the very least, for Quentin to change the subject.

And as if on cue, he did just that. "Now, of course we have even more to worry about, what with the recent string of attacks on women of substance."

"Indeed. It, uh, is a wonder any of us ever leaves the house."

"How many women have been attacked with a stiletto knife now?"

"I don't recall," she lied. However, she knew the number as well as she knew the number of faint scars on her own body. Three. Three acquaintances of hers had found themselves at the mercy of a crazed madman intent on ruining their looks.

"You're looking pale, dear. Forgive me. I'm not usually such a clumsy conversationalist."

"I am perfectly fine." She attempted to smile while peeking over Quentin's shoulder at the orchestra. Would this waltz never end? When it did, if the friends who accompanied her were ready to leave as well, she could quietly make her escape with them and return to the sanctity of her bedroom at home on Sable Hill. Leaving it had been a mistake.

The faint wrinkle that had been marring Quentin's perfect features smoothed. "Please don't be concerned about your safety, dear Eloisa. I'll look after you. This Slasher cannot get to you here."

"That is very kind, but people will talk if I monopolize all of your attention."

He laughed. "I don't care. Actually, my mother would practically start crowing if everyone believed you and I had formed an alliance. I might be this week's most eligible bachelor, but you, Eloisa, have been the focus of every man's attention between the age of eighteen and eighty since you made your debut two years ago."

"You flatter me."

"It's the truth. You are the object of many a man's attentions. Believe me, I've heard."

She shuddered. "Your observation doesn't make me feel any safer."

"How about this, then? My father hired two off-duty policemen to keep watch over tonight's event. I promise, all evening you've been closely guarded—though I would have preferred that they had stayed outside."

"Truly?" She looked around the room.

"Yes. They're right here with us. In the ballroom. One is Detective Owen Howard. You know Owen, of course."

She relaxed. "Of course. Though he is several years older than I am, I've known him for ages." Just like the rest of them had. Though everyone in their circle stayed the same, only growing older year after year, Owen was the exception. He'd reinvented himself, deciding to join the force when most men in their world elected to spend their days in far less demanding pursuits. Owen's decision made her admire him all the more.

"He is a good man, to be sure, though I have to admit to still being somewhat shocked by his chosen profession. He could have done much better."

"Perhaps he enjoys the work?"

"That would be doubtful. His father, after all, is a banker."

"Perhaps banking isn't for everyone."

"Well, he is a third son. With no chance of inheriting much, I understand why he might elect to go into the police business." After a pause, his tone turned haughty. "It's his partner who looks a bit more . . . swarthy. His name is Sean Ryan."

"Sounds Irish."

"Trust me, he's as Irish as a four-leaf clover. He has also been lurking about in an ill-fitting tuxedo. I don't know if the poor fit is from an inferior tailor, a weapon, or the fact that he likely borrowed it from some unfortunate soul."

As Quentin guided her across the marble floor, she scanned the crowd. "I don't see him."

"You will. I promise, once you start looking, you won't miss him. He sticks out like a sore thumb! However, Owen has vouched for his character, which is the only reason my parents allowed him to be in our midst." He leaned closer to drawl into her ear. "So don't worry about a thing, Eloisa. As long as they're here, everything is going to be just fine. As far as I'm concerned, they're worth every penny of their exorbitant fee. If they keep you safe, it will be money well spent."

It took a lot of effort to pretend she believed him. But what Quentin didn't realize was that it wasn't only the threat of being attacked by a stranger that frightened her.

It was the knowledge that much worse than a threat could happen with someone she knew.

"You're staring again," Owen Howard blurted as he reached Sean's side. "If you're not careful, someone besides me is going to notice."

"I'm merely scanning the area," Sean lied. Only through careful effort was he able to refrain from flushing. "There are a lot of people here, you know. Hundreds."

"Yes, but only one Eloisa Carstairs."

"I'm sure I don't know to whom you are referring."

"Of course you do," Owen countered with a wink. "But don't be embarrassed, chap. You aren't doing anything the rest of us haven't done a time or two. Or ten. Eloisa is pure golden-haired perfection. Angelic even."

Sean raised his eyebrows at the descriptor. At times like these he truly wondered why Owen had elected to join the police force. Though he wasn't quite as high in the instep as the majority of the gentlemen and ladies in attendance, he was certainly far and above Sean's social standing.

In addition, Sean was fairly certain if he, like Owen, had made such a social stumble like joining the police force, he certainly wouldn't be showing up at society functions like this. It seemed an odd choice.

Sean, however, was making a small fortune for Hope House this evening. That was what he needed to focus on. His fee would cover the expenses of the women and children who lived there for almost a month. That was reason alone to be standing around in an ill-fitting, borrowed tuxedo, attempting to look vigilant.

"Ready to split up again?" Sean asked. "I'll check the balconies and alcoves while you check the perimeter grounds."

Owen pulled out his silver timepiece. "That suits me fine. Meet back here in an hour?"

As the set ended and the men escorted their partners off the dance floor, Sean watched Owen walk in the direction of the balcony and the outdoor steps that led down to the patio and garden. The patio was decorated with a flurry of white candles.

Then, unable to help himself, he looked for her pale lace gown the color of spring grass. He exhaled as he saw Eloisa being escorted off the floor and toward one of the private rooms off to the side. She was in Quentin Gardner's company, which was reason enough for Sean to pretend he didn't see her. Quentin's father was not only paying his fee, the family was also believed to be above reproach. In short, Quentin was everything Sean was not. He was exactly the type of gentleman Eloisa should be near.

But then Sean noticed her expression had become strained, and she seemed to be trying to pull her arm from Quentin's grip. Her eyes were darting around the room, as if she were looking for anyone to give her assistance.

He stilled and stared at her hard, not caring if his attention was garnering notice.

He knew the exact moment she recognized him—from when they had previously met or merely a fish-out-of-water policeman, he didn't know. He didn't care. Her lips parted. Her pleading look told him everything he needed to know.

It didn't matter who she was or whom she was with. Eloisa Carstairs was looking to him for help.

And he would do almost anything to go to her assistance.

CHAPTER 2

Only with the greatest effort was Eloisa able to keep from crying out. "Quentin, where are you taking me?"

"Nowhere special. Only to one of my mother's quiet seating areas." He stopped in front of a pair of ornately carved chairs framed by heavy velvet curtains. "I never understood why she'd been so intent on designing the perfect alcove. Now I have a very good idea. We'll be able to rest here as long as we like without being disturbed."

When she saw him start to pull the drapery closed, she pulled free from his firm grip at last and stepped away. "I'd rather not sit here."

"Why? I assure you it's nothing no one here hasn't done a time or two." He grinned, but that grin slowly faded as he stared at her intently. "Eloisa? Dearest, you're deathly pale." He reached for her gloved hand and tugged her toward the chairs. "Sit down. Relax. You look as if you're about to faint."

Fearing he was correct, she sat. However, she was very far from relaxing. That same old fear gripped her as she scanned the area. Hoping for someone to come upon them soon. Praying for help. Perhaps the man whose eyes had just met hers.

"D-don't pull the curtains shut. Please."

Immediately, he pushed them back against the wall. As she tried to catch her breath, he knelt at her feet. "Shall I get you a glass of water? Lemonade?"

"I-I don't know."

Concern crossed his face as he picked up one of her gloved hands. "Why not?"

She didn't have an answer for that. Her mouth went dry as she attempted to think of something to say. Of any excuse to explain her skittishness.

But nothing was coming to mind.

Suddenly, the man in the ill-fitting tuxedo—the one who must indeed be Mr. Ryan—appeared. "Miss Carstairs, are you all right?"

Quentin scowled as he got to his feet. "Detective, be off. This is a private conversation."

After looking at her for a long moment, the detective turned to Quentin and replied, "I beg your pardon, sir, but your father was asking for you. I told him I'd find you."

"What did he want?"

"I couldn't say, sir. Only that I told him I'd convey his message." Looking then directly at her, Detective Ryan said, "Sir, it appears Miss Carstairs has gotten overheated. Since you are needed elsewhere, I'll escort her outside."

Quentin eyed him with a decidedly haughty glare. "Detective, you seem to be mistaken about your assigned duties here. My father hired you to make sure the women are safe here, not to interfere in my business."

"I understand exactly what my duties are. Sir." To Eloisa's surprise, the detective didn't look cowed in the slightest. Instead, he looked relaxed, almost at ease. But his eyes never left hers. "Miss Carstairs, would you care to take a breath of fresh air?"

Feeling both men's gazes, Eloisa knew there was only one real choice. The proper, correct thing to do would be to stay with Quentin. She'd known him for years, he was hosting the party, and nothing would make her parents happier than for her to spend time with him.

If she left with the detective, eyebrows would be raised and questions would be asked.

However, she had recently learned that the best decision wasn't always the obvious one. She had also learned that feeling safe was something not to be taken for granted.

Therefore, she stood as gracefully as she could on unsteady feet. "Thank you so much, Detective. I would enjoy taking a turn outside, especially since Quentin has been called away."

Quentin edged forward, just as if he feared she would actually make a social faux pas and take the policeman's arm. "Eloisa, I will escort you wherever you wish."

She inched closer to the detective. "Please don't trouble yourself."

"It would be no trouble." His speech was clipped, his tone hard. Almost frightening.

With effort she kept her smile in place. "But I would feel terrible if I monopolized your company, especially since your father summoned you." Before Quentin could say another word, she turned to Detective Ryan. "Are you sure you don't mind escorting me out to one of the balconies? I really am in need of some fresh air."

"I don't mind at all."

Then, before Quentin could protest again, she wrapped a hand around the policeman's forearm as he led the way out of the alcove.

Quentin was most likely sputtering behind them, but she didn't care. All that mattered was that she felt safe with this man. And, with luck, he would even find a way for her to get home before she burst into tears.

When they were halfway to the balcony doors, the detective looked down at her. "By the way, my name is Lieutenant Detective Sean Ryan, miss. We've met before."

Though she had already recognized him, his words brought back a rush of memories she had tried very hard to forget. "Yes. Um, I remember. The Sloane . . . matter. You were one of the officers who asked me questions about the family." Smoothing a faltering smile, she said, "Would you mind terribly if I acted like I know you better than I do? I don't want anyone to suspect that we're not acquainted."

A shadow entered his eyes. "I wouldn't mind that at all, Miss Carstairs."

She noticed that her walk with the handsome Detective Ryan was earning her a few curious looks, but Eloisa figured the expressions of surprise could have as much to do with the fact that she was in attendance at the ball. She'd hardly been out in society in weeks.

It might have something to do with her expression too. For once she didn't feel as if she were on the verge of tears. In fact, at the moment she couldn't help but smile.

"We seem to be attracting quite a bit of attention," Mr. Ryan said under his breath.

"I don't mind." Feeling daring, she tilted her chin up to gaze into his eyes. "Actually, I was relieved when you happened upon us. It was my good fortune that Mr. Gardner sent you on the hunt for Quentin."

Looking a little sheepish, he said, "I'm afraid I made that up. When I saw Mr. Gardner lead you into the alcove, I noticed . . . Forgive me, but you didn't look entirely comfortable."

"I see." She was embarrassed now. If this detective noticed how ill at ease she was, perhaps others had noticed as well.

He looked at her in a searching way. "Was Mr. Gardner making improper advances?"

"No." When he raised his eyebrows, she flushed, realizing that she had answered fairly quickly. "At least, I don't think so." She bit her lip before continuing. "I'm sorry. You must think I'm a ninny."

"Never that. But perhaps I will allow that you seem a bit nervous?"

"I sometimes have a difficult time being alone with men."

Even her kid gloves and his layers of clothing couldn't hide the fact that the muscles lining his forearm tensed. "Do I make you nervous?"

"No. I mean, I don't believe so." Embarrassed again, she dropped her hand.

They were at the outside doors now. The Gardners' ballroom had two sets of white French doors that opened to a wide balcony. The breeze that beckoned them was bracing. Exactly what she needed to get her bearings.

After they stepped out onto the expanse, she noticed two other couples outside as well. However, they were far enough away not to disturb her and Mr. Ryan's privacy.

For the first time since she'd arrived at the Gardner house, Eloisa exhaled with relief as she turned and rested her back against the balcony's railing. "Thank you again for your escort."

He stepped to her side. "Care to tell me what has you worried?"

"It's nothing."

Facing the balcony, he leaned forward, resting his forearms on the rail. "Sometimes it helps to talk about a fear."

"You think so?"

He shrugged. "I think it can't hurt." After a pause, he added, "You might not know this, but police officers are very good at keeping secrets."

"Even you?"

"Especially me."

"I-I can't seem to shake my fear of being in an enclosed space with a man." She waited to feel a sense of relief, but it was proving as evasive as ever.

Now, as she felt the detective's look become more intense, she wished she'd never said a word. Even though Reid Armstrong had told her he'd told the police a debutante of good character had been violated by Douglass Sloane, Eloisa never meant to actually speak of it. "I meant—"

"I understand."

For some reason, she believed he did understand how she felt. Perhaps his professional experience gave him a sixth sense about how traumatic situations could damage one's psyche.

Or perhaps he knew something of a more personal nature?

"I interviewed many people about the Sloane family, miss," he said quietly. "As well as many people who were witnesses to Mr. Sloane's behavior."

He knew, she realized. Detective Ryan knew Douglass Sloane had raped her. She clutched the railing in a futile attempt to stop her hands from shaking. "I see."

After a moment, he said, "I imagine your family has been a source of comfort during this time?"

She noticed that he'd somehow managed to make his statement sound like a question. And though it was tempting to lie, she found that she could not. "Not exactly."

"Oh?"

This line of conversation was too intimate. Too personal. She was tempted to point out his poor manners, but she didn't dare. At the moment, she was even more frightened of being left alone than of being alone with him and answering his questions.

"I haven't told them anything."

He blinked. It was obvious she'd surprised him.

And just as obvious that he was a man unused to surprises.

Weighing her words slowly, she whispered, "My parents are not aware that anything is remiss. I mean, they are not aware of what happened with Douglass."

"I see." He swallowed. "Have you told anyone at all?"

"Only Mr. Reid Armstrong."

"I see." He said nothing else, letting Eloisa know that he, too, would never betray her confidence. Ironically, his effort made her want to share more. "Reid found me after . . . after the incident."

"Ah."

"Yes."

He was still looking at her intently. "If you will forgive me for prying . . . Why haven't you told your parents? Or anyone else? Why not even a girlfriend?"

"I'm afraid you don't quite understand the propensity for gossip in my circle. I can't let this . . . blemish my reputation."

"If a man overstepped himself, it was his fault, not yours." He still was gazing at her intently. "Never yours."

His words made her shiver. And though she tried to tell herself the response was from the conversation, she had a feeling that was far from the truth. "Not in my world, Detective. May we please speak of something else now?" Now the whole conversation was making her uncomfortable, sparking feelings of pain and embarrassment. They flashed over her in waves, each image that came to mind threatening to overwhelm her.

"As you wish."

"Thank—"

"But if I may be so forward, I hope you have asked for the Lord's help."

"Do you mean pray?"

The lines around his eyes eased as a hint of humor entered his gaze. "You look flummoxed. Is the notion so unfamiliar?"

"Perhaps."

"Do you not believe in the power of prayer?"

"I haven't found all that much comfort in prayers lately."

Now he was the one who appeared taken aback, Eloisa realized. She very likely had just offended him. "I am sorry if I have spoken too freely."

"Not at all."

"Forgive me if I offended you."

"You couldn't." His voice lowered. "I know we don't know each other well."

"Hardly at all," she interjected. Though he already knew her better than most. He knew things about her almost no one else did.

"But if you ever do need to talk, you can always talk to me."

"You?"

To her shame, his cheeks reddened. "I realize I'm not the type of companion you're accustomed to, but as I said, I have been known to keep a secret." He paused until she felt as if she had no alternative but to meet his gaze. "And there is also the fact that nothing you could tell me would scandalize me."

His words were shocking. But even more appalling to her was the idea that she wasn't dismissing his offer out of hand. "You sound certain about that."

"I've been on the police force for years, Miss Carstairs. I'm afraid I've seen my fair share of shocking situations."

Looking into his eyes, noticing how they were so dark yet so filled with emotion, Eloisa yearned to let down her guard. To throw caution to the wind and simply talk without worry of being judged.

Or of having her worst nightmares bandied about as choice pieces of gossip.

But then the wind shifted, and she caught the scent of another woman's perfume. Heard the lilting strains of the orchestra, the faint echo of crystal glasses clinking, and the refined echo of a toast.

And she remembered where she was—and who she was. She would find her parents' friends, the ones who had brought her, and see if they, too, were ready to depart.

Pushing away from the banister, she faced him squarely. "I think not. Thank you again, Lieutenant, for coming to my aid. But I do believe I will join the party again."

Whatever emotion she'd spied in his dark eyes was shuttered quickly. "Of course. Good evening."

She'd just turned around when a woman's shrill scream pierced the night air. After a second's pause, more cries of alarm echoed from the garden below.

She'd just turned toward the stairs when Detective Ryan waylaid her. Gripping her shoulders with both hands, he pulled her to the side. "Stay here, Miss Carstairs," he murmured. "Stay here where it's safe."

Then, just as abruptly, he turned on his heel and rushed toward the iron steps that led to the downstairs patio.

"But—"

He paused. "Promise me, Eloisa," he ordered, his voice thick with emotion. "Promise me so I won't have to worry about you."

Only when she nodded did he rush down the stairs. She moved back to the railing so she could watch him. Perhaps even call out for him to be careful. But he was out of sight, beyond the candlelit patio, before she could utter another word.

Less than five minutes later, she heard more commotion from the garden. After a moment, she walked along the balcony until she saw a group of people below. Some servants had brought lanterns to where Detective Ryan stood in the middle, talking to Owen Howard. She couldn't see their faces. Eloisa craned her neck, moving slightly to the side in an attempt to discover what everyone was staring at.

When the crowd parted, Eloisa gasped. She could just make out that Danica Webster was lying on the ground. Her gown was torn, and she seemed to be bleeding from several places on her face and neck. As a pair of elderly women peered over the railing as well, screamed, and then collapsed into their companions' arms, Eloisa gripped the railing even tighter.

It seemed that even a police presence this evening hadn't prevented another attack.

―――

It took two hours to clear the scene. Sean and Owen had sent footmen for more officers and medical assistance. Miss Webster's brother carried her to one of the Gardners' private sitting rooms. There, she soon came to and was attended by a physician. Fortunately, as with the other victims, none of the attacker's slashes had cut very deep. Only enough, Sean was sure, to leave scars that would never completely fade.

The doctor cleaned Danica's wounds, stitched her up, and at last released her into her parents' care.

While the young lady was being treated, Sean, Owen, and their supervisor, Captain Sawyer Keaton, interviewed everyone from the party they could while uniformed personnel managed the crowd and tried to interview servants.

It was a grueling, almost thankless undertaking for the police. All the servants had been too busy to do anything but their tasks at hand, and all the guests were so highbrow that they were easily offended by even the smallest hint of questioning. After his job and his character had been threatened for the tenth time, Sean knew his temper was brewing.

Their captain knew it too. "Go on back to the station, Ryan," Keaton said. "Your attitude isn't helping anything."

"I'm sorry, sir."

Captain Keaton shrugged. "There's a reason we have Detective Howard here. Owen is not merely decorative; he's also of this class. Face it, Sean. He's far better at soothing ruffled society feathers than you could ever hope to be."

"I agree, sir."

It was also frustrating to learn that, like the previous victims, Miss Webster had little to tell them about her attacker. And there didn't seem to be any witnesses.

He was just about to take a hack back to the station when he noticed Eloisa standing off by herself. What was she still doing here? When the captain was pulled to one side by Mr. Gardner, Sean walked to Eloisa's side.

"Miss Carstairs, are you all right?"

Pain and stress dimmed her clear blue eyes. "I suppose I must be. My friends . . . I was just considering how to get home. Perhaps I should send for a driver . . ."

"May I have the honor of escorting you there?"

After a moment's hesitation, she nodded. "I would appreciate that very much, Lieutenant. I . . . Thank you."

"I'll be right back," he murmured before returning to the captain's side. "Captain, I'll meet you back at the station. Miss Carstairs needs an escort home."

The captain stared at him hard before shrugging. "Sure. That would be fine, Ryan. It's going to be a long night for all of us no matter what."

While Eloisa went to say her good-byes to Mrs. Gardner, Sean asked the butler for her cloak. Owen stepped to his side. "Did I just hear right? Are you really planning to escort Eloisa Carstairs home?"

"What I am doing is none of your concern."

"I think it might be."

"Then you are mistaken."

Owen rocked back on his heels, a mocking smile playing on his lips. "Listen to you. So glacial. So proper. So much so, I can hardly hear the Irish in your speech."

As jabs went, it hit right on the mark. However, it didn't faze Sean at all. He was, indeed, Irish. Once more, he came from the area of Chicago most people tried to escape. But he'd always figured someone had to come from humble beginnings. And he'd never had cause to feel anything but love and affection for his family and old neighbors who still lived there. "Can't be helping my accent, Owen," he mocked, daring to make it a bit thicker than usual.

"And the rest of us can't help but be aware of it. It marks you."

"No harm there."

"There is if you have developed an affection for the elusive Eloisa."

It grated on Sean that Owen could speak her Christian name without censure, and half the assembled crowd acted as if he were not worthy of even breathing the same air she did.

"I'll see you back at the precinct. Let me know if you need any assistance," he said as Eloisa reappeared.

When she looked at him and smiled softly, he realized she was waiting for him to help her on with her cloak. Hoping his hands weren't as clumsy as he feared, he retrieved Eloisa's velvet cloak from the butler and carefully placed it around her bare shoulders.

"This is so kind of you," she said quietly.

Not trusting his voice, he simply nodded. Actually, it took

everything he had not to respond when his fingers accidently skimmed the bare, satin-soft skin at the nape of her neck.

Or when he smelled the faint scent of her perfume.

Yes, he was a cop and Irish. He was scarred from too many fights when he was young and too many scuffles with criminals during his work on the force.

All he knew about good manners was from spending a year as his captain's errand boy just before going to the police academy—and from watching Owen.

At thirty-two, he was twelve years older than Eloisa and far more cynical and hard.

But, as Eloisa again smiled at him softly and placed one white-gloved hand on his forearm, Sean Ryan knew that he was, at the moment, the luckiest guy in the city.

Maybe even the whole world.

CHAPTER 3

I appreciate your escort more than I can ever say," Eloisa said as Detective Ryan guided her around two men loitering under the dim glow of a lamppost. Though both her home on Sable Hill and the Gardner home were in the best of areas, one never knew who might be lurking about on Michigan Avenue between, especially late at night. It was also a comfort to know Detective Ryan was no doubt armed.

"It is very kind of you, especially given the circumstances," she added.

Recalling just what those circumstances were, she shivered. It was doubtful that she'd ever completely forget seeing poor Danica Webster lying on the ground, her pink gown marred by a profusion of tears and stained with blood. Only the knowledge that her wounds weren't life-threatening gave Eloisa any comfort.

"I promise, it is my honor, Miss Carstairs," Detective Ryan replied in what she was coming to understand was his usual quiet way. "It is not often that a man like me gets to walk down the avenue with such a lovely lady on his arm." Though he didn't smile, his eyes warmed. "I'm sure to be the envy of all who know me."

"Hardly that."

Seeing that he was on the verge of stepping a few inches farther away from her, no doubt in an attempt to give her more space, she tightened her grip nervously.

She felt his muscles contract under the thick layers of his suit jacket and wool coat. However, he didn't pull away but simply stayed by her side—and looked at her searchingly. "Are you sure you are all right?"

"I don't know." All she did know was that she wasn't quite ready to step inside her home and spend the next ten hours in the quiet of her bedroom, alone with dark memories. Though it wasn't fair to him, she wished their walk could take hours, not the thirty or so minutes that was the norm. "I keep thinking about Danica."

Anything to hold on to his reassuring presence.

"That's understandable," he murmured. "It was a disturbing sight, to be sure."

She shivered. "I imagine she was terrified." Remembering when she'd been at another man's mercy a few weeks ago, Eloisa privately amended her words. No, she didn't imagine anything.

She knew Danica had been terrified. She remembered the sound of her scream.

"Do you know Miss Webster well?"

Eloisa glanced at his profile. His features weaved in and out of view, all in accordance with the flickering torches on the lampposts that lined Michigan Avenue. To her relief, the detective didn't seem to be questioning her for any purpose. No, he was merely making conversation.

Probably because she was holding onto his arm like it was a lifeline.

And though she knew she should release him to go do his job, she found herself exhaling in relief. He wasn't going to leave her. Not just yet.

Focusing back on their conversation, she answered his question. "We are acquaintances. Good enough friends, I suppose." When she realized she hadn't told him anything he didn't already know, she added, "Danica is about my age. She made her debut two years ago, like I did. We move in the same circles."

For a moment, she was tempted to give nuance to what she had said. While it was technically true, it had not truly described her relationship with Danica. They had, indeed, made their debuts at the same time. They also did move in the same circles. But that was where the similarities ended. Eloisa had been immediately embraced and fiercely sought after by the best families and the most distinguished gentlemen. Danica, however, had merely been politely welcomed into the fold.

But telling the detective all that made her uncomfortable. It sounded too pompous, too disdainful of Danica, and Eloisa didn't feel that way at all. So she remained silent.

Which she then was afraid the detective had misinterpreted.

He glanced her way, but nothing in his expression told her how he felt about her description.

"Seeing someone you know in such a way is always shocking."

His voice was gentle, gliding over her frayed nerves. "I have to keep reminding myself she is alive. That she will be all right." She closed her eyes. "But I have to admit that for those first few seconds, I was sure she was dead."

"I feared the same thing, if you want to know the truth."

He was so composed, so assured. So stalwart. "Does it ever get easier?"

"It?"

"Witnessing the results of violence?" She was already so burdened by her dreams and memories of Douglass Sloane's attack, she couldn't imagine living in a world where she saw such pain on a daily basis.

As he scanned their vicinity, he murmured, "You might not believe this, but I still find it difficult to brush off much of what I see on the job. People can be so cruel."

She'd never thought of that in such a way. "I suppose that is true."

After giving a pair of men passing by them a hard look, Lieutenant Ryan continued. "The job is hard enough when the victims are men. But when I see violence done to the innocent, to women or children? It is never easy to observe, or investigate for that matter."

His words shocked her. Not because of what it revealed about Detective Sean Ryan, but rather by what it revealed about herself. She was acting as if she were the victim, holding onto him, forcing him to converse with her while he was likely more than eager to deposit her at her doorstep and move on.

Abruptly, she released his arm. "Forgive me, Lieutenant. Here I am, all in a dither when you have things to do. I really should let you go. Surely I can get home on my own now. It's not too much farther . . ."

"I shall see you all the way home." His voice was clipped. Definite. "And furthermore, Miss Carstairs . . . there is nothing to forgive. I know many a hardened man at the precinct who would've flinched at the sight of a lovely young lady bleeding on the ground. Violence has a way of preying on a person's soul, I fear." He grimaced. "All I can say is that I haven't become so jaded by my job that I have forgotten about the sanctity of a life." His eyes warmed again, as if he were thinking of something he thought amusing.

She wished she knew what it was.

"H-have you been in the force very long?"

"Thirteen years. I started at nineteen."

"Did you always want to be a policeman?" she asked. Again, she thought he was probably eager to return to the crime scene, but, well, this was the first conversation she'd had in a long while that she found genuinely interesting.

The corners of his lips curved. "It's a long story, Miss Carstairs. Perhaps it would bore you."

"I wouldn't have asked if I wasn't interested. Please, do share."

"It's nothing too exciting," he said as they turned onto the main drive leading to the group of three estates at the top of Sable Hill. "But something happened that was memorable. It changed my path."

"Which was?"

"Let's just say I was a boy becoming rather adept at getting into trouble."

She hated that he was pushing her interest aside. "Don't do that."

"Do what?"

"Please, don't treat me as if I have nothing in my head but feathers."

"I would never presume such a thing."

"Then?"

For a second, he glanced down at his thick-soled shoes, the ones that had looked so out of place in the elaborate, gilded ballroom but looked so right as he escorted her down the side of the street in the open air. As if he were so solid and strong, that nothing was too much of an obstacle.

She prodded. "Detective?"

After a brief pause, he spoke. "First of all, I should say that I am one of eight children, the fourth child. Third son."

"Ah."

"We grew up poor, though by the time my two youngest sisters came into the world, things were better and my parents even moved to a house on Haversham Street. But when I was young? We lived in the tenements."

"I see."

He shook his head, then paused to look beyond her at one of her neighbors' impressive, elaborately carved front doors.

"I doubt you've seen anything of the like. I hope you have not." After a resigned sigh, he continued. "Anyway, one of our neighbors was falsely accused of thieving and arrested," he said at last. His clipped diction had softened, the vowels a little longer.

He spoke of thievery with the same contempt she would imagine people would only reserve for murder. She stopped abruptly. "What happened?"

"Well, the man who was accused—his name was Mr. Tierney—was an old man. A nice man, but forgetful, I'm afraid. Anyway, one day he came home with a very nice watch for his oldest boy, who was going into the family business. He'd also managed to finish his schooling—not an easy accomplishment where we lived. Most every boy I knew had quit school to support his family."

He sighed. "At any rate, Mr. Tierney came home with a fine watch and presented it to his son with much fanfare. All of us were invited, and we came, though I guess I should admit that some of us were not all that impressed."

"Was it not a good watch?"

"It wasn't the watch, Miss Carstairs. It was the fact that Mr. Tierney's son wasn't like the rest of us. While we'd all been working on the streets and docks from the time we were thirteen or fourteen, he'd studied. While we went to work in the cold, he'd learned things. I'm afraid some thought he'd had things too easy."

"Did you?"

He shrugged. "I did. But along with that resentment was a healthy bit of jealousy. He had a life I could only dream about. And the kind of watch I knew I'd never own." He looked down at his feet again. "It was a truly fine-looking timepiece," he murmured. Then he lifted his head and met her gaze.

And, for the first time, truly smiled.

It fairly took her breath away.

"Well, don't keep me in suspense. What happened?" Remembering Lieutenant Ryan speaking of arrest, she guessed. "Had he stolen the timepiece?"

"Not at all. It turned out Mr. Tierney had bought the watch from a street peddler." He shrugged. "Well, that was what he said."

"Is buying from someone on the street illegal?"

He chuckled. "Not at all. The problem was that when the officers came to arrest him, they based it on the fact that a thief had stolen a gold watch from a wealthy man right on the street. When Mr. Tierney showed it off to the neighborhood, someone commented on it, and the next thing anyone knew, half the city knew a lowly Irishman somehow came up with an expensive timepiece."

"What had happened?"

"As far as I've been able to discern, Mr. Tierney bought the timepiece from a street peddler who was actually a fence, someone who made a living selling stolen items."

"But couldn't Mr. Tierney have told the police who the peddler was?"

"He didn't remember much about the peddler. And the man who actually owned the timepiece took one look at Mr. Tierney, who arrived at the police station looking much the worse for wear, and promptly said he looked like he could have been the thief."

Eloisa was appalled. "But how could he say that if the thief got

28

away too quickly for him to know for sure? And how could Mr. Tierney, an older man, get away that fast anyway?"

"The man's word was good enough, I fear. See, the police didn't much care whether or not Mr. Tierney had done it. As far as they were concerned, he sounded guilty. Had the watch, couldn't exactly remember where he'd bought it, and couldn't exactly remember who he'd bought it from." His mouth formed a thin line.

"What happened to Mr. Tierney?"

"He was quickly tried and sent to prison."

Though she'd never known the man, she was dismayed. "That is horrible."

"They lost the family business. His wife and children were forced to move. His boy—Asa, his name was—went to work in the factories and later died in an accident."

"I'm very sorry."

"I am too." He frowned. "But I am just as sorry to burden you with this tale. Now that I have some distance from it, I must admit it sounds even bleaker than I remembered."

"If the police did such a dreadful job, why did you want to join their ranks?"

"Until that time, I had been getting into a bit of trouble. Nothing too terrible, but enough to try my mother's patience. When I witnessed everything that had happened with Mr. Tierney, I realized that crimes do have consequences."

"But he was innocent!"

"I, however, was not quite as innocent as I should have been. Anyway, I started realizing that I wanted to be the person who actually tried to solve crimes. I wanted to be the type of man who actually cared, who solved crimes to make sure the innocents weren't taken advantage of." He shook his head. "I wanted to be the type of man I admired. To catch bad men and bring them to justice." After a pause, he blurted, "I would be lying if I didn't mention that I also noticed that no cops were living how we were. They got paid more, had respect. They'd, uh, made something of themselves. I wanted that too."

"There's nothing wrong with that."

His lips twisted. "Perhaps not."

"So you joined the police force?"

"So I began my path toward improving myself and my situation."

"That's commendable, Detective."

"And you, Miss Carstairs, have too kind a heart."

"Perhaps you, too, have a kind heart. Here you are, spending your evening at a society party and now walking me home."

He frowned. "Unfortunately, my attendance at the party didn't prevent Miss Webster from being attacked."

"But still, I can't imagine you looked forward to standing around the Gardners' ballroom and walking their grounds."

"Mr. Gardner paid me well for my time. One of my sisters is involved with Hope House. I'll be using most of what I earned tonight for that."

"What is Hope House?"

"It's a home for women and children who have nowhere else to go."

She folded her hands in front of her waist and smiled. "It seems my earlier statement was true. You are rather commendable."

A faint breeze brushed the hem of her skirts, sliding through the openings of her pelisse. She shivered, both by the frosty air and Detective Ryan's warm look directed her way.

"Take my arm, miss. I don't want you getting chilled."

She needed no further encouragement. Eloisa wrapped her hand around his arm again. She would never have imagined it, but his companionship was soothing. He wasn't peppering her with questions or filling the silence with lascivious guesses about why Danica had been attacked or malicious gossip about any of the other people at the party.

Instead, he easily walked by her side, keeping his stride shorter in deference to her. Guiding her down curbs. Watching the area around them with a careful eye.

She hadn't felt so protected in a very long time, which was quite a surprise. Of late, she'd had a difficult time leaving her home. Now here she was, walking next to a man she barely knew on an almost-empty street.

Simply thinking about the danger she could have been in—and the harm that had come to Danica that evening—made her tremble.

And just like that, she remembered being held down by Douglass. The sound of the collar of her dress tearing.

The panic she'd felt, followed swiftly by the knowledge that she'd never be the same.

With effort, she tried to tamp down the panic. Attempted to conceal the rush of nerves. However, she was unsuccessful.

He noticed. "Did, uh, you happen to notice the moon, Miss Carstairs?"

She stared at him blankly. "Pardon?"

"The moon. I believe they call this a harvest moon."

Dutifully, she followed the direction of his lifted hand. "Indeed. It's lovely." With relief, she let her gaze skim the night sky and saw that the moon was indeed wreathed in a vivid orange glow. "It's hanging so low tonight, one could almost imagine one could snatch it from the sky."

His eyes warmed again. "Indeed, Miss Carstairs," he murmured, obviously echoing her words on purpose. "If you'd like, we could stop for a moment so you could try."

She was embarrassed now. Wonderfully so. "Thank you, but no."

"I almost wish I could steal it for you. Just to see you smile."

His nonsensical statement did just what she thought he must have hoped it would. "I bet you say that to all the ladies of your acquaintance," she teased.

"Not at all."

However, this evening's events—and her seeming inability to move on from the incident in her past—made the night anything but perfect.

She felt drawn to him, this man who was so different from her in almost every way society said counted. But just as surprising was the way she felt about that. She realized then that she had changed so much she no longer needed the type of gentlemen she used to seek out.

No longer could she feel comfortable with a person who had no knowledge of what it was like to be at another's mercy. Or to fear.

Or, most importantly, to have no choices. This man did.

And with that thought came a frightening truth. She was going to miss Lieutenant Ryan. She was going to regret that their places in life were so far apart that they'd probably never have an occasion to cross paths again.

Hoping to steel herself against further pain, she inserted a bit of distance in her voice. And laced it with the brittle humor she usually went to great lengths to avoid. "I suppose you are wondering how I was going to get home, if not for you. Other than sending for my driver, that is."

After a moment's pause, he replied, "It had crossed my mind."

"I was going to leave in the company of some of my parents' friends. My parents would have been there this evening as well, except my mother was feeling a bit under the weather."

"Ah. I hope it is nothing too serious?"

She made herself continue to face forward. Made herself pretend she wasn't missing their more honest, insightful conversation. "It's nothing my mother hasn't dealt with before and often. My mother has rather a flare for imagined illnesses—and the dramatic. My father likes to say she's never met an ailment she hasn't wished to adopt."

His eyebrows rose. "That's almost unkind."

"Almost."

"More than that, I'm afraid."

"Perhaps you are right." Stealing another glance at him, she gave up her weak attempt at more socially acceptable conversation. She'd rather know more about him. "I suppose your mother is far hardier?"

He flashed a smile. "Yes, but I imagine that's because she has to be. As I said, I'm one of eight children. She had no time to be ill." With a wry expression, he added, "Come to think of it, I don't think she had much patience with any of us being sick, either."

She laughed. "You must have lots of stories to tell about growing up in such a large family."

"Yes, but not too many suitable for delicate sensibilities."

She laughed. "Your house must have been a happy place."

"It was happy. And crowded. And noisy. It was everything, I suppose." He glanced her way. "I'm assuming you are not one of eight children?"

"I have an older brother, Thomas. He is currently traveling abroad. My mother also lost a babe before I came along . . . and from what I have heard, she had a difficult confinement."

"That had to be hard."

"I didn't know anything else. But now that I'm nearly the age she was when she had me? I am realizing that it might be easier if I had more siblings to commiserate with." This time she was the one who looked at her feet. "And I'm also realizing that I haven't had a genuine conversation like this in a very long time."

"I haven't either." His voice was rough and gravelly. His look was solemn as they came to a stop. "I believe this is your house."

She gazed into his eyes. Realized they weren't brown like she had originally thought. Instead, they were a murky hazel, shades of green and brown and gold. Mesmerizing.

He stepped closer, reached out, and gently removed her hand from his arm. "Miss Carstairs, are you ready to go inside now?"

She blinked. Turned. And realized he was correct. "Yes. My goodness, I suppose I was in a daze. I didn't even realize we had reached our drive. Maybe I'm more tired than I realized?"

"I'm sure that is it." He still held her gloved hand. "Take care of yourself, miss," he murmured as he bent over her hand slightly.

She inhaled, preparing herself for his lips to brush her knuckles.

Instead, he straightened and released her. "Good evening."

"Thank you again for your escort."

He bowed slightly. "As I said before, it was my honor." Looking tentative for the first time, he added, "I must warn you that I'll return tomorrow, in the morning about nine thirty, if that's not too early. We'll be questioning most everyone who was at the party again, and most especially those who know Danica."

"I understand." Actually, there was a part of her that felt relief. She wasn't ready to say good-bye to him forever. And it didn't matter to her if he came far too early for the normal routines of her household.

Forgetting she had earlier assumed he would return to his duties, she asked, "Will you be heading home soon as well?"

"I'm afraid not. I'll stop by the Gardners' home to make sure things have been wrapped up for the night before I head to the precinct."

"So you'll be working for hours yet."

"It's my job."

"I hope you will get some rest. Eventually."

After gazing at her a moment longer, he said, "Ring the bell now, Eloisa."

She felt a fluttering in the pit of her stomach at his use of her first name. Dutifully, she rang the bell. Almost immediately, the front door opened. "Good evening, Worthy."

"Miss." Worthy treated the detective to a frosty glance. "Sir."

"Worthy, this is Lieutenant Detective Ryan. He was kind enough to escort me home this evening. I'm afraid there was a bit of a disturbance at the Gardner house."

The tall, thin butler blinked, then presented a slightly less frigid glance to her escort. "Good evening, sir."

"He'll be back tomorrow."

"I see."

This time it was the detective who replied. "Good evening, Miss Carstairs. Sleep well." He left then, before she could return an unsuitable reply.

Worthy closed the door. "I hope nothing tragic occurred?"

"Miss Danica Webster was attacked by an unknown assailant, slashed with a knife, though not fatally. The police were already there, so I suppose things could have been worse."

"What has happened to our town?" the butler murmured. "Miss Carstairs, may I call Juliet for you?"

"Yes, please. And tell her to bring me a bit of tea, too, would you? She'll know what kind."

"Yes, miss."

Eloisa walked up the grand staircase thinking not about the bath and the pot of tea the servants were now going to make sure she received, but instead imagining Detective Ryan walking back to the Gardners' at a brisk pace.

No doubt he'd already forgotten her completely and was concentrating on his duties.

Juliet joined her in the room, and after a brief exchange of pleasantries, seemed to understand that Eloisa wasn't in the mood to talk.

Only when she slid under the cool bedsheets did she remember what the detective had said. When they'd arrived at her house, he'd said that escorting her had been his honor.

She decided she was going to think of that as noteworthy.

Because she knew she had thought his company was a pleasure too. She could hardly wait to see him again.

"You are being ridiculous, Eloisa," she said. "But dear God, if you could, please watch over him tonight."

She fell asleep praying for Sean Ryan's safety.

CHAPTER 4

Gasping for air, clutching the collar of her nightgown, Eloisa woke.

As she attempted to catch her breath, her vision slowly focused. As the seconds passed, each one feeling twice as long as the last, she realized she wasn't trapped in Douglass Sloane's harsh grip.

It wasn't his heavy rasp she heard. It was her own shallow pants. She wasn't pinned beneath him. She was alone. In her bed. In her room.

Heart still racing, fear still clinging to the periphery of her consciousness, Eloisa edged out from beneath the tangle of damp sheets and stood.

Once she was steady, she rummaged through her wardrobe until at last she found a clean, dry nightgown. With shaking hands, she replaced the sweat-soaked one with the other. And wondered how she would ever explain to Juliet why it had been necessary to change her gown in the middle of the night yet again.

Just as quickly, she pushed aside her worry. After all, it wasn't as if Juliet would actually question her. She might have been with Eloisa for some time, they might have a warm regard for each other, but they both knew their places. Juliet would never be so bold as to question why Eloisa did anything.

Therefore, it was a certainty that the offending fabric would be whisked away, laundered and pressed, folded neatly, and would then reappear in her wardrobe by nightfall. As if nothing had ever happened.

And that, Eloisa was beginning to realize, had become the guiding force in her life. She lived each hour of each day pretending that Douglass Sloane had never raped her.

Sometime in the last few years, she'd become marvelously adept at pretending that everything was in order. It was a skill her mother possessed in spades, and it had come in handy when her biggest problems had been centered around meeting the right man.

But now, mere weeks after Douglass had forced himself upon her, Eloisa was wiser. She was not nearly so naïve about the hidden agendas of men, even well-spoken gentlemen. And now, with the monster called the Slasher—the Society Slasher—on the loose, she had even more to fear. Someone in their midst was targeting women of well birth and marking them forever.

Most women of her station pretended to be unaware of that.

Only in the middle of the night, when at last her body settled into the realm of unconsciousness, did she allow herself to revisit her darkest memories.

Sitting at her vanity, Eloisa tied back her damp hair and shivered as she remembered exactly how Danica had looked, bleeding on the ground just hours before.

Danica would now be forever scarred, too, but her scars would be visible for all to see. It was a testament to how far down she'd spiraled that Eloisa was slightly envious of those scars. Yes, Danica would be marked.

There was a possibility that, for the rest of her life, people would notice the marks on Danica's face first and the color of her eyes second. And if she stayed in Chicago, well, chances were great that no one would ever let her forget that she'd been hurt. Every conversation would have that knowledge on the edges of it.

But though Danica would likely be waking up at night, too, reliving the moment she'd been a victim, she would also be free of shame.

Far freer than Eloisa was.

Shuddering, Eloisa got up, crawled onto the window seat, and covered her knees with her hands. As the chill through the glass seeped into her side, she rested her head on her knees, curling into a ball in a weak attempt to shield herself from the cold.

She didn't bother returning to bed, however. It was already half past three. It was going to take her quite awhile to once again slip on her façade for a new day. To pretend for all the world that nothing bad had ever happened to her.

───

Sean would have liked to have said that the Carstairs' mansion looked different in the morning light, but it looked exactly the same.

And because of that, it looked like everything he wasn't and had never been.

Standing on the long, manicured drive, he gazed at the house more closely. As always, it gleamed with good fortune, sitting as it did on top of Sable Hill. As he crossed the meticulously maintained grounds, he was in awe. Five white pillars lined the front porch, greeting the visitor to the white brick home sprawling behind it. The perfectly tended grounds and well-plotted landscape further enhanced the beauty of the elegant lines of the mansion.

It looked as perfect as one of the new buildings of the fair's White City.

He'd seen photographs of Southern plantation houses before the War Between the States. Though the tintypes had been grainy and out of focus, Sean was fairly sure the Carstairs' home would fit right in.

Growing up, he'd never thought much about the great houses in the city. Actually, he'd never thought much beyond his close-knit, one-block neighborhood. Their mix of small houses and rickety tenements lined alleys along with a jumble of storefronts.

Sean had a feeling his whole block might fit into this mansion's expansive grounds.

He had just straightened his hat and was preparing to knock when the door opened and the Carstairs' eminently proper butler, Worthy, faced him yet again.

"Good morning, Lieutenant Ryan," he said around a little bow. "Miss Carstairs is expecting you. Won't you please come in?"

While he handed Worthy his hat and coat, he tried not to stare at the large foyer. Large oil paintings framed in ornately carved, gilded frames lined the cream walls. Beneath his feet was an intricately patterned, black-and-white marble floor. Just beyond were numerous rooms and a wide hallway.

Worthy cleared his throat. "This way, sir."

Sean followed the butler down the hallway covered in a combination of sea-blue, turquoise, and ivory wallpaper. He had only the vaguest sense of a few framed portraits before entering a somewhat stark sitting room.

Where Eloisa and her parents rose to greet him.

Only years of experience helped him not to show his surprise. He had imagined he would be meeting with Eloisa privately. Disappointed that he would have to divide his attentions between her and her parents, he gave in to temptation and let his gaze settle on Eloisa. Concern filled him as he noticed how shuttered her expression was.

Her parents' expressions appeared far more open. Their mouths looked pinched, their gazes solemn. And, it seemed, they were far more suspicious.

He stopped and nodded to the three of them. "Good morning, Mr. and Mrs. Carstairs. Miss Carstairs. I am Lieutenant Detective Ryan. Please forgive the intrusion. I'm assuming that Miss Carstairs told you about the unpleasantness of last evening?"

"I did," Eloisa murmured.

"I suppose we all must do our duty," Mr. Carstairs blustered.

"Yes."

Still, Eloisa's father stared at him as if he were an unfortunate who had stumbled inside. "Must say that it's a bit out of the ordinary to welcome the police into our home."

"I expect that it is, at that." Sean knew better than to point out that he wasn't exactly being welcomed.

"Far more surprising to hear that you escorted our daughter home last night."

"Yes, sir. I wanted to keep her safe. I'm grateful that she granted me the honor." He carefully glanced Eloisa's way, then forced himself to keep his expression neutral and not soften as was his want. Today she was wearing a pale-yellow morning gown. It was intricately detailed and extremely flattering to her coloring, though he supposed there was little in her wardrobe that wasn't.

She was also regarding him discreetly.

It took everything he had not to lose himself in her aquamarine gaze.

"It was very kind of you to trouble yourself like that," her mother said. "Though I imagine one in your line of work is called upon to perform many such services."

"Indeed, ma'am."

Eloisa glared at her mother. "Mother, Lieutenant Ryan solves crimes. He is not part of an escort service."

Mrs. Carstairs sniffed. "Nevertheless . . ."

Sean decided to offer Eloisa's mother an out. "Nevertheless, I was happy to be of service."

Mr. Carstairs waved a hand. "Sit. Sit, Ryan. Coffee? Water?" He turned to his wife. "Is anything on its way?"

"I believe so. I expect Worthy told Mrs. Nelson that a policeman arrived." She worried her bottom lip. "Though I'm not sure if it is proper to serve beverages to police who are here in an official capacity?"

Before he could mention that he actually hadn't come only to question Eloisa, that he'd also wanted to reassure himself that she was suffering no ill effects from witnessing the aftermath of Danica's attack, Eloisa spoke. "Mother, don't be so rude."

"I'm only being honest, dear."

"Regardless of what your deportment classes have taught you, Audra, I would still like some coffee," Mr. Carstairs said.

Mrs. Carstairs picked up a sterling silver bell. "Then I shall make sure it is on the way, Evan."

While her mother rang the bell, Sean glanced back at Eloisa. To his surprise and delight, she smiled for the briefest of moments before schooling her features into one of relative calm.

The bell was answered immediately by Worthy, who informed them that a teacart—with coffee for Mr. Carstairs—was being prepared by Mrs. Nelson and would be arriving within a matter of minutes. After the servant left, Evan Carstairs leaned forward on his elbows. "Have you apprehended Danica Webster's assailant yet?"

"Not yet, I'm afraid."

Not looking pleased with the answer, he shot another question

Sean's way. "Well? Is it the work of the Society Slasher?" Evidently, he was not concerned about offending the sensibilities of his wife and daughter.

"The evidence suggests that," Sean replied, thankful he was adept at answering questions without revealing very much at all.

"Well, then?" Mr. Carstairs barked impatiently. "What is taking you men so long to make an arrest?"

Knowing that Evan Carstairs's harsh tone was a result of worry for his daughter, Sean weighed his words carefully. "There are a great many reasons, including the possibility that the Slasher might be known to the women he attacked."

"Surely not," Mrs. Carstairs said with a decisive shake of her head. "Of course only a madman would be running about, cutting women with sharp objects."

"It is a crime that makes no sense, but please know we are doing everything in our power to discover the attacker as soon as possible."

Before either parent could fire off another question, Eloisa turned to him. "Lieutenant, please, could you tell me how Danica is recovering?"

His voice gentled. "I have not stopped by her house this morning, miss, but from what I heard last night, it seems she will be just fine. She may be slightly scarred, and I am sure she is shaken by the attack, but other than that, the doctors feel she will eventually recover completely."

"Her scars are unfortunate," Eloisa's mother said. "They'll ruin her chances for an engagement this season."

Eloisa winced. "Mother, surely you don't mean to sound so callous?"

"I'm only stating the truth."

Sean kept his silence, feeling helpless as he watched Eloisa clench her hands tightly together on her lap.

"We will have to pay her family a call soon, Eloisa," Mrs. Carstairs said. Smoothing her skirts, she added, "It can't be helped. I will need to do some thinking about what is the appropriate space of time. One mustn't be too eager to visit, you know."

"You will do what is right, dear. You always do," Evan replied. Turning to Sean, his tone turned abrupt again. "Now that that is taken care of, do you need anything else?"

As a matter of fact, Sean felt he needed many other things, the least of which was that he wished to have a moment to speak to Eloisa in private. It was obvious she would never tell him anything of worth in front of her parents.

Luckily, Sean was prevented from answering right away by the arrival of a brass cart filled with a teapot, a coffeepot, a tray of currant scones, and a dish of tarts. All of it looked finer than anything he'd had the pleasure of sampling.

"Looks like we're eating too," Mr. Carstairs stated. "Good. I'm starved."

"Yes, dear," his wife murmured as she began serving. "Detective, what would you like?"

Though the treats looked tempting, visions of his thick fingers maneuvering the fragile china cups propelled him to refuse the offering. "I'm afraid I must beg off. I appreciate your offer, but I must admit that I also came to ask Miss Carstairs more questions about last night."

Her father waved a hand curved around a lemon-curd tart. "Ask away, then."

After sharing a glance with Eloisa, Sean forced a thread of regret in his voice. "Forgive me, but it would be best if I spoke with her privately."

Mr. Carstairs paused in mid-bite. "Surely not."

Her mother sniffed. "You might not realize this, Detective, but it isn't quite appropriate for you to converse with Eloisa privately."

Against his will, his cheeks heated. "All the same—"

"Mother, I will be fine with Lieutenant Ryan," Eloisa interrupted.

Her mother, who had been filling her own plate, paused. "What could you possibly have to tell him that you couldn't say in front of us?"

"It won't take long," Sean said.

Mr. Carstairs's eyes narrowed. "What game are you playing, Ryan?"

Sean hardened his voice. "Not a one, sir. I'm only doing the job the city trusts me to do."

Mrs. Carstairs fussed with the lace bordering her wrist. "I still don't think it is proper for a young lady such as Eloisa to have private conversations with a policeman."

"There is nothing wrong with being a policeman, Mother," Eloisa retorted. "You know Owen Howard is one."

Mrs. Carstairs's cup rattled in her saucer. "Perhaps we could speak about this another time, dear."

Sean was about to point out that he was not there on a social call when Eloisa stood up.

"Lieutenant Ryan, I know it is cool outside, but perhaps you would allow me to show you the gardens in the back?"

Her mother sputtered. "Eloisa, this is not the time . . ."

Skillfully ignoring both of her parents, Eloisa smiled at Sean, the expression lighting her face. "My mother is right. The gardens are not quite the thing of beauty they are in the spring or summer, but they're still quite beautiful."

"Thank you, Miss Carstairs," he murmured as he got to his feet. "I would like to see the gardens very much." Turning to her parents, who now looked like a pair of disapproving statues, he nodded. "Again, I promise I won't be long."

And with that, he followed Eloisa out of the room and back down the hall. Her yellow dress once again captured his eyes and ignited his imagination. It emphasized her delicate features and golden hair. The bustle was ornate and carefully hooked in a cascade of intricate folds. Remembering how one of his sisters had once begged their mother for enough fabric to create such a gown but had been promptly turned down, Sean realized that he finally understood the beauty of such a dress. It was everything feminine in the world.

But, perhaps, that was Eloisa?

She stopped in the foyer as Worthy mysteriously appeared and handed Sean his coat and hat. Another footman appeared with a velvet-lined cloak for her. And then, with a flourish, Worthy opened the imposing front door again, and Sean followed Eloisa out.

Once the door was closed again, she smiled at him. "I'm so sorry about my parents and their blustering. I'm sure it was beyond horrible."

"Not at all." He was tempted to remind her that he'd seen far worse things than protective parents. That she should be grateful that they cared enough about her to do everything they could to keep her safe.

She wrinkled her nose. "How well you lie! I promise, when I informed my parents that you would be returning this morning, I had no idea they'd want to talk to you as well."

"They did everything that was proper," he said as he held out his arm for her to take.

As she took his arm, she gazed at him with a new, far cooler expression. "I am sorry. Am I making you uncomfortable?"

He had a lovely woman—the woman of his very secret affections—on his arm and was currently meandering along the grounds of a magnificent estate. Nothing should be wrong.

But the fact of the matter was that he was indeed uncomfortable, especially because though he would love to pretend that he was there only to chat about flowers and how pretty she looked in yellow, many other things needed to be discussed. "Miss Carstairs—"

"Couldn't we simply call each other by our first names?"

"If that is what you would like, Eloisa. My name is Sean."

Smiling, she nodded. "I know that."

They walked a little farther from the house and entered the gardens, where only carefully trimmed evergreen hedges and some white chrysanthemums decorated their path.

"Eloisa, I didn't lie when I said I needed more information from you about last night. About Danica."

"All right."

"Tell me what else you know of her."

The broad question seemed to make her worried. "I don't know her all that well."

"But she is in your social circle."

"She is, but I'm afraid it's a rather large social circle." After a slight pause, she said, "Danica and I were acquaintances at best. I haven't shared a private conversation with her in some time."

"I see."

"Also, I was with you when we heard the scream, Sean. So I certainly didn't see if she was conversing with someone before the Slasher attacked."

"So you saw no one at the party who was unusual? Who was not part of your usual, uh, crowd?"

"Other than a policeman in an ill-fitting suit?" she murmured, her eyes softly teasing. "No."

Though he knew she spoke the truth, he was still embarrassed about how out of place he'd looked. "I see."

"Couldn't Danica tell you anything?"

"Not at the moment. Miss Webster couldn't give us any clues besides the fact that he was large and wore a black cloak. It's regretful that she chose to be about the grounds alone."

She shivered. "He may very well attack again."

"I fear it is a possibility." Actually, he'd had a frank discussion with his captain about that the evening before. They'd come to the conclusion that the Society Slasher was becoming more aggressive and taking more chances with every victim. Captain Keaton had even predicted he would likely kill his next victim if he wasn't apprehended.

But of course there was no reason to share such a thing to a gently bred young lady like Eloisa.

Her bottom lip trembled. As he watched her fold into herself, keeping her emotions tightly contained, he had a sudden desire to wrap his arms around her and hold her to him.

"Eloisa, when we parted last night, and I said that I'd be returning, I'm afraid I led you to believe that I needed to question you further about last night's incident."

"Don't you? You've already asked me some questions."

"No. We were together when we heard the cry. Even if I thought you might know something—which I do not—you were not near the scene." After glancing up at the house, he stopped near a cove of evergreens. "Eloisa, I wanted to talk to you about your . . . incident."

Her expression turned perfectly blank. "There is nothing more to talk about."

"If it weighs on you, perhaps there is."

"I fear I have been feeling very sorry for myself, Sean. I know I am now . . . ruined."

"Not ruined," he interrupted. Far too roughly for her delicate sensibilities, he was sure.

She didn't say a word, only averted her eyes.

"Forgive me," he murmured. "Owen often says I have the manners of a mule. My cloddish attempt at showing my concern has just proven that to be true."

She blinked, then to what looked like both of their surprise, the corners of her lips curved up slightly. "Manners of a mule might be putting things a bit harshly."

"Still, I am sorry. It's just that I am concerned about your welfare. I certainly don't want to do anything to give you further discomfort." Even as he stumbled over his words, he prayed she at least understood that his heart was in the right place. While he knew it would be best for her to at last confide everything she was feeling to someone, he knew this was not the time. Perhaps he was not the person.

"Lieutenant, your concern could never bring me any measure of discomfort. Not compared to what happened." She stopped in front of him. Stared.

In that moment, he saw the shadows in her eyes, saw pain. And, he guessed, a desire to share that pain. Deciding to err toward bluntness, he said, "Do you want to speak about what Mr. Sloane did? As I said, nothing you could say would shock me, and nothing you tell me will be repeated."

She inhaled sharply.

He let her have that moment, remembering everything he'd heard about Douglass. He also remembered the rumors Owen had shared when they were investigating the wealthy heir's death. Rumors of philandering. Of him forcing himself on maids. And the startling rumor that he'd also forced himself on a young lady.

A young lady with such a spotless reputation, who was so well regarded, that even the idea that someone could treat her so harshly was difficult to imagine.

And as his eyes skimmed Eloisa's face, he noticed she was holding herself as if she could break at any moment. The shame that stained her expression. "You see . . . Douglass, he . . ." Her voice drifted off before gazing at him again, offering a silent plea for help.

And because he was the man, because he'd already privately promised himself that he would do anything and everything he possibly could to help her, he said the words. "Douglass Sloane raped you."

She visibly flinched. Inhaled, then at last nodded. "Yes. Yes, he did."

He turned away as anger coursed through him. He'd grown up on the outskirts of the tenements. So though he'd never actually experienced the life of the truly downtrodden, he'd certainly been aware of women being beaten and injured.

With thirteen years' experience on the force, he'd witnessed first-hand the injuries women could sustain when at the mercy of uncaring, violent men. "Were you injured?" When she paled, he wished he had bitten his tongue. In his efforts to help her move forward, his manner of plain speaking had shocked her. Of course she had no idea what damage could be done. No one did unless they'd seen the evidence for themselves. He still remembered the first time he'd seen a woman who'd been beaten and viciously assaulted. He'd promptly vomited, much to his shame.

Or did she know?

"Eloisa, do you, perhaps, still need to see a physician?"

She pressed her hands over her face. "I cannot even believe we are speaking of such things."

Unable to help himself any longer, he pressed his palms over her hands before gently guiding them away from her face. "This conversation is not the travesty, Eloisa," he said as he gently traced one finger along her jaw. "What was done to you was. Do you need assistance in locating a doctor? I could find one for you who would keep his silence."

She inhaled a shaky breath. "When I spoke of being ruined, I meant that my reputation will be if anyone ever finds out. I don't know what man would ever want a woman with my past."

Sean wished he were naïve enough not to understand what she meant. But of course he did. "That is not who you are. I promise you, you are far more than the results of one night's pain."

"Until very recently, I have been afraid to leave the house. Even though I know Douglass is gone, a part of me is still very afraid of being accosted again. I dream of it."

"That would be a natural reaction, I am sure."

"Perhaps. However, I am also at a loss of what to do with the rest of my life. I had planned to marry, you see."

"Why couldn't you still marry?"

"I would be duty bound to tell any fiancé what happened."

"So?"

"No man will want me when he discovers the truth."

"You are just as beautiful as you ever were," he said, stumbling over his last reticence. No longer afraid of them both remembering their stations in society.

No longer caring that he should never be saying such familiar words to a woman like her.

"But not as innocent."

"Beg your pardon, but I would have to disagree."

Her skin flushed, leaving him to chastise himself again. "I've meant no offense, though I can see now that I have said far too much. Please forget I ever said such a thing." Then to his surprise, she grasped his sleeve. "Lieutenant Ryan, Sean . . . last night, when you spoke of taking an off-duty paying job and giving the money to Hope House, it interested me."

Though he was still reeling from her disclosure, he allowed her to switch topics. "Yes. Hope House is a shelter for orphaned children, as well as some women who have nowhere else to go."

"When you get paid, will you deliver the money there yourself?"

"I had planned to. Or else I will send it along with my sister Maeve. She volunteers there."

Eloisa straightened her shoulders. "I think I would like to volunteer there too. Or at least visit. Or, perhaps, simply give a donation."

"That's very kind of you."

"I'd like to see Hope House. Would you, perhaps, consider escorting me there?"

"It is in the south side. Not at all fashionable." And, though his sister Maeve often worked there, and even his youngest sister, Katie, he was reluctant to expose Eloisa to such darkness. "I'm afraid it might not be the right avenue for you to serve. You might not find it safe."

"If you stayed by my side, would I be safe?"

"Yes." If he were at her side, he would make sure nothing untoward ever happened to her.

"Then I will be just fine."

Thinking of her elegant perfection in the midst of so many coarse persons gave him pause. "If you are certain?"

"I need something more than my fears. I need to think of something more than myself." New emotion filled her voice. "I need this, Sean. Please."

He could never refuse such a request. "Then I will take you, Eloisa."

"When?"

He smiled. "You are eager."

She looked down at her yellow slippers. Slippers that looked so fine and delicate, he was surprised the pebbles under her feet didn't bruise them. "I suppose I am."

"I have a day off on Sunday. Sometimes I stop by there on Sunday afternoons, around two o'clock, during the time my sister volunteers to give the regular staff some time off. Would that be an acceptable time?"

"I will make sure I am available. Could I meet you outside the lending library on Polk Street? If I walk there, my mother will simply think I am doing just that—taking a walk in a safe area with lots of others taking strolls. She is used to my doing that on a Sunday afternoon."

"If that is what you would like, yes," he answered, already regretting his promise. What was he doing, agreeing to spend time with a girl like Eloisa Carstairs? Agreeing to take her to the south side, to walk where trash littered the streets, where dirt and filth and suffering lived almost everywhere.

"Thank you. Would meeting a half hour earlier give us enough time to get there?"

Stepping away, he fastened a smile and nodded. "I need to go back to the precinct, but before I do, I would be very much obliged if you would show me the rest of these gardens."

"We both know that was merely a ruse to talk to you alone."

"Yes, but if I was your mother or papa, I'd be wondering why I haven't seen us in the gardens yet."

"Then by all means, let me show you my mother's pride and joy—her rose bushes."

"Lead on, Miss Carstairs. I can hardly wait to see them."

Her light, melodic giggle floated through the air, mingling with the faint scent of late-blooming roses.

And Sean admitted to himself that he'd never been more enchanted.

CHAPTER 5

So sorry, Mrs. Cameron!" Katie Ryan called out as she almost ran over one of the old biddies gossiping on one corner of Haversham Street.

"Katherine Jean, you will stop right this minute."

Though she would have loved to keep running as far as she could from those ladies and their eagle eyes, Katie turned around and faced her nemesis. "Ma'am?"

Mrs. Cameron—all four feet, eleven inches of her—glared at her imperiously. "Instead of apologizing in such a scattered manner, I would expect you to have learned by now to show some respect for your elders."

Knowing that if she didn't give Mrs. Cameron her due, her mother would never hear the end of it, Katie bit back her pride and proceeded to do whatever it took to smooth things over. "Yes, ma'am," she agreed, attempting to look contrite. "I am sorry. You are right, and that is a fact. I need to take better care of where I am going."

Thick black eyebrows, which Katie always thought looked like unfortunate caterpillars, edged together. "And where might you be going at this time of day?"

Katie stifled a groan of impatience. Mrs. Cameron and her best friend, Mrs. Munro, were always certain everyone's comings and goings were their business.

However, no good would come of being completely evasive. "Just going to have a spot of tea with my brother," she said, smoothing the fabric of her new, smart-looking navy dress. "Which is why I need to go. I'm late, I am. I'm trying to catch the 9:14 train."

Mrs. Munro, the woman who all agreed was only a slightly better version of Mrs. Cameron, narrowed her eyes. "And which brother might that be? Connor, perhaps?"

"I'll be visiting Sean, ma'am."

"Him?" Mrs. Munro curved her thin lips in distaste as her partner in crime leaned a bit forward.

Ah, yes. That was the usual response she received anytime she mentioned Sean. By turns, people in their borough were either proud of the affable Sean Ryan for raising himself out of their midst into the police force—and achieving a lieutenant's position, no less. Or they were holding firm to their distrust of the coppers as well as anyone who ever wanted anything other than what was expected of them.

Even their family was divided on whether to ignore or celebrate Sean's success. Their widowed mother was grateful for Sean's financial help, though she was always careful not to mention it in front of Connor or Billy, their eldest brothers.

Maeve, Michael Thomas, June, and she were nothing but proud of Sean.

And Mary Patricia? Well, it was a known fact that she didn't think about anything but her fiancé, Patrick Kelly.

Furthermore, mentioning Sean seemed to always lead into comments about the rest of her family, spurring speculation about what was going to happen to them all, given that their Da had been gone for some time now.

Which was now a very good reason why she should not touch the women's inquisitive looks and questions with a ten-foot pole. "Good day now, ladies. I really must catch the train. Otherwise I'll have to walk."

She turned and scampered off before they could respond. Then dodged and darted through traffic just in time to pay her ticket and board the train for Michigan Avenue, smack-dab in the hustle and bustle of the city, surrounded by tall buildings, tourists, bankers, financiers, and elegant ladies shopping. It was also the heart of where her brother was currently assigned.

She didn't want to be late, though. Sean didn't even know she was going to be there. But she didn't want to hear about his investigation from anyone else or from anywhere else.

Once she got off the train, she walked at a far more sedate pace to his precinct, a bit off Michigan Avenue. And while it was many, many steps away from the glamour of Prairie Avenue, it was an area most people would agree was a sight far better than hers.

But she still didn't feel completely safe there, most likely because there were no biddies standing guard at the edge of the street. And, of course, because according to the latest paper, the Society Slasher was still on the loose—and not even a great detective like her brother had been able to figure out how to capture him.

She took care to keep her face averted from most passersby as she stepped up the front steps of the precinct and opened the heavy door.

A uniformed officer at the reception desk, with a pair of graying pork-chop sideburns and a good extra thirty pounds, looked up in a harried way when she entered, then set down his pencil and smiled at her far more slowly. "Morning, miss. And what brings you here into our midst?"

Looking first at the nameplate in front of him, Katie nodded. "Good morning, Sergeant Fuller. I am here to see my brother."

After a pause, he winked. "Sorry, miss, but we've got a lot of men here. Who might your brother be?"

"He is Lieutenant Detective Sean Ryan."

Sergeant Fuller's gaze cooled, and her cheeks heated as she realized she said her brother's title with probably a bit too much pride.

However, she couldn't help it. She was so proud of him. He'd beaten so many odds, the least of which had been their brother Connor's constant jibes that Sean was forgetting where he came from. And that he was going against everything they were by joining forces with those who many Irish saw as men who had sold out to the rich and powerful.

And many others in the city thought were beyond corrupt.

"I'll go see if he is available, miss."

"Thank you."

He returned five minutes later, but instead of her brother in tow, another man was at his side.

He was tall, slim, and elegant looking, blessed with dark-blond hair that gently curled around his collar. The collar of what had to be a very expensive suit. Judging by the fit of his suit alone, Katie knew the fine cloth had been cut and sewn to his measurements. He might be standing in the police station, but it was obvious he was a gentleman through and through.

When he turned to her, she noticed he had a slight cowlick just above his right eyebrow. He also had brown eyes flecked with enough gold to remind her of *The Republic*, the famous golden statue welcoming visitors at the front of the World's Fair.

When the gentleman turned her way, she felt his gaze skim over her hair, her cheeks, her modest navy dress. And then, to her disconcertment, he smiled.

"This here is Ryan's sister, sir," the desk sergeant said with more than a bit of dry humor.

"Thank you, Fuller."

Then, at long last—though really all of it had taken mere seconds—he turned to her. "Miss Ryan?"

She stepped forward. "Yes?"

"I am Owen Howard, your brother's partner."

Though she attempted to control her expression, she knew she undoubtedly failed to keep her shock completely hidden.

This was Detective Owen Howard? The Owen Howard Sean had complained about for weeks when they'd first been assigned to each other? Sean had obviously forgotten to add quite a few details about his partner, the least of which was that Mr. Howard looked like one of those fallen angels she'd spied in the fair's art galleries and possessed a voice so cultured and fluid, it sounded like rich buttercream.

"Well, now," she murmured to herself.

When he raised an eyebrow, Katie belatedly realized that some kind of social nicety was no doubt in order. "It is nice to meet you, sir."

He inclined his head. "I'm pleased to meet you as well, Miss Ryan. However, I regret to tell you that your brother isn't here."

"He's not?" Immediately, her excitement deflated. All that rushing had been for nothing. Before she took the time to weigh her words, she blurted, "But I thought the both of you did your calls together. If he's not here, why aren't you with him?"

He blinked at her impertinence, but instead of being irritated, he looked amused. "I see you have been learning all about the way things run in the police department. You are right. We do go together on calls

most of the time. But not today. I'm afraid he had some private business to attend to."

Private business?

Before she could question him about that, Detective Howard
treated her to yet another charming smile. "His loss is my gain, however. If he were here, I would have never had the pleasure of making
your acquaintance."

"Oh!" she said through a gasp. Because who in her life had ever
spoken to her like that?

His friendly gaze turned piercing. "Is there something you need?
Something I can help you with?"

"Oh! Oh, I mean, no. I mean, it was nothing."

He didn't look like he believed her, which wasn't surprising, seeing as she was not good at hiding her emotions. Or lying. Or waiting.
Still staring at her intently, he said, "I see. Are you sure about that?"

"Yes. I merely had a question about the Society Slasher."

His eyebrows rose. "Why are *you* concerning yourself with the
Slasher, Miss Ryan?"

She flinched. Not from his words, but from his tone. His emphasis
on that "you" told her much about how he viewed her. Obviously he
wondered about her worry since all the papers said the Society Slasher
only targeted well-to-do ladies. And that it was apparent that she was
neither well-to-do nor wellborn.

The idea stung.

She took a step backward. "You know, I'll just ask my brother
next time we have supper together. I'll be going now."

He stepped closer, and to her dismay, took her elbow and guided
her away from the sergeant's desk and over to an alcove, where there
was a modicum of privacy. "You look upset. Are you in trouble?"

Trouble? No doubt he was sure a poor girl like her couldn't stay out of trouble. "I am not in trouble, sir. And I am not upset." She was pretty proud of herself. Here she was, just turned nineteen, but she was sounding almost like a grand lady.

A curious expression passed over his features before he looked beyond her shoulder. "Miss Ryan, where is your escort?"

Escort? She turned around and followed his gaze before completely understanding what he was implying. She shouldn't be alone, or at least no lady should be.

"I don't have one."

A muscle jumped in his cheek. "Do you mean to tell me that you traveled here alone?"

"Of course I did."

"Allow me to escort you back home then."

There was no way she was going to let him see where she lived. "Thank you, but as you said, I have nothing to worry about."

Confusion settled in his gaze. "What did I say?"

"You know, since I'm not a lady," she blurted before she remembered to be more refined.

"Miss Ryan, I neither said such a thing nor insinuated it."

He looked so affronted, she was embarrassed. "I meant no offense."

"But you have offended me," he said lightly. "Now, please tell me how you traveled here. Did you take a grip car?"

She didn't want to tell him. Actually, she didn't want to have another word with him.

Actually, she wanted to get as far away from him as she could before she completely embarrassed herself and before Sean returned and took her to task. "I took the train," she blurted.

"Then allow me to escort you to the station and wait with you until it arrives."

"I couldn't allow you to do such a thing."

"Yet, I wasn't asking, Miss Ryan." His voice was firm. Firm like steel.

Katie glanced around the station, noticing their conversation was being observed by Sergeant Fuller, most of his fellow officers, and even the few men and women who were sitting in chairs waiting for an audience.

With a sinking feeling, she realized Sean was going to hear of her appearance at the station, and that he most definitely would not be happy about it. No doubt she was in for a talking-to.

And so, because of that, she pulled away from Owen Howard, bid him good day, and darted out the door before he had the opportunity to reply. Fearing that he might attempt to catch up to her, she raced down the sidewalk, nearly running down a peddler.

"Watch it!" the peddler called out.

Katie ignored him and increased her pace, weaving around pedestrians, flower sellers, mothers with their children, and businessmen buying sandwiches from the street vendors.

Only when she reached the train station did she dare look behind her. But there was no one she knew. Nowhere could she find Detective Howard staring at her in distaste.

Making her realize that she'd done a very bad thing today. For the briefest of moments she'd imagined that they were equals. Though in heaven that might be true . . . on the streets of Chicago?

Nothing could be further from the truth.

CHAPTER 6

Eloisa's hands still felt tingly from where Sean had covered them with his own. Now, a full seven hours since he had left her home, as she sat in her boudoir, supposedly writing a letter to Thomas, she kept looking at her reflection in the mirror. And, yes, still holding up her hands to stare at them.

Just to see if her body could possibly carry any outward mark from the experience. But of course it did not. Just as she bore no outward effects of Douglass Sloane's attack. She looked the same as ever. It seemed it was possible to conceal almost anything.

The briefest of knocks signaled her maid's arrival. Juliet was almost her same age—just a year younger—and had lived and worked in the house since she was sixteen. Two years ago, when Eloisa had made her debut, she'd become Eloisa's personal maid, and they'd quickly formed a warm relationship.

"Good afternoon, Juliet."

"Good afternoon, Miss Carstairs," she replied in the same friendly but deferential way she always had, refusing to ever call Eloisa by her given name.

However, the adherence to rules didn't prevent her from raising her eyebrows at Eloisa after she glanced at her bed. "I came in to style your hair. But that is going to be difficult to do since you haven't selected this evening's gown."

Turning in her chair, Eloisa rested the side of her body against the chair's back. "I will. Eventually."

"Eventually won't be making your mother happy, miss. We both know that to be true."

"I know that it's barely six o'clock," Eloisa said as she rose to her feet and walked to the small chamber just beyond her seating area. Inside were dozens and dozens of gowns, each artfully sorted and organized by color and occasion. Two full-length mirrors flanked the gowns. Bandboxes filled with beautiful hats lined the shelves above the gowns. Slippers and kid boots in a plethora of colors awaited her in a custom-made cubby. It was a beautiful space, symbolic of all she'd been blessed with.

But at the moment it also served to remind her that her parents considered both Eloisa's pleasing looks and the magnificent array of gowns ammunition in their mission to obtain her a perfect match.

"I don't even recall what this evening's plans entail," she murmured. Poking her head out of the room, Eloisa looked at Juliet, who was pulling out Eloisa's silver-backed set of combs and brushes. "What am I doing, again?"

Clucking her tongue, Juliet said, "You are dining at home this evening, miss."

"Am I?" She was pleased about that. Pleased and surprised, and now very confused. "Well then, surely there's no hurry to arrange my hair or select a gown?"

"Miss Carstairs, you are staying home because your mother is hosting a dinner party." Looking amused, she added, "Your head must really be in the clouds today."

She'd forgotten. How could she have forgotten? "For what reason?" she asked hopefully. Maybe it was for her mother's ladies guild? Or another soiree to celebrate the fair?

"It's in your honor, Miss Carstairs," Juliet replied with barely concealed impatience. "Don't you remember last week when it was all arranged?"

"Now I do." With a sigh, she added, "It was just after Mother read Reid Armstrong's engagement announcement." Oh, her mother had been disappointed that Eloisa and Reid had never reached an agreement.

"To a housemaid." Juliet sniffed.

Eloisa knew Juliet had very definite ideas about not only gentlemen falling in love with domestics but also mere housemaids in general. Housemaids were only a step above kitchen maids, but below parlor maids and her own position, a lady's maid to one lady—Eloisa. Furthermore, Juliet took her position as the personal maid to the season's reigning debutante very seriously. She felt she was a step above most other domestics.

But even she wouldn't deign to step across the line and imagine herself engaged to a wealthy gentleman.

Still staring blankly into her dressing room, Eloisa murmured, "Who was invited? Do you recall?"

"I only remember Philippa Watson, James Nolt, Avery Kerrigan, Martin Upton, and Owen Howard."

Eloisa rolled her eyes. "I find Philippa tiresome. And Martin? Martin has moist lips." She still cringed as she remembered how it had felt when he'd kissed her bare hand.

Wisely, Juliet held her tongue as she joined Eloisa in the space. "Perhaps you'd like to wear your new lavender gown tonight? It's fetching and will set off your pearls to perfection."

"That will be fine." She stood in front of Juliet and let her unbutton her day gown, turning this way and that as her maid deftly helped remove the dress and its assortment of petticoats.

Then, after quickly washing her face and arms, she inhaled as Juliet placed one silk corset around her and began to tighten the stays. Once her bustle and crinolines were fastened in place, Eloisa found herself gazing at her fingers again.

And remembering the detective's touch.

"Juliet, are you even going to ask me about my caller?"

"The detective?"

"Of course."

Juliet carefully arranged the lavender gown so Eloisa could step into it. "Worthy says we're not to speak of him," she said as she began the process of fastening the gown's back.

"And why not?"

"Because he is common. And because your parents are suspicious of his presence here."

The stilted way Juliet was phrasing her assessment gave Eloisa pause. "Surely they don't think he's dangerous? He's a policeman on the hunt for the Slasher."

"I believe they're more concerned about the way he looks at you, Miss Carstairs."

Now Eloisa noticed Juliet's tone held more than a touch of humor. Once again, she gave the Lord thanks for putting Juliet in her life. Always, Juliet had her back and could be counted on to help Eloisa find humor in almost anything.

Even things that weren't all that humorous.

"I don't believe Lieutenant Ryan has done anything that could be construed as disrespectful."

"Worthy overheard your parents talking about him. They're worried about you."

"They really should find something else to think about besides my every move."

"Beg pardon, miss, but we both know different. I watched the two of you stroll through the gardens. He was gazing at you like you were the stars and the heavens combined."

"You thought so?"

"I know so." Juliet chuckled. "You look pleased."

"I can't help it. There's something about him that has caught my attention, though of course I know it shouldn't have. But yet . . . I think he's handsome."

"He's more than that, I tell you." For a second, Juliet's usual proper demeanor slipped, and she turned as girlish as one of the young maids in the kitchens. "He is so tall. And his eyes are so appealing. And a fine form of a man too. If you don't mind me saying."

"Now I am the one who is shocked," Eloisa teased. "I didn't know my proper Juliet even noticed anything beyond silk and taffeta." Or that she had crept close enough to clearly see Lieutenant Ryan's eyes.

"Oh, I notice things. All us girls do, if you want to know the truth." Smiling brightly, she added, "The Palace of Fine Arts is showing all kinds of marble statues. We girls got an eyeful, we did."

"Yet another reason to blame the fair for the downfall of our ladylike sensibilities," Eloisa teased. "And guess what? Lieutenant Ryan is going to escort me to Hope House on Sunday afternoon."

"Hope House? What's that?"

"It's a refuge for women and children who have nowhere else to go."

"It sounds like a commendable place. Is it for society ladies?"

"Of course not. For women of the lower classes."

"Poor doves."

"I aim to volunteer there."

"If your parents allow it," she pointed out.

"No, I'm going to go even if they don't."

"Miss Carstairs—"

"Juliet, I know what is expected of me, and I will . . . try. But I also want to do something for my heart and soul. It's important to me."

"For your heart and soul," Juliet echoed. She paused in her efforts to carefully hang up Eloisa's day gown. "Miss Carstairs, is this policeman the reason for all of your restless nights?"

Looking into her maid's eyes, Eloisa realized her night terrors hadn't gone unnoticed after all.

She also realized that she was not going to let anything interfere with her burgeoning friendship with Sean Ryan. Though she hardly knew him, he made her feel safe. More importantly, he also gave her a sense of peace.

And that was something she was not going to give up, at least not without a fight. Especially since he knew—and understood—what had happened to her.

"No," she said shortly. "But he might just be the reason I survive them."

"Is there another reason why you can't sleep?"

For a moment, Eloisa met her dear maid's gaze. Compassion shone through. And for a moment, Eloisa considered telling Juliet about Douglass's attack. About how she still dreamed of his hands on her. Dreamed she was trapped.

But if she told Juliet, there was always a chance that someone else in the house could find out.

And she could never risk that.

Crossing to her vanity, she sat down on the cushioned stool and stared at herself in the mirror. "Hurry now, Juliet. I find myself eager to get this evening's event over with."

"Oh. Yes. I mean, yes, miss. Of course, Miss Carstairs." After a pause, Juliet moved behind her and began taking down her hair.

And for the first time in weeks, it seemed that neither of them could think of anything else to say.

CHAPTER 7

Though his body was bone tired, Sean was finding that his head, on the other hand, was more than ready to spin at top speed over the day's events.

He couldn't control everything. That was the Lord's job, not his. He knew that. But even knowing that truth didn't always enable him to resist interfering when he shouldn't. Even his mother had always enjoyed reminding him about this time and again when he'd attempted to navigate not only his own life but those of his seven siblings as well.

"Ordering people about ain't going to make them mind ya, Sean," she always said with a wry shake of her head. "I told you that yesterday, I did."

He'd nod. Say he understood. But then ten minutes later, he would be trying to get his eldest brother, Connor, to stay out of the pub on his way home from the factory or struggling to convince his next oldest brother, Billy, to stay in school a little bit longer.

Of course, they hadn't listened. He hadn't completely believed they would, either. But he hadn't been able to stop trying to help them follow the right path. Sometimes it was near impossible to take a step back instead of attempting to help the way he saw fit.

As soon as he'd arrived at the station after his visit to Sable Hill, Sergeant Fuller had stopped him in his tracks with the news that his youngest sister, Katie, had taken it upon herself to visit him on her own.

While he tried to process that hard bit of information, Fuller kept talking away, as annoying as a magpie. He told him all about how Detective Owen Howard—their precinct's very own "gentleman detective"—had ushered Katie off to the side of the front office, chatted with her for a few moments in private, and then allowed her to dart out of there like her feet were on fire when he had offered to escort her back to the train station.

Yes, she'd set off alone, again—even though Sean had told her incessantly to never, ever go anywhere in the city without the accompanying presence of one of her brothers.

For the life of him, he couldn't imagine why his nineteen-year-old sister would have taken it upon herself to travel to the police station to see him at all.

He was still trying to make heads or tails of Katie's visit when he realized he needed to get to the bottom of why Owen Howard had decided to become so friendly with her. She was no lady, which meant she was far away from anywhere near his usual type of company. And she was a full twelve years younger than Owen's thirty-one.

All sorts of ideas filled him, none of them especially good. Katie was in need of a talking-to, Owen needed to be reminded that his sister was not available for conquest, and perhaps someone in the Ryan family had given her poor advice. Then, of course, there was the matter of Owen allowing Katie to run off. Had he upset her in some way?

He needed to get all the answers he wanted as soon as possible, if not sooner. But because that was unlikely, by the time Sean made his way to his desk, which was located directly next to Owen's, he was in something of an irritable mood.

Owen looked up from the report he was writing and smiled. "Glad you finally showed up. I've got news for you."

"I bet. Care to explain what happened with my sister?"

Owen lifted his chin and stared right back, all trace of good humor vanishing from his dark-brown eyes. "Care to explain why you're using that tone with me?"

"Sergeant Fuller told me Katie came here to pay me a visit."

"She did."

"Fuller also said you took it upon yourself to chat with her. Privately."

"I spoke with her near a pair of filing cabinets ten steps away from the sergeant, not that Fuller needed to feel compelled to tell you all about it."

"He seemed concerned."

"He needn't have been. I took it upon myself to speak with her for two reasons," Owen continued, his speech clipped and cultured, and his tone full of icy indignation. "One, since she came here uninvited and unannounced, I was worried about her welfare."

Sean couldn't argue with that reasoning. He was worried too. "Yes, well . . ."

With a frosty glare, Owen continued. "Secondly, because I am your partner, I assumed you would trust me with your sister. And that you would know I would keep her safe and take care of her for you." Raising a haughty eyebrow, Owen looked everything like the wealthy gentleman he was.

The look was also just cold enough to inform Sean that he'd been more than a little rude and ungrateful. "Sorry. I, uh, meant no disrespect."

After treating Sean to another long, meaningful glare, Owen nodded. "It's all right."

"It's just that I've told her over and over not to travel around the city by herself. It's like she didn't hear a word I said."

"No, it's like she's a female," Owen said with a wry twist of his lips. "It used to be a woman wouldn't enter any establishment without a proper escort. Now they'll barge into a fancy department store and spend a pretty penny without so much as a by-your-leave. Times are changing."

Sean refrained from pointing out that the shopping reference only pertained to women of Owen's station. Girls like Katie? It seemed they only barged into police stations. "So what did she want? Was she upset?"

"Not at all. She came here looking for you, but not because she was upset about something. She said she came here to speak with you about the Slasher."

"*What?*"

His utterance was so loud that he imagined more than a couple of men looked up from their desks in the other offices on their floor.

Owen leaned back in his chair and crossed his arms over his chest. "It seems she's been reading about the Society Slasher in the newspaper."

"I told her to give the *Tribune* a wide berth."

"Unfortunately, it doesn't seem as if she's listening to you about choosing her reading material either, Ryan. I feel the same way you do, of course. Especially since some of the editorials are especially lurid and inappropriate for gently bred females." He paused. "However, I'm sorry to share that your sister didn't appreciate my weak attempt to shield her."

"Katie always was obstinate."

"She also didn't appreciate my offer to see her home, or even to the train station. And I did try."

"I'm sure you did."

Owen pressed his lips together. "I'm sorry, Sean. But she's rather a stubborn force of nature."

"You don't know the half of it. Thanks again for seeing to her. I should have known from the start that your intentions were true."

"If she were my little sister, I'd be protective too. She's lovely."

"She is."

"She's rather lively too. Definitely no wallflower."

Sean noticed there was something new in his partner's voice. "She's a good girl, Owen."

"Of course."

"She's impulsive, strong-willed. I know that. But she also has my heart," he warned.

Casting a chiding look his way, Owen straightened. "You might be my superior, but I don't appreciate your insinuation. I wouldn't think of being anything less than a gentleman around her."

"Of course you wouldn't."

Still looking at him closely, Owen said, "Care to tell me how your visit to Miss Carstairs's house went?"

Thinking about how beautiful Eloisa had looked in her morning gown, the way she'd taken his arm in her gardens, and the earnest look in her eyes when she'd revealed that she wanted to visit Hope House, his throat felt tight. "She didn't have anything useful to add to our investigation."

"But how did your visit go?" Owen pressed, something new glinting in his eyes.

"Like I said, uneventful."

"No, you said—"

"Let's review what we have on the Slasher so far. Anything new?" Impatiently, Sean brushed a stray chunk of hair away from his eyes and reached for the report Owen had been writing when he'd arrived.

Owen lifted a handful of letters, each written on exceptionally fine-looking stationery. "Beyond the latest batch of angry correspondence, demanding that we become miracle workers and apprehend the man, oh, yesterday? No."

Though it was difficult, Sean did his best to put all thoughts of his sister and everything that had come to pass with Eloisa behind him and concentrate on what everyone in the city was counting on him and Owen Howard to do: locate and apprehend the Slasher before another innocent got hurt.

They'd spent the rest of the day at the station, focusing on the case. Time really was of the essence, and that meant that no matter how difficult and frustrating it was, they needed to go over all of their information again. And then again.

It was only by chance that he'd learned Katie was staying with Maeve that evening, and Maeve had already invited him for supper. Since he also needed to speak with Maeve about Hope House and Eloisa, Sean took both as signs that his evening would be exponentially more productive than his day had been.

Because any time spent in Eloisa Carstairs's company was not only a foolish idea and a prescription for trouble, but also a waste of investigative time. When he was with her, his work seemed to disappear.

CHAPTER 8

It took Sean forty-five minutes to get to his sister's home from the precinct station, but by the time he was halfway there, his body began to relax and his dark thoughts started to lift.

Instead of expansive lawns like the ones on Sable Hill, with each large, imposing home framed by well-manicured and meticulously maintained lawns and gardens, Maeve's neighborhood was composed of lines of neat row houses built of red brick and limestone. Instead of sparsely filled streets where elegantly appointed carriages toured behind matching horses, the narrow lanes were filled with children as their mothers, aunts, and grandmothers watched over them while gossiping over mugs of coffee and hot tea.

The contrast to Eloisa's world was as clear as night from day. It was also more than a few steps above where he and his seven siblings had grown up on Haversham Street. Where his mother and Connor still resided with twenty-year-old Mary Patricia and Katherine Jean, who'd only recently become all of nineteen.

No matter how many times he, Billy, Maeve, and Michael had encouraged them to move, his mother and eldest brother refused. They would never hear of the idea that the three youngest girls in the family would be better off somewhere other than the ramshackle area.

Instead, Connor would remind them that their father had worked tirelessly on the canals and tunnels and construction that built the city of Chicago, then in turn rebuilt it after the Great Fire. And that their neighborhood had been good enough for him, and therefore it was good enough for them all.

It seemed to look worse every time Sean visited. More than once he'd attempted to talk his mother into moving even a few blocks to the north. Maeve and Michael Thomas had done the same thing. But their mother had always refused, saying it was home and that Connor would protect them. Sean knew Connor would protect them. But he also knew Connor would encourage their mother to stay there out of sheer stubbornness rather than a real fondness for the place. No matter what, Connor was determined to show the rest of them that he knew best, even when he was being uninformed and narrow-minded.

Obviously, Katie wasn't the only Ryan with a stubborn streak a mile long.

Now, as Sean turned the corner onto Maeve's street, he felt the weight of a dozen pairs of eyes watching his arrival. He'd long ago stopped being surprised about the varying degrees of curiosity and contempt for his chosen occupation. His job on the police force was a source of talk in the neighborhood where they'd grown up, and here in Maeve's as well. A varied combination of suspicion, pride, and disdain was directed at him, especially given his success in his job.

When he saw his sister's neighbor, he tipped his hat. "Afternoon, Mrs. Henry. I hope you're doing well this fine evening."

She leaned her elbows up on the brick balustrade, her faded-chestnut curls neatly pinned up under a serviceable gray cap. "Well enough, I suppose. And what brings you here to our neck of the woods?"

"My sisters."

"You here to see the two of 'em?" she asked with good humor.

He wasn't surprised that she was aware Katie was staying the night. "Hard to pass up an occasion to see them both. I'm hoping they'll indeed take pity on their bachelor brother and feed me a hot supper."

"I seem to remember hearing something about Maeve cooking a roast this evening."

"If that's the case, you've just made me a happy man, Mrs. Henry."

Corrine's gray eyes softened. "Maeve's little Jemima is the spitting image of your aunt Molly, God rest her soul."

He crossed himself, the mirror image of Corrine. "If Jemima becomes half the lady our Molly was, the angels would be pleased."

Corrine smiled. "You always were a charmer, Sean." She made a shooing motion. "Out with you now. You know by now half the neighborhood has told Maeve you're coming her way. If you don't hurry, she's apt to think something happened to you."

He gave a look of mock horror. "Can't have that. I'll get over there double-time then." Tipping his hat again, he said, "And please do give my best to your man."

"I will do that." Almost grudgingly, she added, "Take care of yourself, Sean Ryan. It's dangerous work, what you do."

"I'm always careful." He winked.

"I'm sure you are." She chuckled. "Except when you are not."

He was still smiling about Corrine's quip when he arrived at Maeve's house. He could hear her silly dog barking up a storm and her daughter, Jemima, egging him on, followed by Maeve's reprimand.

So many things in his life never changed.

After the briefest of knocks to signal his arrival, he opened the front door. The entryway led directly into a rather cramped living room, where the dog was playing with Jemima on the floor.

When both Jemima and Maeve looked his way, he said, "Maeve, you really should stop being so cruel to my niece."

"Uncle Sean!" Jemima cried as she scampered over to him and wrapped her arms around his thighs. "Mama didn't tell me you were coming by."

"That's because I wasn't sure if he'd actually show up," Maeve quipped. "Every time we try to make plans, you break them, Sean Ryan."

"Lot of things to take care of in the city, Maeve," he murmured as he looked around the room, then at last met Katie's gaze. His mouth tightened when he saw his younger sister blush.

Looking from him to Katie, Maeve raised her eyebrows. "Looks like I've discovered the reason you decided to take me up on my offer of supper."

"I do need to speak to Katie, but I have a favor to ask of you too."

Maeve paused, the damp kitchen towel that had been wrapped around her waist now in her hands. She smiled, though there was a look of worry in her eyes. "A favor?"

"I hope you won't mind me asking." He sniffed the room in an appreciative way. "I'm hoping your offer of a home-cooked meal is still on the table?"

"Jemima has already set you a place."

"Thank you, Maeve."

"Now, your hint of a favor has sparked my interest. Do tell."

"I will," he said before turning to their youngest sister. "As soon as Katie and I have a little chat."

Crossing her arms over her chest, she turned and glared at Katie, then turned back to Sean. "What's she done?"

"Nothing," Katie said.

"We'll see about that," Sean murmured.

Maeve glanced at their sister again. "How about I join you both and we discuss it, the three of us? You know I'll hear about it sooner or later."

"I'd rather speak to her privately, if you don't mind." When Maeve looked ready to argue, he lowered his voice. "I understand how you feel, but let me talk to her first."

"All right then." Turning to her daughter, she clapped her hands once. "Come along into the kitchen, Jemima. I want you to help me work on supper."

When they were alone, Katie's expression became more shuttered. "I should have known you would come by here."

"Yes, you should have. I heard quite a story when I returned to the station today," he said as he led her to a pair of chairs near the fireplace. "Care to tell me why my little sister visited a police precinct?"

"I wanted to see you."

He looked her over carefully, taking in her features, the expression in her eyes. Only then did he realize he was breathing more fully. He'd been worried about her.

"Why did you decide to come see me, Katie?"

"It doesn't matter."

"We both know it does. I recall telling you quite distinctly that I don't want you there."

"Is it because you're embarrassed of me?"

Where on earth had that come from? "It is because the police station is a place for criminals, Kate," he corrected gently. One would hardly want one's little sister in the midst of those folks. It had been bad enough when she'd convinced their mother to visit him at the precinct station once or twice when she was a little girl.

Her eyes widened, but she remained quiet.

And so he tried another tack. "Detective Howard said you arrived there by yourself." His voice hardened. "And that you left by yourself."

"That is hardly noteworthy." She tilted her nose up a bit.

He wondered when she'd adopted that move! Struggling to maintain his patience, he said, "It is noteworthy when Detective Howard told me you refused his escort. And when I've cautioned you to never go about by yourself, especially now."

"Your reasons were silly, Sean. Everyone knows the Society Slasher is only going after ladies. Not girls like me."

"What do you mean, girls like you?"

When she blushed and looked down at her feet, he knew he had touched a nerve. "Was Detective Howard rude to you?"

"Of course not."

Of course not. "Then why wouldn't you allow him to see you back to the train station?"

She gazed at him for a long moment. Then she uttered, "Because I know he doesn't think I'm worth much."

"Say again?"

"When I told him I was there to talk to you about the Slasher, he told me I shouldn't have to worry about him, Sean."

There was a bitterness in her voice, but he couldn't quite understand its source. For a second, he wished he had taken Maeve up on her offer to join them for this discussion. He had a feeling only a feminine mind was going to be able to navigate Katie's glares, utterances, and half-formed statements.

"And why did this bother you?"

"Because it was obvious he thought I was very far from a lady."

"I don't think that was what he meant."

"It is what it felt like."

"What do you know about the Slasher?" he asked, deciding it would be better to concentrate on that instead of Katie's grievance with his partner.

"I know there was another victim last night, and I read that you were there, investigating."

"That is true."

"I wanted to make sure you were okay."

"Katie, there is no reason for you to worry about me."

"But the papers say all kinds of things about him."

Knowing just how merciless this assailant was, how hard it was to view his damage, made Sean's tone harsher than he intended. "You shouldn't have been reading about the Slasher in the first place."

"I'm not a child, Sean. I am nineteen now, you know." She tilted her head in that way she was now so fond of doing, so full of sass. "Plus, I'm interested in the papers."

"Because?"

"Because I might want to be a reporter one day."

A reporter? Oh, but he really should have had Maeve stay in the room. He decided to close this conversation, and soon. "Let me tell you this one more time, Kate. Stop traipsing around Chicago on your own."

"Sean—"

"And don't continue visiting police stations, either. If you have a need of me, send word. I'll come find you as soon as I can."

"But—"

But he wasn't done. His voice getting louder, he bit out, "And since I'm giving you advice—"

"Which I did not ask for."

"I sincerely hope you reconsider any idea about writing for the newspapers. You know how the writers of the papers sensationalize everything. Even things that don't need to be sensationalized."

Her eyes widened. "The Society Slasher does things that are really, really bad, doesn't he?"

There was no need to prevaricate. "Yes."

"Sean, the last two times the Slasher has attacked, you've been in the area."

"So have other men on the police force."

"You might get injured. What if he tries to attack you?"

"No one is going after Irish policemen, Katie."

She slumped. "I suppose even a serial criminal knows the difference between the fine ladies and gentlemen of Chicago society and the likes of us."

Now he understood where her hurt lay. And he ached for her. It was a hard lesson to learn, that no matter how good a person's character, no matter how strong a man like him might be or how beautiful a girl like Katie was . . . for some people, those things would never be enough.

He drew in a deep breath. "Kate, I promise, Detective Howard wasn't saying you shouldn't have to worry about the Slasher because you aren't a lady. He said that because he couldn't imagine a sweet girl like you reading about such disturbing events in the newspapers."

She perked up. "Truly?"

"Really. In his world, women are kept away from the newspapers. The men in their lives filter everything. He was trying to do that."

She swallowed, then slowly looked at him in wonder. "Detective Howard was trying to protect me this morning, wasn't he? He was trying to look out for me, just as if I was someone special. Just like I was one of those ladies shopping on Michigan Avenue."

Sean privately thought Owen was looking out for her because

she was his partner's little sister. Because she was young and fresh and innocent looking. Probably also because he thought she was beautiful—and she was.

But Sean also knew what Katie needed to hear.

And so he said the words that he ached to be true. "Yes, dear. He wanted to protect you because he considers you a lovely young lady."

When her blue eyes sparkled with happiness, Sean forced himself to smile too.

She didn't need to know that he would beat up Owen Howard in a heartbeat if he even thought twice about having designs on Katie Ryan.

No, she didn't need to know that at all.

CHAPTER 9

Do I want to know what happened with you and our little sister?" Maeve asked Sean when he entered her kitchen, feeling mildly uneasy by the conversation that had just taken place with Katie in the other room.

"Probably not," he said.

On his way over, he'd been prepared to discuss Katie's reckless behavior with his older sister and get her assurances that she would help him redirect their youngest sister's energies. He'd been ready to tell Katie how disappointed he was in her behavior and do anything he could to make sure Maeve was on his side.

He knew he was justified in his feelings too. Even without the Slasher wreaking havoc all over the city, there was plenty for a young girl to be worried about. Especially a pretty girl like their Katie was.

And though at nineteen he'd already been on the police force and Maeve had been married, Sean had been determined to conveniently forget those things and focus on just how young and naïve their Katie was. He'd been willing to risk her tears and anger if he could be assured that his adored sister would stay safe.

But after talking to her, he'd had a change of heart. He wasn't Katie's father, and she already had one brother acting as a father figure. Sean was also coming to the conclusion that the two of them were a lot alike. Both he and Katie had always had a desire to be seen for what they were beyond a first glance. He knew that was a hard enough road to navigate without him stifling her further.

"Sean?" Maeve waved a hand in front of his face. "Hello? You know I'm expecting more of an answer than that."

"Katie is fine."

"She is not fine."

"All right, then how about this? At the moment, I don't feel there's anything to worry about."

A line formed between her eyebrows. "Truly?"

He shrugged. "She's being a bit impetuous. Again."

"More than that."

He nodded, giving Maeve her due. "Even so, I think in the long run it might be best to not make a big deal out of it. You know how June was at that age," he added, even though he knew Maeve didn't need any reminders of just how flighty their recently married sister had been at nineteen.

"I didn't think any of us were going to survive June's eighteenth year, let alone her nineteenth."

"She just about drove all of us to drink," he teased. "Mom threatened to lock her in her room more than once. I wish she actually had."

"It wouldn't have mattered if she had. June would have simply climbed out the window." Rolling her eyes, she added, "Which she did."

"Billy caught her once. Threatened to paddle her backside."

"That, too, might have settled her down. But, of course, our Connor wouldn't hear of it." Grabbing a fresh dish towel, Maeve wiped off a mixing bowl she'd just washed. "June always was our eldest brother's favorite."

"And from the time she was born, she's also had him wrapped around her little finger."

Remembering how each of them caused a fair bit of drama over the years, Sean said, "If we could survive June, I imagine we'll survive Katie too."

"I hope so. I've got my own children to raise now. Jemima and Jack Junior are enough for me at the moment."

Walking closer, he leaned against her kitchen cabinets. "Before either of them claims your attention—I assume Jack is out with his friends somewhere until supper—I think I'd better get to the other reason I'm here."

Maeve picked up a baking pan and dried it. "I was hoping you'd get to that."

"I'm here to beg a favor."

She looked him over closely, her perceptive gaze seeming to take in whatever emotion he was wearing on his sleeve. "Ask away, but I'm afraid I don't have time to sit and chat while you take your sweet time getting to the point. While you get your thoughts together, I'm going to keep working on supper. I sent Jemima outside."

"You sure you don't mind me staying?" He didn't want to take any food her family needed.

"Positive. I invited you, didn't I?" Maeve looked over her shoulder as she began washing carrots and potatoes. "We've got plenty tonight, brother. We'd love to have you join us."

"Thank you for that."

Maeve waved a hand. "It's nothing. Now, how about you stop

dragging your feet and tell me a little bit about this favor you'd be needin'?"

"I've met a young lady who is interested in visiting Hope House."

Setting down a potato, she frowned. "What happened? Did she lose her man? Is she homeless?"

He held up a hand. "It's nothing like that. She wants to volunteer there."

"Volunteer? What, she got an excess of time on her hands?" she joked.

"As a matter of fact, she does. But it's more than that," he added quickly. "She intends to help Hope House financially. Or become a benefactress or something like that."

"A benefactress?" Maeve tilted her head to one side, staring at him hard. "What kind of girl is this?"

"A nice one." *A special one*, he added privately.

A look of pure gladness crossed over her sister's features. "You've met someone? When did this happen? And where? Do I know her?" She paused. "Is it Jamilyn Mikenney? She's always had her eye on you, but I've never been of the mind that she was good enough for you. Did she finally get her claws in you?"

"Stop, Maeve. It's not Jamilyn."

"Is it Trinny Jamison?"

"It's no one you know."

"If I don't know her, how do you know her?"

"I met her through work, but over time she's become my . . . friend of sorts." Of course, this was exaggerating things a bit much. He'd only really talked to her three times—all in the last twenty-four hours.

And he couldn't exactly say they were now friends. Actually, he felt it was impossible to categorize his relationship with her. She seemed to trust him, while he was basically smitten.

Yes, their relationship was an interplay of disparities, he pre-sumed. He thought she was beautiful and refined. Enchanting. She was everything he always imagined a woman could be, and he counted the moments spent in her company as some of his most gratifying.

For Eloisa, however, there was a very good chance that when she did ever think of him, it was only as someone who was a bare step above a butler. Though, now that he thought about it, the Carstairs' butler, Worthy, was no doubt two steps above him on the social scale.

Still looking at him intently, Maeve wrinkled her nose. "What did you mean when you said she was your friend? What kind of woman would take up a friendship with you?"

"With me?"

"Sean . . ." She gritted her teeth.

Enjoying the novel experience of teasing her—really Maeve was the last person to ever enjoy being teased—he said, "I'm sure you didn't mean that in quite the way it sounded. At least, I hope not."

"Oh, away with you. You know what I meant. Who is she?"

Suddenly, he was rethinking his idea. How could he describe Eloisa Carstairs so a woman like Maeve would understand? "She's simply a young lady I met while working on my current case."

Maeve glanced at him sharply. "On a case, you say?" After a moment, she looked horrified. "Sean, you are trying to uncover the Slasher! Was she attacked?"

"No, but she has been places where he was."

"Truly?" Another line formed between her eyebrows. "But I thought you said this man stalks society girls. I mean, that's what the *Tribune* has been saying."

"They're right in this case."

"So she is part of society. And she is rich too. And she has struck up your acquaintance. I'm finding this a right bit intriguing."

"Maeve, there's no reason for us to go down this path. I came to ask you a favor, not to divulge details about my personal life."

"I wasn't aware you had a personal life."

"I do, and I'd like to keep it that way. Personal." Well, he hoped he would have one eventually.

"Your cheeks are flushed. That means something. What is it about this girl?" she continued, her manner as feisty as a Doberman's. "Is she special to you?"

"Perhaps she could be if our circumstances were different. However, I doubt Eloisa would ever even be permitted to be special to a man like me."

"Eloisa is her name?" she asked slowly.

"Yes. Eloisa Carstairs."

Her lips turned up. "That's a pretty fancy name. And what do you mean by 'be permitted'?"

"About what you would think. She has more than one person overseeing her."

"Overseeing her? Whatever for?"

"You know, to make sure she doesn't suffer a social mishap." Inwardly, he rolled his eyes. Since when was he an authority on such things?

"A social mishap," she repeated under her breath.

Sean could have kicked himself. The last thing in the world he wanted to do was reveal his feelings for Eloisa. But he didn't seem to be able to do anything in a half-hearted way where she was concerned.

After tossing her sliced vegetables in with her roast, Maeve turned to him. "This Eloisa sounds like a very grand young lady. Very high and mighty, she does."

"She is." Was that a note of pride in his voice? A mistaken note, undoubtedly. "She's very pretty. And a young lady of some repute."

"And you are seeing her?" This time, she wasn't even trying to hide the incredulousness and humor in her voice.

"Not like that. As I told you, we've become friends, of a sort. Which brings us back to Hope House. Would you please meet us there Sunday and show her around the place? She's interested in learning more about it."

"Hope House ain't that kind of place, Sean. The last thing those girls there need is some uppity rich lady looking down their noses at them."

"She is nothing like that."

"They're all like that."

"Maeve, will you do this for me?"

"I don't see why I should. I got far better things to do than show a spoiled rich girl how the other half lives."

"Because I've asked you to. Could you do that, Maeve? Could you meet us at Hope House on Sunday afternoon? She wants to take a look around."

"Sean—"

"Please, Maeve? Eloisa needs something more than I can give her. And I hate to admit it, but I've already told her you would be there."

"Sean." She glowered, but little by little her exasperated expression lifted, and she slowly smiled. "I'll be there at two o'clock. If you two come traipsing in a quarter after four, don't expect me to still be standing around."

"Never."

"I hope she's worth it."

She was. Though they'd only had a few conversations, Eloisa was fast becoming someone very important to him. Not that it mattered, of course. It wasn't as if they would ever have a future. "She's just a friend, Maeve. Just a friend who needs to give a helping hand."

She sighed. "Now that that's settled, is there anything else you'd be needing, besides a home-cooked meal and me helping out your lady-friend?"

"Only a pretty smile from you."

"Jack would say you'd have to earn those."

"No, sister. Jack would say you should smile a lot more, seeing as he's such a good man and takes good care of you."

At last her posture softened, as it always did when she talked about her husband. "I smile at my man when it's warranted. And it ain't always warranted, you know. He's a good man, but he's only a man."

"You're a hard woman, Maeve," he stated, thickening his Irish accent so he sounded like one of the dock workers fresh off the boats.

She chuckled low, letting him know the tension between them had been broken. "Oh, Sean. I promise you this. You don't know the half of it!"

CHAPTER 10

Hope House was located in a section of the city Eloisa had only passed through by bus or elevated train. The area wasn't a particularly dangerous one, but it was certainly not a place she'd ever had the occasion to visit.

Though now, as she walked up the narrow lane where the old house resided, Eloisa came to the realization that her existence had been even more sheltered than she'd previously thought.

The more she ventured out and about, the more she realized that she really hadn't been to many places in the city at all. The more she gathered her courage and ventured beyond Sable Hill and its surrounding areas, the more it was apparent that she had much to discover about her hometown.

It made her excited and optimistic for her future. Made her wonder if the Lord had decided to enter her life again. Maybe even possibly leading her onto a new path where she could learn to see everyone and everything with his eyes. See that there was beauty everywhere . . . she'd only need to be brave enough to look.

Sean glanced her way, concern flashing in his hazel eyes. This, she was learning, was a frequent occurrence. From the moment he'd met her at the lending library, he'd stayed firmly by her side, even going so far as to glare at men on the grip car who had eyed her just a little too closely. Knowing that he took her welfare so seriously made her feel safe.

In fact, the longer she was in his company, the more she felt at ease.

No, it was more than that. She felt free. Free to be herself.

When she glanced his way again, she was surprised to see that a hesitant curiosity now shone in his eyes.

"So, what do you think of it, Miss Carstairs?"

Forcing herself to look back at the house, she attempted to come up with the perfect descriptor. "It is intriguing."

To her pleasure, he grinned. "Now there's a polite way to describe it."

She couldn't resist smiling as well. Eloisa was slowly coming to realize that when the lieutenant relaxed, his faint Irish accent grew a little stronger, and his smiles became more frequent. Unfortunately for her, those things made his already handsome features mesmerizing. One warm look from him made her heart beat a little faster and tugged at her carefully built defenses.

With a firm resolve, she turned away from him and back to the house.

What an architectural muddle it was! A sprawling structure, its two stories and attic were a bohemian blend of limestone, whitewashed bricks, and old-world charm. She imagined that one could easily get lost inside it. Perhaps not even be found for days.

At one side of it lay a small park, really little more than a mass of abandoned land and weeds. On the other side rested a row of cramped houses, each looking in danger of falling apart during the next winter storm.

"I'm not merely being polite, Sean. I truly am intrigued by its possibilities. This house has character. Potential too."

"I suppose it does have potential."

Eloisa turned to him, then felt her neck flush as she realized he was looking at her and not at the house. Another rush of nervousness coursed through her. Something was happening between them that she wasn't sure she was ready for.

Clearing her throat, she asked, "Uh, what was Hope House originally, Sean?"

"It was originally constructed as a home for some high-and-mighty banker. When the area started to decline, he sold it to a developer. It was then used as a hospital. Later, an asylum."

She shuddered. The house's history was indeed varied and, she decided, somewhat dark. Imagining the cluttered rooms inside, and what the occupants who had lived in them must have been like, she wondered if it really could become worthy of its current name—Hope House.

Sean continued. "Eventually, this place became a boarding house. Then, just three years ago, a widow from Maine decided to give it its new identity." He flashed a quick smile. "Next thing we knew, she was telling anyone who would listen about this place of refuge. Before long, women and children were moving in. My sisters—especially Kate and Maeve—volunteer there."

"And the women and children are doing all right?"

"Maeve says they are." He clasped his hands behind his back. "It goes to show you that almost everything and nearly everyone can rise out of the ashes."

She liked how he'd used the words *almost* and *nearly*. It made his statement more believable. "That's a lovely sentiment, don't you think?"

Her escort scoffed. "Lovely?"

A cool wind blew down the street, rustling leaves as she shrugged. "It's nice to imagine that almost anything or anyone can be repurposed. Become useful."

"I believe that to be true. But, uh, I feel I should warn you that only small miracles are being done here." His voice was full of doubt as he glanced around the rather rundown area and then stepped a little closer. "Miss Carstairs, are you sure this is where you want to spend your time? I can't help but think that other places in far better areas would be just as pleased to be at the receiving end of your attentions and money."

"Your suggestion is a bit premature, don't you think? I haven't even stepped foot inside."

"I merely don't want you to feel like this is the only place where you might do some good." Before she could say a word, he rushed on. "For example, I have heard that many women do good works with their church. Or serve on committees. Or, um, attend teas."

"Perhaps I should point out that I have more experience than you with charity work and volunteer opportunities for young women."

He flinched at her tart tone. "Forgive me. I meant no disrespect."

"I know you want to protect me, Lieutenant, and I'm grateful for your concern. But I already am quite active in the ladies' auxiliary club at my church. Furthermore, our city's library already has a large share of benefactors. The last thing it needs is someone like me to get involved. But this place certainly does."

"But—"

"No buts." She cut him off as she started up the home's front walk. "This is a place that has reinvented itself several times, much like its occupants."

He scratched his brow. "You might be romanticizing things a bit. The women and children here are starting over. However, they are much like this area. They didn't have a whole lot to begin with. Now they're only more rundown."

She was surprised he didn't see the bigger picture.

Or was it that he didn't think she was capable of seeing it? "No matter what the history, here this house still stands, in all its glory. Giving hope."

"Such that it is." The lieutenant cast a wary eye her way. "I still feel that you might be imagining that things are a bit too rosy."

"Will your sister be here?"

He grimaced. "Maeve promised she would." He held out his arm. "Shall we go inside?"

"Yes. Yes, of course." A flutter of nerves filled her stomach as she lightly placed her gloved hand on his forearm. The muscles under his coat bunched, stiffened, as if preparing to bear her weight.

Or maybe it was just a simple reaction from her touch.

Looking at her hand on his coat, she couldn't help but notice the differences between them. Her glove was white and one of many specially made to her measurements. His coat jacket was made of inexpensive worsted wool, undoubtedly slightly scratchy to her touch.

At that moment, as they ascended the steps, she was suddenly very worried she was overdressed. Her gown of pale-blue worsted wool, which seemed so plain and utilitarian in her elegant bedroom, now seemed far too fancy and pretentious for the work her heart hoped to accomplish. A tremendous wave of apprehension flowed through her.

She might not know this area, or what exactly the women and children had gone through, but she'd made it her life's work to study her surroundings and the people within them. Always, she'd been able to fit in.

Unfortunately, she had a terrible feeling she was about to be disregarded without saying a single word, simply because she looked so out of place.

"Do I look all right?" she blurted when they were almost at the door. "I mean, do I look appropriate? Or terribly overdressed?"

Sean's head whipped toward her. First he met her eyes, then, with a long, slow look, his gaze slowly fluttered downward, skimming her lips, her neck, her shoulders, her clothes.

She stood straight and proud, unsure, and too conscious of the new flutters that filled her. This time, though, they had nothing to do with her insecurities and everything to do with a handsome man's appraisal. This man.

At last he exhaled. "You look beautiful, Eloisa." He cleared his throat. "I mean, you look fine."

"You don't think I will stick out like a sore thumb?" She fingered the fabric of her sleeve. "Perhaps I should have worn a different dress."

"A different dress wouldn't have made a difference. Nothing would have."

"You sound so certain."

"I am." As if he couldn't help himself, he ran a thumb along the length of her jaw. "I think even in burlap you would look beautiful. It simply cannot be helped." While she digested his words, realizing that she'd just received one of the sweetest compliments in her life, he rested his hand on the door handle. "Come now. Let's go inside before my sister gets too impatient."

When she felt him rest his palm on the small of her back, carefully guiding her forward, she smiled. "Well, that mustn't happen. I never thought I'd see a man like you afraid of his sister's wrath."

"Maeve has two children of her own and could easily manage a family of twelve," he said dryly. "She certainly did her best to manage me when we were growing up. Believe me, you don't want to get on her bad side."

A giggle escaped her just as Sean opened the door and motioned for her to precede him.

As he closed the door behind him, she realized their arrival had indeed been anticipated. A handful of scrubbed boys and girls dressed in utilitarian dresses and shirts and trousers were watching her the way so many people examined the curiosities at the World's Fair.

Several women stood behind them or off to the side. Those women's expressions showed nothing but unease and suspicion.

And right then and there, Eloisa knew Sean Ryan's words had been correct. Nothing she wore was going to make her fit in here. She was out of her element, and everyone in this entryway knew it. Including her.

Hoping to show that she wanted to make friends, she met their eyes and smiled softly. "Hello."

Not a single person responded. If anything, Eloisa's weak attempt at friendliness seemed to arouse even more disdain. She tried again. "I'm pleased to meet you all. My name is Eloisa Carstairs."

One of the younger women's eyes widened, then the corners of her lips lifted. "That you are."

Eloisa wasn't sure what that meant. She certainly wasn't sure what she was supposed to say. Confused, she glanced at Sean.

A curious mixture of resignation and irritation tugged on his features. After gazing at her softly, he turned to the cluster of women. "Come now, everyone. No need to be putting on airs, right? I told Miss Carstairs here that you were a friendly group," he continued in the same tone of voice. It was a bit coarser than his usual tone with her. A bit deeper.

Little by little, the postures of the assembled women relaxed. One almost smiled.

"Sean's always been a charmer, he has," one lady said as a dimple appeared in her cheek. "So much so, it's a wonder that he hasn't been snapped up by a whole host of eager girls on Haversham Street."

"Those days were a long time ago," he mumbled.

"Not so much," a dark-haired woman snapped, giving Eloisa a very strong impression that she'd just met his sister.

"Maeve, thank you for meeting us here," he said.

The woman he was speaking to, a striking brunette with blue eyes the same color as Lieutenant Ryan's, raised her eyebrows. "I told you I would be here. 'Course, you didn't tell me you would keep me loitering about in the entryway while the two of you chatted on the front stoop for a good ten minutes about Lord-knows-what."

Eloisa had no idea why Maeve was needling him, or why all the women there were looking at her like they hoped she would turn away and leave them in peace as soon as possible.

However, she was determined to make a good impression. Not wanting to wait for Sean to formally introduce her to his sister, she stepped forward and held out her hand. "Mrs. O'Connell, it's a pleasure to meet you. Thank you for having me here. I don't wish to inconvenience you too greatly. I just wanted to get a tour, and your brother was kind enough to offer his escort."

Maeve stepped forward and grudgingly shook Eloisa's hand. "It weren't too much trouble, miss. We don't get cause to put on our Sunday best and mingle with our betters much, anyway."

"Maeve, mind your tongue," Sean warned from behind her.

"I'm only speaking the truth."

"And then some." His voice gentled when he looked at Eloisa. "Given that this is a shelter for women and their children, I am not allowed to go any farther than this entryway. But I'll wait for you here until you're ready to leave."

"Are you sure you don't mind? I could get home on my own." At least she hoped she could.

"I don't mind at all," he said, his eyes warm and impossibly kind. "It would be my pleasure."

"Aren't you the gent, Sean?" Maeve muttered. "Well, Miss Carstairs, I suppose we must get on with this. First of all, these ladies come from all over the city. They live here free of charge while they heal from whatever injuries they might have sustained or until they decide where to go next."

Stunned that Maeve would speak so plainly in front of the residents, Eloisa glanced at the women. Some of them would hardly look at her. But one or two of them were gazing at her shyly.

Smiling gently, she asked, "How did you all hear about Hope House? Did the police bring you here?"

A lady with curly, blonde hair cleared her throat. "Not me, miss. I heard about the place from one of my old neighbors' sisters. She said the women who worked here treated people real nice. Like it weren't their fault they were here."

Eloisa swallowed back a cry of dismay, afraid to say the wrong thing. But inside, a dozen comments and questions bubbled forth. She was both curious and filled with the need to offer as much assistance as possible.

But also in that mix was a burgeoning notion that everyone in the room was only humoring her, that they all thought of her as nothing more than a simple-minded debutante with too much time on her hands.

It was disheartening to realize that in many ways that may be the truth. She was, indeed, looking for an escape from her everyday concerns—and from the haunting memories that threatened to overcome her when she had nothing else to occupy her mind.

"May I have that tour now?" she asked. "And please, do call me Eloisa."

Maeve stepped forward. "I'll be glad to show you, Miss Carstairs. Let's start in our drawing room, if I may? It most likely pales next to what you're used to, but we're mighty proud of it."

With effort Eloisa bit back a reply, both to the rather judgmental tone and the continued use of her last name. She decided not to offer her first name again. She had a distinct feeling that it would be ignored. With a peek over her shoulder at Sean, who was watching her with an impassive expression, she followed Maeve and entered the maze of rooms.

The drawing room was an open space decorated in shades of gray and blue. The furniture was obviously a cluttered compilation of cast-offs from other places. But even to Eloisa's discerning eye, it had a calming aura.

Continuing on, they crossed into another area, this one with two desks and a shelf containing no more than a paltry dozen books. "This here is the library," Maeve said.

"It looks to be in need of books."

"Well, some girls can read, others can't. So I guess it's fair to say that a reading tutor would come in handy too."

"Perhaps I could help with that in some way?"

Maeve shrugged. "How you wish to help is up to you."

After following Maeve down a dark, narrow hallway covered in faded, rose-colored wallpaper, they came to another small room, really nothing more than a large closet. It held a couple of dolls and a bin of wooden blocks. "This here is the playroom, such that it is. Some of the children like to have a space of their own. It's their mothers' saving grace, it is."

Eloisa peeked inside, intending to merely smile at the little girl she'd suddenly spied sitting on the rag rug in the corner. But when the little girl gazed at her with hope in her eyes, Eloisa couldn't resist trying to make a new friend. Walking in, she said, "Hi. I'm Eloisa."

"I'm Gretta."

"What game are you playing in here all alone?"

"I'm pretending."

"Oh?" She kept her voice low and encouraging, though she could sense Maeve's disapproval. "Who are you pretending to be?"

"A daughter."

Stunned, she knelt down beside the girl. "You're pretending to be a daughter, dear?"

"She don't have a family," Maeve said in her brisk, no-nonsense way. "Gretta here is an orphan."

It took everything Eloisa had to suppress the flinch that had risen up inside her. Surely there was no need to speak so bluntly. Or was Mrs. O'Connell's tone a result of how she felt about Eloisa?

Keeping her eye on the child, she said, "I like your name, Gretta. How old are you?"

"Six."

Eloisa was surprised. Gretta was small and rail-thin. She wouldn't have guessed her age much more than four. But then she noticed the weariness in the little girl's brown eyes. "How long has Gretta lived here, Mrs. O'Connell?"

"Seven months, or thereabouts. When her mum died of the tuberculosis, a couple of her neighbors tried to take her in, but they couldn't afford another girl, especially one so young. Luckily we had space here for her. Otherwise she would have gone to the workhouse."

A flash of fear appeared on Gretta's face. Then, to Eloisa's amazement, she valiantly attempted to hide it.

"Well, I'm pleased to have made your acquaintance, Gretta."

Gretta's nose wrinkled. She paused, then reached out and gingerly ran one finger along Eloisa's sleeve. "Your dress is pretty."

"Thank you."

"You're pretty too."

Eloisa gently covered Gretta's hand for a second. "I think you are prettier. Next time I come, perhaps we can visit some more?"

Gretta smiled but said nothing, leaving Eloisa with the feeling that she was far too used to grown-ups not following through on promises.

After getting to her feet, she followed Maeve out of the room and up the back stairs.

"Up here are the sleeping quarters. As you can see, everyone shares. Most of the residents take a stroll on a Sunday afternoon with decent weather, or a lot of them would be in their rooms."

There were at least two if not three beds in each room. Each was made up neatly. Also in the rooms were bowls and pitchers of water, hooks to hang dresses, and shelves where the women's belongings were stored. It was all very utilitarian and very sad. However, none of the women she saw downstairs had looked especially dejected or displeased to be there. Unlike the women in the entryway, the two in the room smiled when Eloisa greeted them.

At the end of the hall on the second floor was a children's room. "This is where the orphan girls live. The boys are in the attic."

Eloisa felt tears prick her eyes as she imagined sweet little Gretta lying on one of the cots that lined the floor, each with one thin blanket. There were no toys or extra blankets to be seen.

"It's very sparse, isn't it?"

"To someone like you, I suppose it is. These women are grateful for their blessings, however. And the children grow up learning not to expect much."

The meaning was clear. That Maeve was certain Eloisa had never had the occasion to go without something she wanted . . . and that she obviously took everything she had for granted.

Eloisa knew she should have expected Maeve's disdain. But the distrust that emanated from her came as a surprise.

And there, in the darkened hallway, she realized that not only did Maeve not think much of her, but she actively disliked her too.

"Why do you dislike me so much?"

Maeve's expression soured. "I don't *dislike* you, Miss Carstairs. It's simply that I have no use for young ladies like you." Her tone hardened as she continued. "I have no desire to be a part of your miniscule effort to do charity work, to temporarily fill some gap in your life, deal with something that's been missing."

"That is not why I am here."

"Oh?" That one word told just how little she believed that statement. "Oh, I see. Well, maybe you're on a mission to give yourself some experiences. Perhaps it is to impress my brother? What is it today, Miss Carstairs? Do you have a little desire to see what the other side lives like? Are we going to be fodder for your next dinner conversation?"

Eloisa was taken aback. "Of course not!"

"If I'm wrong, then I'll eat my words. But I must tell you, if I'm right? Well, all you're going to do is hurt any number of people who aren't wise enough to see your true motivations. Especially my brother. I'm not sure where Sean picked up this soft spot for you, but I am here to tell you if you so much as make him feel even an ounce of regret for befriending you, I'll make it my business to make sure you regret it. We might not mix in the same company, but I have enough influence over Sean to make sure he sees you for who you really are."

A warning and a threat. Eloisa would have laughed if she wasn't feeling so hurt by Maeve's accusations. "You don't know me, Mrs.

O'Connell. Just as you are saying I don't know you, you certainly do not know me."

Maeve's eyes cleared as she stared at her. "We'll see." Her expression looked like she was seeing Eloisa for the first time.

"You really shouldn't presume so much," Eloisa said.

"I know enough about your like." She looked away. Ran her fingers down the seam of wallpaper on the wall. "More than one woman from your side of the tracks has turned our lives into something out of a Dickens novel. And done nothing of use."

"That is not who I am," she said again. For a moment, Eloisa was tempted to confess everything that had happened to her. To tell her all about how she'd trusted Douglass Sloane and he'd abused both her emotions and her body in the worst way imaginable.

To share how alone she was at the moment. About how much pressure she was under, because her mother was determined that she make a suitable match within weeks, not months. As if any match were possible since . . .

And how she was so disgusted with so much in her life that she was willing to go against everything she knew to make something feel right for a change—if even for only a few minutes out of the day.

But, of course, Maeve wouldn't believe her.

Or even if she did, what would be the point? Eloisa's story was regrettable, but it certainly wasn't a cause for tears. No matter what had been done to her, she was still the pampered daughter of one of the city's leading families. She had been blessed with physical features and a temperament that others found pleasing.

She'd never been truly cold, and she'd never gone a day without food in her life. She'd never even had to worry about being looked after. A houseful of servants and her parents were ready to see to her every need.

"Thank you for the tour," she said before turning around to walk back down the stairs. "I sincerely appreciate your time."

She heard Maeve grumble behind her as she followed, and saw Sean's eyes fill with relief at the sight of her, then darken with worry as he took in the obvious tension that was flowing between her and his sister.

Sean strode forward to meet her, and lifted his hand slightly. It was obvious that he would have taken her arm or her hand if they had a different sort of relationship—or perhaps if his sister wasn't there, probably looking as though she was eager to interfere between them.

"Is everything okay?" he murmured, looking from her to his sister.

Before Maeve could reply, Eloisa painted a bright smile on her face. "Everything is perfectly fine. I'm so grateful for your time, Detective, and for Mrs. O'Connell's time too." Slowly, she turned and met Maeve's sour expression. "Words cannot express how illuminating this visit has been."

Sean's eyes darted to his sister's. "I look forward to hearing your impressions, Miss Carstairs. But for now, I should take you home."

Still aware of Maeve glaring at her with no small amount of distrust, Eloisa ventured, "Or perhaps to the train station? I know you are a very busy man."

He offered his arm. "As I said before, escorting you is my pleasure." Glancing just beyond her, his voice turned far less gallant. "I'll see you later, Maeve."

"That you will, Sean. That you will."

Only after they exited the house and started walking down the street did Sean speak again. "Care to tell me what that was all about?"

"It's nothing you need to worry about, Lieutenant Ryan," she said, briefly returning to formal address. Her conversation with his sister was absolutely nothing she wished to discuss with him. Not until she could calm herself. Not until she could understand for herself what had just happened. And what she'd just done. It certainly felt as if she had done so much more than meet his sister and visit a house for the disadvantaged.

No, it was obvious that she had done so much more.

"I know I said I'd take you directly home. But would you care for a light lunch? I didn't eat much before . . ." He flushed. "Or tea? Ice cream?"

Accepting wasn't the wise thing to do, just as his offering probably hadn't been the best choice he'd ever made, given his sister's obvious disapproval of their friendship.

But now it didn't really matter. All that did matter was how she felt, and what she wanted.

And right that moment, she didn't want her time with him to come to an end. "I'd like that very much, Sean," she said with a smile. "I didn't eat much before coming either. I was too excited about seeing Hope House. Thank you for the invitation."

CHAPTER 11

Sean could hardly believe Eloisa had accepted his clumsy invitation. For a second his mind froze, for what had just occurred was so far from his expectations that he wasn't quite able to process it.

Much to his dismay. He'd thought he was made of sterner stuff.

Then a buzzing directive filtered through the chaos. *Say something*, it practically shouted. *Say something before she realizes you're a feebleminded idiot and she reconsiders her acceptance.*

"There is a small café up ahead. It's nothing special, but it's open on Sunday afternoons, and they do serve good soup. The woman there also bakes fresh bread every day."

"A bowl of warm soup sounds delicious."

Now that they had a destination in mind, his feet began of their own accord. After half a block, he realized he was walking too fast and he shortened his steps.

She beamed. "Thank you. I was afraid we were about to enter a race and I knew I would come out the loser for sure."

"Pardon me. My manners are not usually so clumsy." Of course, it had been a very long time since he'd escorted any woman in a social situation like this.

Walking her home from the Gardners' party certainly didn't count.

Luckily, they arrived at the café before he had to think of something else to say. He opened the door with a flourish, and they were immediately surrounded by a burst of warm air scented with the smell of the fire in the hearth and the tangy aroma of pork, thyme, and rosemary.

Mrs. Kirkpatrick herself came over to greet them. "Afternoon, Sean. It's been a long time." She eyed Eloisa curiously. "Glad you decided to stop in."

"Yes, ma'am. It's a perfect day for some of your home cooking."

"That it is." After darting another curious glance Eloisa's way, Mrs. Kirkpatrick smiled warmly. "We always have a bowl for you, Sean. Free of charge, of course."

"That's not necessary." Feeling Eloisa's attention firmly on him, his cheeks flushed. "You know I never asked for such things."

"It's our pleasure, you putting yourself out in harm's way and all. Speaking of which . . . I trust you are staying safe in the streets? All the papers talk about is you and your gentleman partner on the trail of that Society Slasher. We worry about you, you know. I pray for you every night."

"I appreciate your prayers. Uh, I was just telling this lady here how good your soups are. I'm hoping that delicious scent is what I'm smelling?"

"It would be, indeed. We've got two choices today. Potato with leeks and bacon, or pork with white beans, onions, and carrots." With a laugh she said, "And I just happened to have made a loaf of honey wheat bread today."

"It all sounds wonderful," Eloisa said with a smile.

Before they'd walked inside the cozy café, Sean had intended to keep Eloisa's identity a secret, fearing she might not want anyone to ever know that she was out and about with him.

But since it was obvious that she had no desire to be ignored, he turned to her. "Miss Carstairs, you are in for a treat. Mrs. Kirkpatrick here makes some of the best bread in the city."

"It sounds heavenly. I'll have a thick slice of bread, and perhaps a bowl of the potato soup too. If you please."

"And I'll take the pork."

"It will be right out," Mrs. Kirkpatrick said with a new gleam in her eye. "Now that your order is settled, why don't you two take a turn at that table near the fire? It will keep you toasty until I bring your order. There's a new chill in the air. It seeps into my bones."

Sean smiled his thanks as he gestured Eloisa toward the table. "After you, Miss Carstairs."

She sat down with a rustle of skirts and crinoline, looking as graceful and elegant as ever. With effort he looked around the room, afraid to stare too long at her.

The cheery fire next to them felt calming after their walk in the brisk air. Giving in to temptation, he pulled off his gloves and held out his hands, enjoying the heat licking his fingertips. After watching him for a moment, Eloisa carefully began unfastening the buttons on her wrist. When she fumbled with one of the fastenings, he reached for her hand. "Allow me," he murmured. He carefully unhooked each one, telling himself that the slight tremor in his own fingers had everything to do with the delicate nature of the glove and nothing to do with the nature of the task.

At first she looked at him as if she'd never had such a kindness done to her before. Then he realized that he'd probably just broken some special sort of society rule. Maybe gentlemen weren't supposed to ever help a lady with her gloves?

But it was too late to go back now. Besides, he wanted to help her. And, if he were being completely honest, he wanted to hold her bare hand in his. Glide his thumb along her smooth skin to see if it really felt as soft as it looked.

Telling himself that he mustn't think about such things, he focused on his task at hand. With care he freed another button.

"You look as if you have a lot of experience with disrobing women's hands, Lieutenant Ryan."

He couldn't contain his bark of laughter. "Hardly that. I've just been sitting here thinking that my fingers are too thick and clumsy for such a delicate task. I am trying hard not to accidentally break a button."

"If you did, it wouldn't be a tragedy."

"If I did, I would feel even more like a clumsy fool than I already do."

Tilting her head, she stared at him. "I wouldn't have guessed such thoughts ran through your head."

"Even policemen need a break from thinking about cutthroats and thieves, miss," he murmured, taking care to lay on his accent a little thicker than usual so she would smile.

And when she did, he smiled right back. Suddenly hoping that she would never guess everything else he was thinking.

After sliding the glove off, he promptly unfastened the other one. When they were bare, he gave in to temptation and examined her hands. Her fingers were long and slim. No scars or veins or spots marred the skin. They were perfect. Actually, she had the prettiest hands he'd ever seen. He ran a finger along her knuckles. Her skin was, indeed, just as soft as he'd imagined it would be.

"Lieutenant?" She tugged on her hand. "May I have my hand back?"

Of course, his actions made him feel like twice the fool.

Right away he let go. "Forgive me."

"There's nothing to forgive."

"I, uh, was just noticing that your hands are very pretty," he blurted before realizing that he shouldn't be saying such things. It would be better to keep such thoughts to himself.

"Thank you."

"Sorry. I imagine you've never been around a man with such cloddish manners."

"You're right. I've never been around a man like you before, Lieutenant."

"Sorry. I don't always know how to act around you."

"Is there a certain way you feel you are supposed to act?"

"I don't know." He smiled as he shrugged. "I'm used to keeping company with gamblers and thieves, you know."

True interest entered her eyes. Leaning forward, she said, "You know what? I really don't know. What is your job like? What do you do all day?"

He was prevented from replying by Mrs. Kirkpatrick's arrival of a tray filled with their steaming bowls of soup and a half loaf of bread. A small crock of butter accompanied it. With great fanfare she set a bowl in front of each of them.

"You two eat up now," she commanded. "Especially you, miss. You look like a strong wind would blow you away."

"I'll do my best," Eloisa said with a smile. When their server left, she carefully dipped her spoon into her bowl, skimmed off a small portion, and said, "Now, as you were saying?"

He shrugged. "My days are about what you might expect. I report in to the precinct. Once there, my captain usually has a case for us to follow. Or we continue the one we are working on."

"We?"

"Detective Howard and I. We've been partners for about a year now."

"Do you ever get scared?"

He swallowed a spoonful of soup, taking the time to think about it. "Sometimes," he said with a shrug. "I've gotten into some sticky situations, especially back when I was on a beat."

"Beat?"

"An area I used to have to patrol. Now I follow cases, but back when I started, I would patrol assigned areas and attempt to keep the peace." Remembering some of those hours, the ones when he felt like there was only him against the rest of the world—and all of it lasting far too long—he grimaced. "I don't think I've ever prayed so much before or since."

"I am glad you survived."

"Me too." He smiled at her as they concentrated on their soups. Then, when they were about done, he asked a question of his own. "What did you think about Hope House?"

"I liked it." She paused, obviously wanting to expound on her thoughts.

"Was it what you imagined?"

"Yes and no." She flushed. "I'm sorry. I have so many thoughts running through my head, I seem to be having a difficult time organizing them."

"Take your time."

Something new entered her gaze. It was filled with surprise and, perhaps, gratification? "You really are interested in my thoughts and impressions, aren't you?"

He nodded. Since he was in no hurry to leave her, he leaned back and watched her. Patiently eager to see what else she was going to say.

"First of all, I didn't imagine the house would be so small."

"You found it small? I would have thought it would have seemed large to anyone."

"I didn't mean it looked like a small home. I meant that I had assumed it would look more like a dormitory or a boarding house. Something far more functional and sterile, less homey. Instead, Hope House looked like a home. I was so glad about that."

"I've been glad the residents are living in a place that feels like a home. It is pretty worn down around the edges and could use more elbow grease and tender loving care. But overall, it is a good resting place for those women and children. I've always been fond of it."

"I'm glad you told me about it. Already I am looking forward to my next visit." Smiling, she said, "I've already decided to go through all of our linen closets. I'm sure we have plenty of extra sheets, quilts, and blankets to spare at home."

She sounded so eager, so ready to fix all those women and children with kindness, he felt that he should give her a small word of warning. "Don't feel obligated to give more than you are able."

"I simply want to do something. I want to buy fabric and ask some of our maids to help me fashion some warm dresses for the little girls." Quickly she added, "Maybe the cook could make a few batches of cookies too. I'd love to bring them a treat."

Sean thought her enthusiasm was adorable. This was the first time he had seen her so animated. She looked younger, more vibrant, more approachable.

However, he also knew that seeking to help those residents could be terribly difficult. They didn't trust others easily, and might even be suspicious of Eloisa if she showed up with too much at one time. "The women and children didn't arrive there overnight, Miss Carstairs. It takes time for them to get on their feet. You mustn't expect that some warm blankets or a new dress will make much of a difference."

She blinked. "I know that."

"I'm relieved to hear you say so." He also didn't quite believe her. Either she was under the misconception that change could be brought about quickly, or she hadn't quite grasped that the people she would be helping were needy on so many different levels.

Her naïveté worried him, but it also made him appreciate her tender heart. "What do you hope to accomplish at Hope House?"

"I'm not really sure." Looking stung, she folded and refolded the napkin in her lap. "You're probably going to tease me, but I don't expect to do too much."

"Oh?"

She nodded. "I'm just me. I don't have much experience with any of the things they are struggling with. All I do know is that I am hoping to do something." She shrugged. "Whatever I can. Maybe I can work with some of the children there. I met the sweetest little girl named Gretta. She was just sitting by herself. My heart went out to her."

Thinking of the many children living on the streets, most never having the shelter Gretta was now enjoying, Sean was struck yet again by Eloisa's naïveté. "Please, do be careful. You don't want to form attachments."

"And why is that?"

She looked so confused, so completely at a loss to understand what he meant, that he hastily amended his words into something less blunt. "Miss Carstairs, I am worried that a child like Gretta might misunderstand your motives. She, uh, might imagine that you want to get to know her."

"And what is wrong with that?"

"I can't imagine that a lady like you . . . would really have time for that." As soon as he heard his words, he ached to snatch them back. He sounded unforgivably full of himself. Superior. It was the last way he wanted to come across.

But, to his amazement, Eloisa didn't seem hurt. Instead, she took his words seriously. Her head tilted to one side. "I think I do have time for her. If one day Gretta wants to spend any time with me, I can't imagine anything that would make me happier. Definitely not any other pressing engagement." She paused. "Why do you look so surprised? What else do you think I do?"

"I couldn't begin to guess." All the things he was going to mention sounded rather demeaning.

"But you have, Lieutenant Ryan. How do you think I fill my days? By simply going to parties?"

"Yes." He held up a hand before she could find exception with his reply. "Miss Carstairs, please don't misunderstand me. I don't think there's anything wrong with you attending parties. I am not judging." Furthermore, he secretly liked the idea of a lady like her never being subjected to the filth and danger he saw on a daily basis.

"Forgive me, but you do sound judgmental."

"If I do, it wasn't my intention. I'm only basing my thoughts on my experience with some other ladies of your social circle, which, of course, would be the barest of acquaintances in the line of duty. I guess that's what I usually think of young ladies of your class doing."

"Some days I feel that all I ever do is shop, primp, try to better myself, and attend social gatherings." She grimaced. "Sometimes it feels like that's all I do. But there's a reason for it, you see. My mother . . . those parties are some of the only acceptable ways for me to meet men." She paused. "But I'm sure you wouldn't understand." She wouldn't mention again that she knew she could never marry.

"I don't. Not at all." And to his surprise, he meant it. "I can't imagine having that kind of pressure on my shoulders. But I must tell you that I don't wish you were denied some light moments. I think you should try to grasp all the happiness you can. You've had enough pain, I think."

"Yes, but I'm not alone in feeling pain. No one is immune to that." Carefully, she dabbed at the corners of her lips with the corner of a napkin, then placed it on the plate under her bowl. "This was delicious. Thank you."

"You're welcome." When he saw her reach for her reticule, he shook his head. "This is my treat."

"I couldn't let you."

Pride, his old, true friend, caused his tone to turn hard. "Even cops like me can afford to buy a girl a bowl of soup."

She looked down at her hands. "Of course."

He'd embarrassed her. Injecting a note of humor in his voice, he teased, "Besides, I'll have you know that Mrs. Kirkpatrick never charges me full price for my meals—that is, when I convince her to let me pay for them at all."

When her chin lifted, he could have sworn there was something new and fresh in her eyes. Was she, too, feeling a new awareness rise between them? He wasn't sure.

Getting to his feet, he said, "I'll be right back." He turned and went to settle the bill with Mrs. Kirkpatrick, who had been unabashedly watching them from a spot near the back counter.

CHAPTER 12

Katie had just finished doing some shopping with her sister June and was heading toward the train when she saw *him* up ahead. Owen.

No, she cautioned herself. *Not Owen. Detective Howard.* She needed to stop thinking of him in such a familiar way. Especially since there was nothing between them.

Nothing but a shared concern about her brother.

She paused, wondering what to do. Should she simply walk by, pretending she didn't see him? Avert her eyes? Simply smile?

Stop and say hello?

It was all so confusing. She not only didn't have any experience with men, but she didn't have any experience at all with gentlemen like him.

In the end, he took the dilemma out of her hands. "Miss Ryan?"

She turned her head to face him, and attempted to appear surprised. "Oh, hello, Detective Howard. It's so nice to see you again."

By his expression, it was obvious her ruse had failed miserably. "I am relieved to hear you say that. For a moment I feared you were going to ignore me completely."

What could she say to that? Nothing . . . nothing came to mind. "I trust you are having a good day?"

"I would, if I wasn't currently wondering if you are walking alone. Yet again."

"I was just out doing a little shopping with one of my sisters and her husband. June is recently married and needed a new hat."

"They didn't see the need to make sure you returned home safely?"

"They knew it was a mere block from where we parted to the train station."

Something crossed his features before they smoothed again. Before she knew it, he had his hand curved around her upper arm. "Please, allow me to escort you."

"That's unnecessary."

"It would be my honor," he parried as he guided her through the throng of people.

A flicker of unease rushed through her. His comment felt odd, artificial. Combined with the grip on her arm, she was beginning to wish she'd taken up June's husband's offer to escort her down the street. "There's no need to grip me so securely. Please, release me."

"Not yet."

Though they were darting through the maze of people, his hand on her arm linking them together, she allowed herself to gaze at him again. "I don't understand why you are treating me this way."

"No? Well, let me make this easier to understand. The last time we saw each other, you entered the police station alone, barely spoke with me, then ran out of the lobby when I asked to escort you safely home. Then, while you apparently traipsed down the streets without a care in the world, I, on the other hand, was left to stand on the pavement like a fool."

"There was no need for you to have left the lobby."

"There was every reason. I was beside myself with worry."

"I'm sorry for that. But, now—"

He smoothly interrupted. "Are you going to the station on Elm?"

"Yes. And I must hurry or I'll miss my train."

However, he didn't increase his pace. He didn't allow her to race ahead. Instead, Owen kept his hold steady on her arm and his pace sedate. Foiling her goal.

She became resentful. Who was he to come out of nowhere and start ordering her about? He was a coddled and very wealthy man. He had no right to impose his ways on her. She was so far from the ladies of his class, she feared she wasn't even refined enough to get a job as a lady's maid in one of their mansions.

Why, he likely had no idea what it was like to be a poor person living in the heart of the city.

"Sean told me you have your own coach," she said with more than a slight touch of asperity.

"That is true. I do."

"If you roam about the city in your own carriage, I'm surprised you even know where the train stations are."

"Watch your tongue. You know everyone in the city takes the elevated when they can." Leaning a little closer to her ear, he added, "I'm sure you also realize that we are not that far apart in circumstance."

He was so far above her in the world, she was surprised she didn't need a step stool to converse with him. "Only someone like you could think something like that."

Impatiently, he muttered, "I'm a cop, first and foremost, Miss Ryan."

Looking up, she noticed they were standing outside the train station. She now had mere minutes to purchase her ticket, skitter up the stairs, and be waiting at the platform before her train came.

With a jerk she pulled her arm from his clasp. "No, Detective Howard. First and foremost, you are a gentleman."

"I'm trying to tell you that places in society shouldn't matter."

"It matters to me," she replied before running into the station.

Once inside, she practically barreled down everyone in her path. She was desperate to get that train. Staying in the vicinity of Detective Howard would be a terrible mistake. If she wasn't careful, she was going to start imagining that his concern for her welfare meant something.

After that, it was only a matter of time before she'd start dreaming that he could actually care about a girl like Katie Ryan.

That he could actually want a girl like her in his life.

—

Two days after he had escorted Eloisa to Hope House, Sean returned to Maeve's, grateful for her offer of another home-cooked meal. Besides, he was wondering what she had thought of Eloisa.

From the time he'd escorted Eloisa home, he'd replayed every conversation, every warm look, every feeling he'd had in her presence. Now he was feeling like the biggest fool. He had a serial slasher to catch, along with a whole host of other cases and crimes to concentrate on. The last thing in the world he needed was to spend almost every waking second thinking about a woman who only saw him as her conduit to the needs of the lower classes.

Maeve was in the kitchen, slicing an onion to within an inch of its life when he entered.

"Who is winning, you or the onion?"

Wiping her eyes with the edge of her apron, she grimaced. "The onion, I'm afraid. Every time I make scrapple, I promise myself I won't do it again. I hate dicing onions. Don't know why."

After quickly washing his hands, Sean gently pulled the knife from her. "I'll do this, then."

"You don't mind?"

"Not at all." Actually, cutting a defenseless onion into small pieces sounded like exactly the type of mindless activity he needed. "I need something to occupy myself. It's been quite a day."

"Mine too. Jemima fell and scraped her knees something awful, and then I ran out of milk and had to ask Jack for some milk money."

"Do you need some money?"

She waved a hand. "It weren't the money he got excited about. It was the fact that he figured out I spent too much at the fabric store the other day. He weren't real pleased with me. I'll tell ya that."

"Hmm," he said in his best noncommittal way. Sean had always thought Maeve's husband had the patience of a saint to put up with his bossy, opinionated sister. When she handed him another onion, he carefully sliced it in half, then started chopping again. "Almost done."

"Ta."

"Anytime, Maeve."

Her usual caustic demeanor sweetened. "This is like old times, it is."

"Not hardly. When we lived at home, Ma kept you in the kitchen and me out of the house."

She laughed. "Right you are. But I'm still glad you came by." Her expression still bright, she said, "You and me standing here in the kitchen, chopping onions, what a sight we are."

He laughed. "I'd say so."

"My life is a far cry from the likes of Eloisa Carstairs, it is."

Now he knew what had really been bothering her when he'd walked through her door. She was thinking about Eloisa's days and comparing them to her own. "Maeve, just because Miss Carstairs doesn't chop onions, it doesn't mean she's all bad."

"I'm not being critical of her."

"'Course you are." Since he'd come over wanting to hear her thoughts about Eloisa as much as a meal, he dug in. "What did you think of Eloisa?"

"Are you speaking of Miss Carstairs?"

"Of course I am."

"So you are calling her Eloisa now?"

"Maeve. Don't be like that."

"I'm not being any certain way. All I'm doing is wondering what had made you decide to develop a friendship with her."

"I wouldn't call us friends. Merely acquaintances."

"Sean, if I believed that, I'd be a sight less smart. No need to lie to me, you know. I saw the way you eyed her the entire time."

He'd had no idea his regard was so apparent. "And what way was I eyeing her?"

"You know."

"Maeve, I promise, I do not."

She blew out a breath of air. "You were looking at her like she was the stars and the sun and the moon, all wrapped up into one glorious, high-society package."

He glared at her. "If I was looking at her often, it was purely out of concern for her welfare. You ladies certainly didn't make her feel welcome."

"We aren't *ladies*, brother. Some of the women there are hardly respectable. Some aren't respectable at all. We all knew that too."

Looking mulish, she glared at him. "It was awkward, it was." After a moment, she added, "She stopped by again yesterday."

"She did? Did she stay for a time? She didn't arrive alone, did she?"

"No, she had her driver with her. And from what I heard, she only stopped by to drop off some linens and books." Almost grudgingly, she added, "The women were appreciative of her efforts."

Sean didn't miss the slight disdain in her tone. "Miss Carstairs was there for a good cause. No harm would have come to you for trying to give her the benefit of the doubt. Or from giving her a little less of a bitter attitude. She's had a difficult time of it lately. I would appreciate it if you could spare her a bit of compassion."

"A lady like that needs compassion? For what?" Her voice rose. "What could she possibly have that has necessitated her needing a helping hand?"

"It is her private business. I'm afraid I can't share."

Maeve thrust one of her hips out as she glared at him. "What happened? Did one of her maids not iron a ball gown just so?" She snapped her fingers. "Oh, I know. Maybe she had a small, unsightly blemish appear on her cheek. That would certainly mar her perfect life."

"That's enough."

"Or did one of her many beaus not save a dance for her? I've heard that a hurriedly filled dance card can be a terrible thing in her social circle."

Sean stood up. As he did so, he looked down at her with something akin to scorn in his eyes. "For the record, you used to be far nicer. You used to think of other people."

"I do think about people who need my concern. I help out at Hope House, don't I?"

"I came over here the other evening to ask you to show some Christian charity to Eloisa. To try to look beyond her wealth and privilege to the person she is inside. Years ago, I wouldn't have even thought that I would need to do that. I would've assumed that you would be there for her, no matter what. But now I'm not even sure you would be willing to reach out to her again as a favor for me. What's happened to you?"

"*Life happened*. As well as the fact that I, for one, am more than willing to accept the reality of our situation."

"And what is that supposed to mean?"

"It means, Sean Ryan, that you may mix with society by moonlighting at balls and galas. You might even know a couple of gents because Owen Howard has decided to go slumming. Some people might even give you the time of day because you're a fancy police lieutenant, and a good one at that. But the truth of the matter is that you are no closer to being friends with Eloisa Carstairs than I am with President Cleveland. You're just too different. And if you think differently, you're fooling yourself, Sean. She's going to hurt you something awful too. Mark my words."

His sister's words stung, mainly because they had a grain of truth to them. "You have things all wrong."

"No, brother. It's you who has things all wrong. Anytime Eloisa Carstairs says good-bye to you, she'll go home to her mansion. She'll go into a bedroom that's likely bigger than half my house, and a maid will attend her. Servants will bring her tea on carts. Other servants will prepare her food, serve it up to her, remove the plates, and wash them. And then she'll change for bed by getting into a nightgown that someone else washed and pressed, and slide under sheets in a bed that someone else made. But first her lady's maid will take down her hair. And when she looks in the mirror, she's going to see herself. And she's beautiful."

Her voice cracked. "She has *everything*, Sean. She has everything and she wants more. She's going to want to marry a man who can give her more. No matter what you might think, she is not going to want to marry someone like you."

"You sound as if you've thought a lot about how a lady like her lives." Of course, the moment he said those words, Sean ached to take them back. She certainly didn't deserve either his words or tone.

"Of course I have, Sean," she replied with more than a trace of bitterness laced in her tone. "I've got me a cozy home, a good man, and two healthy children. I'm blessed, and I don't mean for the Lord to think I'm not appreciative of that." She lowered her voice. "But I'd be lying to both you and myself if I acted like I was never envious of a lady like her."

He shook his head. He didn't know everything there was to know about Eloisa. Far from that. However, he now knew her well enough to realize that it would be a grave mistake to believe that Eloisa Carstairs was only the sum of her appearance. "No—"

"She has everything, Sean," she repeated. "Everything. And the sad thing of it is, she is still looking for more, even for someone like you."

"Like me?"

"Stay away from her. Knowing her will only do you harm. I mean it."

"I'm going to leave now."

She slumped. "Yes. Yes, I believe that would be a fine idea."

He turned, but not before whispering, "Maeve, I hear what you're saying, I do. And if we were talking about a different woman, I would say you were exactly right."

"But?"

"But I know Eloisa. And I know what she's been through and I know what her dreams are. And I can promise you that it would be a grave mistake to judge her only on her looks and wealth. The Lord gave us full lives, made us whole people, Maeve. We're not simple paper dolls that can be bent and prodded and transformed with a twist and a pull. We have hearts and souls and dreams and feelings. Even people like you and me. And even wealthy women like Eloisa Carstairs."

Maeve's lips parted. Obviously she was stunned by his small speech. "I'm sorry, Sean," she murmured.

"I'm sorry too." He knew he should step closer and promise her forgiveness. But at the moment he was too angry with his sister and too struck by the feelings that were coursing through him to do anything but step into the dark evening.

He'd just defended Eloisa with everything that he was, he realized. Because she was important to him.

Far too important to give up. Even if that was the smart thing to do.

CHAPTER 13

Another evening, another formal affair. As Juliet picked up another hairpin and artfully arranged her chignon, Eloisa gazed at her reflection in the mirror and tried to drum up some enthusiasm for the evening's event.

She couldn't do it.

Yet again, her plans included dressing up in a very expensive gown to spend the evening in the home of one of her parents' very particular acquaintances. Once she arrived, admired every other lady's very expensive gown, she would converse with several suitable gentlemen.

After that, one of those men would escort her into a warm—because too many people would have been invited—extremely fragrant—because too many artfully arranged flower arrangements would be on display—dining room.

She would then smile, make scintillating conversation, and appear interested in whatever the gentleman at her side wished to talk about while eating mere bites of each offering during a lengthy, seven-course meal. This, of course, would be preceded by aperitifs and followed by forced banter with some of the same fifty people who always attended these events.

She was likely to be seated with an eligible bachelor, someone of social standing who was in the market for a wealthy bride.

Or, perhaps it would be a gentleman of somewhat lesser rank who was a close friend of the hostess, or to whom the hostess owed a favor. This man would be more charming, more effusive in his compliments, more attentive. And because of all these things, infinitely more desperate.

Two years ago, when she'd made her debut, her mother and father had sat her down on a settee in the formal drawing room and systematically explained the truths that would now govern her life.

The first truth was that Eloisa must always, *always* be aware that there were few people as wealthy as the Carstairs family.

Eloisa had been stunned.

Oh, not by the announcement, of course. For most of her life, she'd realized that most everyone in Chicago did not live like the Carstairs family at the top of Sable Hill. Their estate encompassed more than two acres. Dressmakers and milliners delivered their creations to their home for perusal. Almost twenty servants were employed by the family to see to their every need.

However, she'd also learned at a young age never to speak of such things. "There is nothing more bourgeois than speaking about one's wealth, dear," her mother had intoned again and again.

The second truth was that even without their wealth, the Carstairs family enjoyed a stellar reputation. That meant not only were they well thought of, but they were somewhat lauded by others.

And that meant that under no circumstances could Eloisa do anything to taint this hard-earned status.

And that meant that Eloisa could not forget to always look her best, behave her best, and never, ever forget that she was being watched.

"People are always waiting for you to make a fool of yourself, Eloisa. Take care not to give them something to talk about," her father had warned. "Remember, once a reputation has been lost, it can never be regained. Ever."

The third edict was both similar to and quite different from one given to her brother.

Thomas, being a boy, had been told not to let some desperate girl encourage him to make foolish choices. Soon after his lecture, he'd been sent back to boarding school, then Yale, then given leave to tour the continent for a full year.

She, on the other hand, had been told her duty was to marry well. Very well.

She'd also been repeatedly warned that her name, combined with her beauty and their wealth, would attract all sorts of nefarious men. Men who would do or say almost anything to reap the benefits of marriage to her.

"Just because you're available, it doesn't mean you are available to just anyone, Eloisa," her mother advised.

Years ago, when she was fifteen and sixteen, and perhaps more enamored of herself than she should have been, Eloisa had been hurt that her mother had never taken into account her personality or her humor or her grace, or anything that made her Eloisa, not simply a Carstairs.

But now that she'd made her debut, she'd learned that the core of her mother's words had merit. Some men did, indeed, strive to marry into her family. Some attempted to lie about it.

Now that she was older?

Most leaned toward honesty.

She leaned that way, too, and toward entertainment. Which was why she was secretly hoping that tonight's event would entail a favor owed to the hostess. She could use a laugh. She could use a few minutes of meaningless flattery. Anything to take her mind off the fact that she'd been measured up and found less than desirable by a group of destitute women in a charitable home.

For a woman who had always been taught that she was the epitome of everything that everyone else wanted? It had been a blow to her ego.

Juliet met her gaze in the mirror. "Any idea with whom you'll be paired this evening, miss?"

"Not a clue."

"Maybe it's that handsome Mr. Gardner."

Eloisa felt a faint tremor course through her. For some reason, she never felt comfortable around Quentin. "I hope not."

Juliet looked at her closely, then shrugged. "Well, I'm sure your mother has someone special in mind."

"She always does," Eloisa said with a wry smile. "I just hope it isn't Baron Humphrey again."

"Remind me who that is?" Before Eloisa could think of an appropriate adjective to describe just how boring Baron was, Juliet held up a pin in each of her hands. "The pearl or sapphire stick pin tonight, Miss Carstairs?"

She didn't care. She wasn't sure if she ever had. "What gown am I wearing tonight?"

"Your mother wanted the sea foam, miss," Juliet said with a hint of a smile.

Eloisa knew that gown. Its hue complemented her coloring exquisitely, making her look even more delicate than her blonde hair, light-blue eyes, and slim frame already did. Its cut was demure, and its fit was forgiving enough that Juliet wouldn't even have to cinch her corset strings as tight as she usually did.

The dress was everything proper. Everything boring. Everything that would cause a man to notice her but then forget about her easily. She would blend in with the rest of the room. Look pretty but not stand out.

Exactly how her mother believed she should always look.

Exactly the opposite of how she'd been feeling lately.

Perhaps it was the constant nightmares, the lack of sleep? Perhaps it was her time over at Hope House, or even her burgeoning friendship with Sean Ryan.

Whatever the reason, she knew she was tired of being relegated to the shadows. She was eager to be bold. To stand out, at least for a time.

Thinking quickly, she said, "Juliet, what about the ivory gown with the black lace overlay? Is it in poor shape?"

Juliet's eyes filled with hurt. "Of course it's not in poor shape."

"I meant, I don't want you to have to press it."

"I wouldn't have to press it, Miss Eloisa. It is in perfect order." Her lips curved up, making Eloisa realize that Juliet, too, was eager to shake things up a bit.

"In that case, I would like to wear that gown instead of anything sea foam. And I think the sapphires in my hair."

"And your black lace fan?"

"Yes, and the black gloves."

Juliet's eyes sparkled. "Miss Eloisa, you know your mother prefers you to wear white gloves. She doesn't feel black gloves are proper for a young lady. Most especially not at a dinner party."

Privately, Eloisa didn't think they were either. But she wasn't a young girl anymore.

"I know she doesn't. However, the gloves will be on my hands and arms, not hers."

Their eyes met in the mirror. Slowly Juliet smiled, giving Eloisa what she needed, an ally in asserting her independence.

"I don't know whether to praise your courage or warn you to prepare yourself, Miss Carstairs. Your mother won't hesitate to make her displeasure known."

"We should probably be ready for anything, then," she said as she watched Juliet carefully place the pair of blue sapphire pins into her chignon. As she imagined, the jewels stood out like fireflies against her hair, drawing one's attention to how shining and golden it was. "Tonight I find I'm tired of simply doing what is expected of me. There has got to be more to me than just a pretty face."

"There is much more, miss. And begging your pardon, Miss Carstairs, but it does my heart good to see you smiling and to see you've got some of your spunk back. It's been awhile. I mean, from what I have observed it has been."

Though Eloisa had never shared with Juliet what had happened with Douglass, sometimes she feared Juliet had guessed. For weeks after her attack, Juliet had stayed close, taking longer on Eloisa's toilet, brushing her hair with a little more care, fussing over her just a little bit more than she used to.

Juliet was nothing if not an extremely talented lady's maid, but, still, it had been an odd thing. Though Juliet never said much about her life before she came to service on Sable Hill, and though she was a year younger than Eloisa, Eloisa imagined Juliet was far more knowledge-able in the ways of the world than she could ever hope to be.

All of that was exactly why Eloisa had known her behavior had worried her sweet lady's maid to no end. "Yes, it has been awhile. But perhaps it is time."

Crossing to the bed, Juliet carefully gathered the sea-foam gown in her arms. "I'll be right back."

"Take your time, Juliet."

And for the first time in many weeks, she was actually looking forward to the night out. Surely it wasn't simply because of the change of gown.

Perhaps, instead, it was because she'd finally gotten herself back. She was going to be a little bit more daring, a little bit more bold. A little bit like the person she thought she'd be . . . before she'd understood what it meant to be Eloisa Carstairs.

And what it meant to be at a man's mercy.

Eloisa's new resolve lasted just until the time she walked down the staircase and saw who was waiting for her. Owen Howard. Detective Owen Howard.

Immediately, her thoughts turned to Sean's warnings about how women still weren't safe in the city. Had the Slasher struck again?

"Detective," she said when she reached the bottom step. "Is everything all right?"

Owen, all golden good looks and good manners, strode to her side, clasped her hand, and helped her down the last step.

He'd always been polite. Always exceptionally debonair.

But rarely had he ever looked at her the way he was at the moment—a mixture of adoration and admiration.

"Owen, what is going on?"

He also smoothly ignored her plea. "Eloisa, may I say that you look beautiful this evening? I'm simply captivated."

She blinked, then became aware of her mother watching them from the edge of the foyer.

Raising her voice, she played her part right back. "You are too kind, Detective Howard."

He leaned closer. "Please call me Owen. After all, we've known each other for a long time."

She almost smiled. "You know I cannot call you that in public."

A dimple appeared. "You know what that does, don't you? You are giving me hope that we'll be together in private."

A bolt of alarm shot through her. Though, of course, he meant nothing nefarious, she couldn't help the shudder of revulsion that coursed through her. Afraid he noticed, she forced herself to giggle. "I am shocked, Owen."

Yet again, he directed their repartee. "No worries," he whispered as he bent his head closer to hers. "You have to know half of what I say is all for your mother's benefit."

"Of course."

As if her mother knew she was being summoned, she stepped forward. "Eloisa, I saw Owen's mother at a charity event not a week ago. When we realized that the both of you had received an invitation to the Lawrences, we decided it would be a wonderful thing for him to accompany you."

"It is wonderful. So wonderful." Eloisa barely controlled her temper. This, this . . . date had been planned for days, and her mother had never found it necessary to inform her of it? Of course, on its heels was the awareness that she'd told her mother time and again that she had no interest in either her social calendar or who escorted her to events.

Wisely ignoring Eloisa's sarcasm, her mother gazed at her dress with a critical eye. "I wanted you to wear the sea foam this evening. I spoke to Juliet about that myself."

"Juliet did have that gown laid out. However, I changed my mind."

"Black lace is almost inappropriate for the occasion. Dear."

"But not quite," Eloisa returned, her voice firm.

Just as her mother was drawing in a breath to continue their pointless squabble, Owen interrupted.

"I, too, was just informed of our partnership for the evening, Eloisa, but I must admit to being relieved. We know each other well enough to be able to relax, don't you think? Accompanying you is my honor."

Ignoring her mother, she gazed at Owen and realized that she felt the same way. Owen was different from the other gentlemen of their circle. His insistence on having a job—and a dangerous one at that—created quite an aura about him. One of confidence and mystery.

He also knew when to speak, when to gloss over things, and how to go about doing so in an unobtrusive, refined way. He was the antithesis of Sean Ryan.

Eloisa didn't mind Owen's company. He was a family friend, knew Sean, and could be depended on to keep her safe in any sort of situation.

But she still was confused as to why anyone thought she needed such protection beyond their driver, who would take her to and from the Lawrences' home. And why Owen was looking at her in such a protective way.

"Has something happened?"

While Owen averted his eyes, her mother spoke up. "The Slasher has struck again."

"What?"

Owen placed his hand on her waist. "Easy, now. Everything will be okay."

"How do you know that? How can you know that?"

"Because you have me by your side, and I refuse to let anything happen to you."

Looking into his eyes, Eloisa knew Owen was being completely sincere. Though they'd never been more than friends, she trusted him implicitly. "Who was it?" she asked, pleased that she was getting her bearings again. "Who was attacked?"

"Millicent Bond."

Eloisa felt dizzy. "Millicent? Is she . . . is she alive?"

"Eloisa, control yourself," her mother cautioned. "Millicent's misfortune is none of your concern."

"Of course it is. Mother, the girls being attacked are my friends."

"Millicent was hardly that."

Eloisa inhaled sharply. "Was?"

"Millicent didn't survive the attack," Owen said quietly as he wrapped his arm more tightly around her, pulling her closer to him in a way that was completely inappropriate. However, his body's warmth served to remind her that she was not alone. As his brown eyes skimmed over her face, he frowned. "You're not going to faint on me, are you?"

"Of course not." Though she was having difficulty catching her breath.

"Forgive my familiarity, but do we need to loosen your corset?" he whispered into her ear. "Can you breathe?"

She was tempted to admit that she was having difficulty breathing, to say she needed to summon Juliet and return to the safety of her room. She ached to retreat to someplace within herself and forget about everything. But she'd learned the hard way that leaving reality for a little bit was a double-edged sword. A few hours of blissful relief made the return to reality even harder.

"Thank you for your concern, but I am fine."

"Of course she is," her mother said, her tone now filled with ice. "Mr. Howard, I wouldn't have thought a gentleman like you would have ever stooped so low as to start discussing such things."

Eloisa's patience broke. "Mother, such things hardly matter. After all, Millicent was murdered."

Owen didn't even bother to respond to her mother's comment. Instead, he smoothly ignored her protests and escorted Eloisa to the small receiving room. After helping her to the chair, he knelt in front of her. "Are you sure you're all right?" he asked. "I can ask your mother to summon your maid, if you wish."

She smiled softly. "There's no need for that, though I'm starting to regret my choice of gowns. This one was definitely not made with comfort in mind."

"If it's any consolation, please know that you do look lovely. Exquisite."

His kindness and compliments warmed her. She placed her gloved hand on his arm. "Owen, are you certain you aren't needed elsewhere?"

"You worried I can't do my job?"

"I'm worried that you are too much of a gentleman to cancel at such a late date."

"I didn't want you to have to go out without an escort."

He truly was so very gallant. "How about this? How about I stay home?"

"How about you desist in attempting to send me away?" he countered, humor lighting his eyes. "I promise you, there are several officers on the case. I know, because I was with everyone earlier. If I was needed, my captain would have requested I stay."

"If you're sure."

"I am more than sure. Lieutenant Ryan will continue to work the investigation tonight."

"He's at the scene?"

"Ah, yes. When I told him we had this evening already planned, he said I could have some time off. I'll catch up with him either late tonight or tomorrow morning."

"That sounds terribly inconvenient for you."

"Maybe it is for Sean." He smiled. "For me, however, it is a stroke of luck."

Escorting her still didn't seem like the best use of his time. "I am honored by your kindness, but if you need to be someplace else . . ."

"I spoke to Sean. He and I both agree that you are a person worth looking after, Eloisa. Please let me do this."

Sean knew Owen was with her. He not only approved but supported it. Unaccountably, she felt disappointed. She could have sworn there was something special between them.

"I'm only going to let you because, if you did leave, I know my mother would send me on my own."

Her mother stepped forward, a mixture of kindness and new resolve in her features. "Eloisa, even though you're wearing black lace and ivory, you do look beautiful. You are on the arm of one of the most sought-after men in your circle of friends. Plus, he has the added benefit of being someone who can take care of you no matter what happens. Will you go?"

She could sit in her room and imagine all the worst things that could have happened to her friend.

Or she could move forward, smile, and know that no matter what happened, she wasn't going to be either unsafe or bored on Owen Howard's arm.

Perhaps if she gave him half a chance, their familiar friendship would change into something deeper. Perhaps they could even fall in love.

If her mother had arranged his escort, it was a sure sign that Owen's suit would be accepted.

Though she was answering her mother, her attention lay on him. "Thank you, Owen. It would be my honor to go to the dinner by your side."

Lifting her hand, he pressed his lips to her knuckles. She could feel the heat from his touch all the way through her satin kid gloves. "You honor me, Eloisa. Thank you."

And so, shortly after Worthy appeared with her black fox stole, Owen took care placing it around her shoulders. His bare fingers brushed against her bare skin, leaving chill bumps up her spine.

When she lifted her head, she wondered if perhaps he was the one for her. Had everything with Sean merely been a dream, a chance for her to experience something more?

A way to enable her to realize she wanted a life that encompassed more than going to balls and parties? Dare she dream that one day she could teach her daughter the very same thing?

And now, on Owen's arm, she realized he would be perfect for her. He knew her social class because he was of it. He knew the perimeters of her experiences because he'd experienced those very same things.

But she also was about more than all of that.

And, by the look in his eyes, he was also very amenable to not only continuing their friendship but taking things to another level.

In short, if he could bear knowing what Douglass Sloane had done, she had a future with Owen.

And that, she realized, fully encompassed the Carstairs family's last and most important rule of life: no matter what, never forget that everything generations of their family had accomplished could vanish in an instant.

What had been always taken for granted could vanish.

And though being Eloisa Carstairs was something of a burden, it was also all she knew.

And was she really ready to abandon everything to experience freedom?

She thought not.

CHAPTER 14

Have you ever seen the like?" Barnaby, one of the precinct's greenest constables, asked Sean as they walked toward the illuminated entrance of the Lawrence home. "It looks like something out of a fairy tale, it does."

"Hardly that, Constable," Sean muttered. "It's simply a very big house."

Barnaby stopped walking. "No, it's more."

Sean had to give Barnaby that. The Lawrences' home was a beautiful structure—ornate and elegant and large enough to be referred to as a mansion. It was also a place he would never be allowed to enter under normal circumstances.

The realization added a bit of contempt to his voice. "The family members who live here are citizens of the city, just like you and me. No better, no worse."

Barnaby pivoted on his heel and met Sean's eyes. Only this time he was the one who looked far more world-weary. "Hardly that, sir. I've lived in these parts all my life, as did my parents. And I promise, there's been hardly a time that anyone even wanted us north of the river, let alone out of Bridgeport. So, yes, they might be citizens of Chicago, but they've never been just like you and me."

Perhaps Barnaby wasn't the naïve one of their pair. "Point taken."

And Barnaby definitely did have a point. Over the years, the gap between the haves and the have-nots in Chicago grew wider exponentially. Most men and women of the working classes didn't look at the mansions with anything approaching awe. Instead it was with a jaundiced eye, influenced by too many years of sickness and hunger. Too many moments of being made to feel less than worthy.

But his burgeoning friendship with Eloisa had changed that for Sean. Now when he looked at a lady dressed in fine silk and jewels, he thought of her. And now when he gazed at a large house, he couldn't help but be glad there was a place like that for a woman like Eloisa Carstairs.

She was too fine to live like he did.

"It's time we stopped our staring and got to work. Look smart, now," he added as they started walking again, toward steps that led to the magnificently carved door lit with gas lights on each side. Clear, shiny windows lined both sides of the entrance as well, and they could see servants inside, all dressed in severe black-and-white, starched uniforms, aprons, and caps.

And just beyond them was a kaleidoscope of colors—gorgeous women dressed in beautiful clothes, each gown likely costing more than a month's rent for a new recruit like Barnaby.

And perhaps even for a lieutenant detective like himself.

They climbed the half-dozen limestone steps, the front door looming even bigger and looking more impressive. The constable raised his hand to knock but stopped himself. "You feel sure Detective Howard is inside, sir?"

"I am sure of it." Even if they had not agreed earlier that Owen should accompany Eloisa tonight, he and Owen had had a long-standing tradition of informing each other of their off-duty schedules. Sean smiled to himself, remembering the first time Owen had handed him a sheet of thick paper, listing his "engagements," as he'd called them. They were the stuff of society papers and his sister Maeve's secret dreams.

And those engagements were far away from Sean's list with church, parks, cheap amusements, and his mother's address. Sean had never been the type of man to feel ashamed of his roots or his family. In fact, the complete opposite was true. He came from good stock. His father had been a decent man, his mother warm and giving.

They'd never had much. And while he'd be lying if he pretended he had never wished for more, he'd been raised to always be thankful for God's blessings.

But the first time he'd held that substantial piece of stationery and read about Owen's life, he'd been ashamed of his own rather meager existence.

Owen, of course, had never mentioned his feelings about Sean's activities. Not that he would. Perhaps he would never be as much the decorated, well-respected detective Sean was in the police department, but he was certainly every inch the gentleman. And therefore, he drew respect and acclaim all over the rest of the city.

He'd been a good partner, however—one Sean felt blessed to have.

Which is why he'd felt little to no compunction about arriving on the doorstep of the Lawrence mansion to pull Owen away from a society dinner party. They were partners, always.

Murder always took precedence over their personal lives, and Owen would be the first to agree about that.

"Go ahead and knock, Barnaby. Time's a-wasting."

"Yes, sir." But still he stood motionless. Barnaby, all twenty-one years of age and hailing from some farm out of the city, was indeed as green as the fields he talked so fondly about. Sean knew Barnaby would give just about anything to switch places with him.

Sean felt for him. It was a difficult thing to confront the rich and famous in the city, especially when one didn't even feel especially confident in the first place.

However, he must remember that they had an important job to do. He also wanted the boy to remember that their job and duties were far more meaningful than the pursuits of most men in the upper levels of society.

"Go on, Constable," he fairly barked.

"Yes, sir." At last Barnaby rapped smartly on the door.

Instantly it was opened by a distinguished-looking butler dressed in a well-cut black suit. If he was shocked to be opening the door to two men like them, he didn't betray a hint of it.

Instead, his dark-blue eyes flickered from Barnaby's uniform to Sean's best tweed suit before bowing slightly. "Yes?"

"I am Constable Barnaby and this here is Lieutenant Detective Sean Ryan," Barnaby more or less squeaked out. "We are here on police business."

The butler blinked. "And why are you on the premises? No one has called for you. At least not that I'm aware of."

Before Sean could smooth things over, Barnaby raised his voice and infused a new, stronger note of confidence in it. "Sir, I'm sorry to disturb things, but we need to see Detective Owen Howard immediately."

"I'm sorry, but I cannot—"

Out of patience, Sean interrupted. "I'm afraid you're going to have to. It's a matter of some urgency."

The servant looked askance. "You'll have to come back at a more convenient time. This is a private party."

To Barnaby's credit, he straightened his shoulders and lifted his chin. "Like I said, we're here on police business. Detective Owen is needed. Immediately."

The butler glared at Barnaby, then let his gaze drift to Sean. Sean met the servant's eyes with a cold look. It was one he'd mastered at a young age when he'd learned that being seen as weak was a recipe for disaster in the schoolyard.

Whatever the butler saw must have given him pause, because he muttered, "Come inside, then."

Sean was pleased to have been let in at last. After they crossed the threshold, he stared at the butler to make it clear he expected him to find Owen.

"I will go see if Mr. Howard is available," he snapped before turning on his heel and walking smartly into a drawing room.

As soon as they were completely alone, Barnaby scowled. "Man's got a bug up his frame, wouldn't you say? He was looking at me as if I was ready to nick his silver."

"At least he let us inside. It was looking doubtful for a moment there," Sean said dryly.

"Yes, sir."

Almost immediately, the butler followed a gray-haired gentleman into the foyer. The man looked harried, like their appearance was the last thing he needed during an already-too-busy day. "Good evening. I'm Mr. Lawrence's secretary. How might I be of assistance?"

"You can't," Barnaby said.

"Our business is not with the Lawrence household," Sean interjected smoothly. "We're only here to ask Detective Howard to join us. I'm sorry for the disruption, but it cannot be helped. As we already told the butler, this is a matter of some urgency."

"Would you care to wait in another room? Perhaps you might like some refreshments?"

Barnaby's eyebrows rose, though Sean wasn't sure if he was shocked by the idea of being served while they waited or curious as to what the food would be.

"Refreshments are unnecessary." Sean finally lost patience. He stepped forward and glared at the butler. "We need to see Detective Howard. Now."

"Yes, sir." His voice was thick with sarcasm, but he did immediately open the door to a room just to the side of the entryway. "Please wait in here. I'll go see if Mr. Howard is available."

Sean stepped forward, invading the personal space even accorded a servant. "You will tell Detective Howard that Detective Lieutenant Ryan has requested that he come immediately."

The butler blanched. "Yes, sir."

Keeping his face impassive, Sean stared at the man until he turned and walked out. The secretary went with him. Less than five minutes later, Owen strode in.

"Sean. Can't say I'm glad to see you tonight."

"Can't say I'm glad to be cooling my heels at one of your engagements," Sean teased.

"What happened? I thought we had everything handled with Miss Bond."

"Turns out there has been more than one victim tonight."

When the butler inhaled sharply, Sean said, "We had best be going. I'll fill you in on the way."

"Was it the Slasher?" Owen's expression was intense, and he already looked prepared to hear the worst.

"Looks like that."

Turning to the butler, he raised his chin. "I'll need my topcoat and hat, if you please."

To Sean's amusement, the butler bowed deferentially. "Right away, sir. And please, let me know how I might be of any further service."

"I will, Jamison. Thank you."

Yet again, Sean was struck at how easily Owen Howard could meld his society demeanor with the qualities in him that made such a good policeman. Sean couldn't think of another man in his acquaintance who could connect the two so seamlessly.

But, of course, they'd worked together for a year now. That was to be expected.

What wasn't to be expected was the appearance of the lady who never seemed to be far from his thoughts—the beautiful Eloisa Carstairs. He had assumed she would remain with her friends and not be aware he had come for Owen. Her hair was swept up in a mass of curls. She was clad in a form-fitting, black lace gown and sinfully smooth, black satin gloves covered her delicate skin all the way to her elbows.

The stark color against her blonde hair, blue eyes, and exquisite skin was a breathtaking sight.

"I'm sorry to intrude," she blurted as soon as she was within speaking distance. "I couldn't simply sit in the dining room and listen to Carlotta talk about the latest dress displays at Field & Leiter."

"Miss Carstairs." He stepped forward. Then, before he could stop himself, he reached out a hand.

To his delight, she clutched it with her gloved hand. Holding his palm firmly, almost as if she were afraid he would vanish if she let him go. "Lieutenant Ryan, what has happened?"

"We'll speak about this later." Aware that Barnaby was staring at Eloisa like she was one of the seven wonders of the world, Sean decided it would be best for them to keep some distance.

Privately, however, he couldn't blame his constable's awestruck expression. Eloisa looked especially fine this evening, dressed as she was with jewels threaded through her golden tresses.

"Please?" she asked.

"You know I cannot speak about a case," he said carefully.

"Please. I have to know. Does it have to do with Millicent?"

Stifling his impatience, he glared at Owen. "What have you told her?"

"Only the barest of facts."

"You shouldn't have said a word."

"She knew the moment I arrived at her door that something was wrong. I didn't see any need to withhold the information completely. After all, I am her escort for the evening, Ryan."

Sean digested that, hating both his jealousy and the fact that it was obvious Owen realized it. "We really need to leave."

Owen stared at him a long minute before nodding. "I see." Turning to Eloisa, he spoke, his voice softer, infinitely more gentle. "I'm sorry, Eloisa, but I'm afraid I'm going to have to leave you."

She looked pained. "I see."

"Now, what would you like to do, my dear? Return to the table?" He lightened his tone. "If you do so, it will break my heart, but I'll forbear and ask another gentleman to escort you home safely."

"Is there another option?"

Owen flicked his gaze to the constable, who was still staring at Eloisa like she was a Greek goddess suddenly come to life. "If you'd like to leave now, I can have Barnaby here escort you home."

Barnaby visibly gulped. "Me?"

"Constable, I can trust you to look after Miss Carstairs, I hope?"

"'Course, sir, but—"

"You'll do fine," Sean said.

But Eloisa didn't look pleased with that idea any more than their young constable. "Owen, I don't need a police escort," she whispered.

"You do," Sean said before Owen could draw a breath.

"Couldn't I come with you? I promise, I'll do my best to stay out of the way."

Even imagining Eloisa in the midst of such tragedy—or possibly being in danger—made Sean's tone harsh. "Absolutely not."

"But—"

"That is not going to happen, Eloisa. You know we would never even consider putting you anywhere near such a thing," Owen murmured, his tone as patient as Sean's was harsh. "I am sorry, dear, but I need to leave. Ryan wouldn't have come here if it wasn't a matter of urgency."

"If I return to the table, I'll be forced to answer a thousand questions about you, your job, and our alliance." She drew a breath. "I believe it would be best if I left."

"I understand." Leaning closer, Owen pressed his lips to her cheek. "I did enjoy what time we did spend together. You made it bearable. We'll have to do this again, and soon, dear."

She smiled softly. "You always do say the sweetest things."

He winked. "Not at all."

Sean had had enough. Owen and Eloisa looked so perfect together, so right, he could hardly tolerate their proximity. He was also more jealous than he could ever remember being in his entire life.

And it wasn't just that he knew he would never be escorting Eloisa anywhere like this dinner party. It was also the fact that he wouldn't even know what to do at such an event. At that moment, he felt he might as well be speaking to her from one of the tenements south of the river.

"Barnaby, escort Miss Carstairs home. Her house is at the top of Sable Hill." He turned to Owen. "Do you have your carriage here?"

"Of course. I'll summon the driver on the way out. Good evening, dear. I'll call on you soon."

Eloisa rushed forward. "Wait! Sean, can . . . can you at least tell me if this . . . if this has to do with the Slasher?"

He shouldn't have said a thing. He should have ignored her question. But because he knew it was only a matter of hours before the news would spread like lightning, he nodded.

She paled. "Can you tell me who else he attacked?"

"You know I cannot, miss," he said, finally using the sense God gave him and remembering his place.

"But—"

"All you need to know is that it is not you, Miss Carstairs."

"Lieutenant, that means nothing. That is not enough."

"On the contrary, I think it might mean everything," he said before he could stop himself. "Now, don't ask me any more questions. You know I can't tell you anything further. Howard, are you armed?"

"Of course."

Sean nodded. "All right, let's go. Barnaby, don't leave her side until she walks through her front door."

"Yes, sir. And then?"

"And then, go to the precinct. If we need you further, I'll send word."

Eloisa reached out and wrapped one gloved hand around his forearm. "Sean? I mean, Lieutenant, would you stop by tomorrow and tell me what happened?"

"Miss Carstairs—" With everything he was, he wanted to be the one man she could trust. But he'd seen her with Owen. They were right together. Moreover, her family must think highly of him. Otherwise he wouldn't have been her escort to the dinner party.

"I mean, if you could? Please?"

Doing his best to avoid Owen's interested gaze, Sean at last nodded. "I'll do that, miss."

"Thank you." Turning to Owen, she held out her hand. "Please do be careful, Owen."

Pressing her palm between his hands, he said, "Always, my dear. Now, you must promise me to not let your imagination run away with you. Let Barnaby see you home and try not to think the worst."

"I don't know if that will be possible."

"If you let your mother see your trepidation, she'll never give you a moment's peace," he warned.

"This is true."

"That's why you must try to not worry, dear," he murmured as he lifted her hand and pressed his lips to her knuckles.

Before Sean's eyes, Eloisa nodded, her body conveying her absolute trust in Owen—and reminding Sean that his infatuation with the heiress needed to end—and quickly too. If it didn't, he was going to embarrass them all.

He turned around and motioned for Owen to follow. His partner did, buttoning his overcoat as they walked out, then crawled into the waiting hack and rushed toward the scene of the crime.

"Where are we going?" Owen asked.

"Fairgrounds."

Owen started. "I assume you found another of the Slasher's victims?"

"I did. She was in an alley behind the Women's Pavilion. Not only stabbed twice but garroted as well. She bled out before anyone spied her. Now we have not one but two murders."

Owen shuddered. "What is our world coming to?"

He didn't dare answer. As it was, there were too many questions, both about himself and Eloisa and even Owen's relationship with her.

Too much was going wrong in their world.

"I'll be glad when this God-forsaken fair is over," he stated.

"For me it can't happen soon enough. Though we are both likely fooling ourselves, Sean. There's a very good chance our murderer isn't one of the thousands of visitors overtaking our city. There's a very good chance he's someone women might know or trust."

That was the second time in an hour someone had proposed that possibility in his hearing.

"I've started to think that too. The women being targeted are cosseted and protected. Like Eloisa, they are gently cared for and rarely alone. A stranger would never get the opportunity to get near these women to speak to them, much less attack them in private."

"I agree. Unless the person is a type of person they might trust."

"Such as?"

Owen shrugged. "I don't know. Perhaps a person dressed as part of the clergy."

"Surely not."

"Okay, how about a servant?" Owen thought some more. "Perhaps even someone on the police force."

Sean thought about that, then shook his head. "I don't know if ladies are going to stay in a policeman's company without a reason."

"The ladies at the party were perfectly comfortable in my company," Owen quipped.

And it was the second time he realized with every bit of his soul that, though he and Owen Howard might have been brought up mere miles from each other and were both detectives, that was where their similarities ended.

CHAPTER 15

The crime scene in the distance was illuminated by several kerosene lanterns. Some looked planted on the ground, some raised, no doubt in various officers' hands. The scattered beams cast an otherworldly glow to the already eerily quiet fairgrounds. As Sean walked with Owen past the lagoon and horticultural building, a terrible feeling of dread settled deep in the pit of his stomach.

He knew he was being weak, but the fact was, he wasn't eager to view another woman sliced open. Especially not a gently bred one . . . like Eloisa. Especially not the second body found that evening.

"This isn't going to sound right, but it's harder to see the Slasher's victims than the other female victims we've seen over the years," Owen murmured. "Every time I see another woman of my acquaintance with her throat cut, it makes me physically ill."

"I hear what you're saying. After doing this job for thirteen years, I thought I'd become numb to such sights. But each time I see such acts of violence, I still feel shocked." What Sean didn't dare mention was that he had been starting to fear he would one day see Eloisa lying on the ground. He honestly didn't know how he would recover from such a sight.

Owen nodded, the muscles in his face tense. "Whenever I see one of our Slasher's victims, I have to force myself to look at her face. I'm always afraid I'll know her."

"That's to be expected. You've known every one of the ladies so far. Anyone would be rattled."

"Every time, I hope and pray it will be the last young lady I see in such condition." His voice turned heavy. "Sean, what are we going to do if we don't find this assailant soon?"

"We'll step up our presence at society events and interview even more people who have anything to do with them. Not just servants but flower sellers on the corner, vendors in the alleys. Livery workers. Someone has seen something of import. We simply need to ask the right people the right questions."

"And if we still don't find our killer?"

Against his will, Sean flinched. "It doesn't bear thinking of." Never would he admit that he'd wondered the same thing.

As they continued walking toward the scene, Owen said, "It certainly seems as if the two of you have developed a friendship of sorts."

The change of topic was jarring, but Sean knew what Owen was doing. They both needed to calm down. In their current state, it was likely their emotions would interfere with thoughtful police work. "She is interested in Hope House," he said at last. "My sister Maeve helps out there, and I was able to escort Eloisa for a tour."

"Tonight Eloisa acted as if you might mean a great deal more to her than a simple escort."

Glad for the dark, Sean flushed. "You know as well as I do that only one of us is escorting her to dinner parties. You have nothing to worry about."

"I don't recall mentioning that I was concerned."

Owen sounded amused. Confused by that, Sean elected to keep silent. When they got closer to the scene, he increased his pace, suddenly eager to concentrate on a crime instead of his personal life.

Or of the image that he knew was etched in his memory—the sight of Owen clasping her hand in his own. And of Owen bowing and pressing his lips to Eloisa's knuckles. There had been a familiarity there, a warmth between the two of them that seemed to have less to do with romance and everything to do with a common familiarity of norms.

And when Sean had seen it, he'd been not just jealous but spellbound.

It wasn't that their behavior was unseemly. It was everything proper. Yet it was also smooth and fluid. Owen had known exactly how to lift her hand. How much pressure with which to press his lips.

Sean would have fumbled his way through such a parting, most likely either holding her hand too tightly or kissing her knuckles with an ill-concealed enthusiasm. It would have embarrassed them both, just like when he'd helped her remove her gloves and she'd noticed his thumb was caressing her bare knuckles.

It was a certainty that Sean would never be genteel enough for a woman like her.

Until Eloisa he'd never given much thought to his class, not beyond the random wish for more money, perhaps. But now he was wishing he were someone more high in the instep. Someone a lady like Eloisa Carstairs would never be embarrassed to introduce to her friends.

"You all right, Ryan?" Owen asked.

"Of course. Why?"

"No reason. You just seem a little off."

"Must have something to do with traipsing around at night in the cold, looking at another dead body." Of course, the minute he said such a thing, he ached to take it back. He'd always done his best to give any victim of a violent crime as much dignity as possible.

Owen's eyes widened. "Sorry, sir."

"No, I shouldn't have snapped at you. I was thinking of something I shouldn't have. That's all."

Owen rolled his shoulders. "No worries. And believe me, I feel the same way. Even though I was about to die of boredom in the Lawrences' dining room, I still would have rather been sitting in warmth eating some really excellent food than come here."

"Escorting Miss Carstairs was no hardship either, I presume," he blurted before he remembered he didn't want to think about Eloisa and Owen together ever again.

Owen's lips curved. "Not at all. She's not only one of the prettiest women of my acquaintance, but she's also one of the easiest to be around. I was so glad I accompanied her this evening. Her mother is about to drive her to distraction, she's so determined that Eloisa get engaged soon."

"I had no idea the two of you were so close." He hoped he didn't sound as jealous as he feared he did.

"We are close enough, but we're merely friends, Sean," Owen said slowly. "I'm fond of her, and I think she feels the same way about me. Though our families might love a match between us, I frankly don't see it happening. There is camaraderie between us but nothing more."

"It's none of my concern."

"Ah."

Like a drunken sailor, Sean couldn't seem to control his tongue. "I mean, it's not like she and I would ever have any reason to know each other better. I'm an Irish cop."

"I'm glad you said that. For a moment there you had me worried.

Eloisa is at the top of the spectrum, you know. We can all imagine that such things don't matter. But that would be in a different world than the one you and I live in."

"At last!" one of the officers called out when they came into view.

And right then and there, all thoughts of romance and class distinctions faded from Sean's mind. For the next few hours they were going to be viewing another casualty, visiting with her family, looking for clues, and stoically taking all the blame for the fact there even was another victim.

Though there had been hardly any clues and no witnesses to speak of, he knew he was to blame for the Slasher's continued rampage. He'd sworn to both his captain and himself that he would do everything possible to catch this Society Slasher. Instead, it seemed he was constantly mooning over the unobtainable Eloisa Carstairs.

"We're here now," Sean replied, his voice all business.

"Thank the Lord for that. We've been waiting on ya for over an hour. What took you so long to return to us, Lieutenant? Waiting for our gentleman detective here to get his valet's help dressing?"

Knowing that the teasing was good-natured, Sean tipped his hat in Owen's direction. "Our society gent was dining with the toffs this evening. It took me awhile to convince his peers that some of us have to work for a living."

"Now that we're all here, how about we get to business?" Owen retorted. "Now, what do you have?"

"Ain't nothin' good," Sergeant Fuller said, immediately becoming serious. "This one's another lady, slashed at the throat. And if you don't mind me saying so, she's far too fine to be spending her last minutes in a place like this." He shook his head as he looked around the narrow walkway between the White City's buildings. "For the life of me, I can't imagine how she ended up here."

"Perhaps her name solves that mystery. Do you have a name?" Sean asked.

"I do. Turns out ladies like her get their names embroidered in the linings of their cloaks." The officer glanced at his notepad. "So unless she was wearing a borrowed garment, our victim is Miss June Redmond."

Owen blanched. "This is June?"

Sean looked at him sharply. "You know her?"

Owen nodded, his expression ashen. "She, uh, used to be good friends with my sister Charlotte. She was a pretty girl. Lively. Sweet. Played the piano." Looking as if he were literally forcing out each word, he cleared his throat. "She was also considered quite a catch."

"Well, she ain't nothin' but dead now."

Sean hardened his tone. "Fuller, watch yourself." Though he knew why the captain had ordered even desk sergeants like Fuller to the scene, it was obvious that Fuller was out of his element.

"Sorry, sir. And I'm real sorry for you, Detective Howard." He wiped his face with a handkerchief. "I keep thinking it's going to get easier one day, but each one of these incidents makes my heart bleed, it does."

"We don't know for certain that this woman even is Miss Redmond," Sean pointed out. "Let's go take a look."

Luckily, Owen was already leading the way. Since Sean had already looked at the victim closely before he went to retrieve his partner, he kept a few paces behind, wanting to allow him a small amount of privacy to look on the body.

Even Fuller, never one to pass up an opportunity to either make a joke or tease Owen about his reputation, looked subdued as he lifted the corner of the worn blanket covering the woman's face.

Owen knelt down, flinched, then closed his eyes. When he

opened them again, his whole expression had changed. Cold, hard, ten years older.

And when he raised his head to meet Sean's eyes, Sean knew that the woman had been Owen's sister's friend. And that somehow, someway, this investigation had just reached a very dark, very personal stage.

Because at this moment, Owen Howard looked mad enough to pass out judgment himself. He looked as far from a suave and elegant gentleman who had kissed Eloisa's hand as Sean did.

So much so that Sean wondered if Eloisa would even recognize Owen as the same man.

When Constable Barnaby appeared at Sean's office a little after eight the following morning, his ears were red. After the briefest of knocks on the molding surrounding the door, he sputtered, "Lieutenant, sorry for interrupting, but you've got a caller."

Sean had gotten home in the early morning, fallen into an exhausted slumber for three hours, then had gone back to the fairgrounds to look over the site of the murder in the light of day. June's appearance at the fair had been something of a mystery. As far as they could tell, she had gone to the Midway Plaisance with a group of men and women who bordered on the fringes of good society.

Owen had even been disturbed when they'd pieced together the names of many of the crowd she'd been with. Only when Owen told Sean most of the men had been friends of Douglass Sloane had Sean understood. If June had been keeping company with men like that, it stood to reason that she wouldn't have been as closely protected or sheltered as a woman of shining reputation like Eloisa Carstairs.

Sean was groggy from lack of sleep, stressed from the vision of cement stained with June's blood—which seemed determined to be forever embedded in his mind—and was currently doing his best to catch up on the latest crime reports with his sergeant before Owen came in.

Which was why he was in less than a charitable mood to be interrupted in such a fashion. "Protocol, Constable."

"Sorry, sir. But—"

Sergeant Fuller interrupted. "Now, obviously, the lieutenant is busy, Barnaby. Tell whoever has come calling that he will see him in his own time."

"It's not a *him*. I mean, a woman is here. I mean, it's a lady."

From time to time, they received visits from some of the more wily prostitutes near the shipyards. They'd come in with a story about a pimp or a young gent, usually in the winter, as an excuse to warm up a spell. Sean had no idea why Barnaby would call one of those women a lady.

However, today was not the day for that. "Tell her I don't have time for that," Sean said. With a wink at Fuller, he added, "But you can listen to her grievance, if you want."

"Just beware, lad," Fuller said with a wicked smile. "Most likely she'll be riddled with pox."

As expected, Barnaby's entire face lit up like a flame. Then he blurted, "Lieutenant, your caller is Miss Carstairs. Sir."

At once, all thoughts of ribald humor fled. He straightened. "Pardon?"

"The lady downstairs is Miss Eloisa Carstairs, sir, and she's sitting in the main lobby with a pair of thieves and about half the uniforms on duty. And when I tried to tell her this station weren't no place for the likes of her, she said she wasn't going to move until you had time to meet with her."

Sean got to his feet. "Good Lord." Already walking toward the door, he said, "Sergeant, we'll have to finish this discussion later."

Fuller sauntered down the hall, trailing behind him. "Didn't know you could still hop to your feet so fast. Looks like I had better take a peek at this lady."

Sean ignored the teasing as he reached up and made sure his collar was buttoned on straight and his tie was securely knotted. By the time he rushed down the flight of stairs and entered the main lobby, his heart was beating fast.

The moment he saw her, dressed in a sapphire-blue, wool day dress, wearing smart black boots on her feet and a fussy hat that drew the eye to her beautiful face, he was barely aware of Sergeant Fuller inhaling behind him.

Sean knew from experience that Eloisa incited that reaction from most men.

She was sitting on one of the wooden ladderback chairs, chatting with one of the uniformed officers. Sean was glad the man had had the sense to stay close to her side. When he was roughly a dozen feet or so away from her, she turned her head and smiled. "Hello, Lieutenant."

Before he knew what he was about, he found himself reaching for her outstretched, gloved hand and helped her rise. However, he wasn't able to prevent himself from scowling. She had no business being in such an area.

"Miss Carstairs, please tell me you are all right."

Confusion swam in her eyes before she nodded. "Of course I am." She looked down at her hands, at her dress, then raised her chin in confusion. "Why do you ask?"

"Because you should know better than to be anywhere near here. I believe Constable Barnaby indicated as much to you."

"I'm sorry if I worried you. I was merely hoping to have a few moments of your time." Gazing at him prettily, she asked, "Do you have time for me?"

Sean did his best to ignore Fuller's chuckle behind him. Completely aware of every man in the room, even the pair of peddling thieves, listening in unapologetically, he leaned closer. "If you wished to speak with me, you should have sent word with a servant."

But to his surprise, she ignored his cool tone and stepped a little closer. Close enough for the faint scent of gardenias to tempt him. "I didn't want to cause you any more trouble than I already have."

He hated the idea of Eloisa's visit becoming a topic of conversation and gossip. She was too sweet, too fragile for that. However, he also knew if he shook his head every other man in the vicinity would volunteer for the privilege.

"Come with me," he said, his speech clipped and his concern for her making his voice harsh. "Sergeant Fuller," he said, looking at his shadow, "please see that I am not disturbed." Unable to help himself, he gently rested a palm on the small of Eloisa's back as he guided her through the room and back up the staircase.

As he passed Fuller, the sergeant's gaze flickered toward him. "You picked the right man to seek help from, miss," he said politely. "Ain't a better man on the force, and that's a fact."

Eloisa met the grizzled man's gaze. "I am beginning to realize that, Sergeant. Thank you."

The moment they reached the stairs and started their ascent, Sean could hear the low murmurings begin behind him. No doubt this visit would be a topic of conversation for the next year.

When they reached the second floor, he stepped to her side and led Eloisa into his office at the end of the hall. Aware that men in the other offices had begun to step into the hall, hoping to catch the unusual sight of a gently bred lady in their midst, he snapped the door shut behind them the moment they were inside his small, cramped space.

Her eyes widened as she gazed around the room.

He tried to look at it from her perspective. He smelled the musty odor of books and files and saw the windowsill in need of cleaning. Chairs with scarred wood and frayed cushions. His desk, if not Owen's, littered with too many papers. An empty coffee cup.

And Sean wasn't sure if she was suddenly worried about being alone with him in close quarters or if she'd finally come to the conclusion that he was no one she should ever know—even if Owen worked there too. But she looked a little taken aback.

Then she exhaled softly, gazed at him with a soft expression, and almost smiled. "May I sit down, Sean?"

And that was when he realized at that very moment, he didn't care that they shouldn't know each other. That she shouldn't be in a police precinct office.

All he was able to do was brush off the chair Fuller had been sitting in and gesture toward it. "Of course. Please, do sit down."

But he had to make her understand. Her safety was at stake.

CHAPTER 16

Little in her life had prepared Eloisa Carstairs for her current situation. At the moment, she was sitting in a rather rickety chair across from Lieutenant Ryan. He was sitting behind one of two desks in a small, cramped office. From what she'd had the chance to observe as they walked down the hall, there were several such offices like his in a confusing maze on the second floor of this police station.

After stopping by Hope House with Juliet to drop off some small toys and blankets for the children, she'd sent her maid to do some shopping with their driver, leaving them to assume she had never left Hope House when they returned to find her still there. Then she had come to the precinct unescorted, which was an experience in itself.

When Constable Barnaby, who had escorted her home the night before, saw her and suggested she should not be there, she informed him she would stay until Lieutenant Ryan was available. Looking exasperated, he asked her to take a seat in the waiting area and went to find Sean.

Furthermore, it seemed as though a woman sitting in the lobby was an unusual occurrence. Every man in the room—and there were a great many—stared at her in a bold, assessing way. She'd dealt with this by pretending she wasn't bothered by their stares in the slightest and chatting with the kind officer who came to stand by her side. All the while wishing she'd, perhaps, been a little less impulsive when she'd decided after a light breakfast of tea and toast to visit Sean. Perhaps he was in no hurry to see her.

In the few minutes she waited, as more men came out of the woodwork and stared at her in a rather rude way, Eloisa realized she had indeed been terribly foolhardy and capricious. This was a scary place, and she was worried about what Sean was going to say when he saw her. So nervous that several times she'd even considered darting out of the police station and hurrying away.

And she would have done that, too, except for one thing—she felt more alive and more in control of her life than she had in years.

Years.

When Sean did appear in the waiting room, a dark scowl on his face made everyone in the room scatter like roaches blinded by light, and Eloisa knew he probably wasn't going to want to hear about how her new taste of freedom felt.

He had not. Instead, he strode to her side, glared, asked her a few questions, and then bit out three words. "Come. With. Me."

As a couple of men chuckled under their breaths, Eloisa did as she was bid, following Sean up the stairs, down the hall, and into this office.

When he stopped, he pointed to yet another rickety, wooden ladderback chair. "Sit."

She sat, attempting to shake out her blue wool skirts in a pleasing way as she did so. It seemed some old habits die hard.

Now, as she stared up at Sean, who, instead of walking around his desk and sitting, had decided to perch against the edge of the desk, she realized that something had happened that had been completely out of her hands.

She was developing an affection for this Irish police officer with the handsome good looks, rough hands, and absolutely mesmerizing hazel eyes.

He, on the other hand, was no doubt beginning to wish he'd never come to her aid in the Gardners' ballroom.

When it was apparent that he wasn't going to lead the conversation, Eloisa began. "Lieutenant Ryan, forgive me for intruding upon your time."

"Forgive you for intruding?"

"Yes." She swallowed. "I know you asked me to wait at home until you had a moment."

"You remember that, do you?" His accent was thicker than she'd ever heard it.

"Of course I remember." She attempted to smile. "And, well, I know you are very busy. And, um, I also know it's technically none of my business . . . but I need to know who last night's victim was."

He raised an eyebrow. "Technically?"

She wasn't sure if he knew what the word meant. "Yes, I meant, um, theoretically."

"I knew what you meant."

She felt her cheeks heat. "All right. Well, what I am trying to say . . . is that while the Slasher's latest victim isn't any of my business, it hasn't stopped me from worrying."

He took a fortifying breath. "Miss Carstairs—"

"Eloisa."

"Pardon?"

"Please, could you call me by my first name? I thought we'd agreed to that." She needed to be close to him again. Needed the warmth in his eyes, the tenderness in his touch. She needed it as much as she needed the answers she'd come for.

"It isn't—"

"At least when we're alone?"

To her dismay, he looked even more uncomfortable. "Miss Carstairs, I would rather not share anything with you at this time."

"Why not?"

"It's been my experience that sometimes when we think we want to know the worst, discovering the truth doesn't make it better."

"Please," she begged again, hating that she sounded high strung even to her ears. Wary. Bordering on manic. "I wouldn't have come here if it wasn't so important to me. Please—"

"The victim was June Redmond, Eloisa."

She exhaled. And just like that, all the fight and gumption left her.

The Slasher had gotten to June. Images of June, with her dark-blonde hair and ditzy attitude and easy laugh, suffused her. Along with the knowledge that June had recently been feeling as stifled as Eloisa had lately. They'd been kindred spirits of a sort.

Rumors had recently abounded about June. Gossips claimed she had begun to frequent some of the more unseemly salons and cafés in the city. Some women whispered that they'd heard June had been seen on the arms of some of the businessmen in the city. Men who might have a lot of money but little else in their favor.

Finally, Eloisa recalled the time June and she had been guests of Veronica Sloane a little over a year ago. Veronica had been in fine form, lashing out at any woman she'd deemed a rival for the gentlemen's attention.

The whole evening had been so exasperating—and never-ending—that she and June had stayed close together. They told jokes and made a few rather snide comments about their hostess as the night wore on.

Eloisa wasn't proud of her behavior. But it was an evening she remembered with more than a touch of true fondness. After all, there were so very few other girls in their situations. And now June was gone.

Sean leaned forward, his expression intense. "You knew her."

She inclined her head. "I did. Quite well."

"Is there anything you could tell me about her?"

How could she attempt to describe June so someone who had never met her would understand the type of person she was? It seemed an impossible task. "I'm not sure what I could say that would be of use."

"Come now. Surely you can think of something. Anything that might be of interest to this criminal? We are learning he seems to be targeting not only wealthy women, but those who are at the height of popularity."

"That wasn't June." Thinking of Danica, she added, "That wasn't Danica, either. Both of those girls hadn't been popular. Before they made their debuts, everyone thought they would be very popular. They were not."

"Why was June not well received?" His speech turned even more clipped. "Eloisa, I need to understand the kind of woman she was. And, it seems, the kind of lady she wasn't."

"I don't want to speak poorly of her."

"Eloisa, please. So far, all we know is that she was beautiful and rich."

The offhanded comment burned. "She was more than that," she said quickly. "June had a delicious sense of humor. Stinging."

"Bad enough that, perhaps, she might have inadvertently stung someone's pride?"

"I don't know. I knew her, Lieutenant Ryan. But though we were friends, I didn't know her well enough to guess what might have upset a murderer."

Sean pressed his knuckles onto the flat surface of his desk.

"Detective Howard is with her family this morning. I'm sure he'll get some information, but they might not be very forthcoming. I know you feel disloyal. I know you're upset. But I need your honesty. Eloisa, I need your help."

For the first time, she saw real fear in his eyes. Fear for her, fear for the other ladies in her midst.

"June has been out as long as I have. She, like me, has also not made a match. She was tired. Tired of the pressure, tired of the sameness that makes up our days. She . . . she began to become a bit . . . reckless with her time and her companions."

His gaze was so intense, she was sure an explosive could be set off behind him and he still wouldn't blink. "Tell me."

"Some of the men were from the fair. Others new to Chicago. Men with a great deal of money, eager to spend it, to make a grand entrance." Weighing her words, she continued quietly. "Make a statement."

"Did you know these men?"

She shook her head. "I am comfortable with few men."

"Yet you came down here by yourself. Unescorted," he bit out.

"Coming here was different." She took a deep breath, intending to tell him more about why it was different, but she couldn't find the words to tell him that she'd instinctively known she would feel safe around him. That she was sure he would make her safe.

As her words lay between them, sinking, his gaze turned hard. Accusing. "That is your explanation?"

It wasn't, but what else could she say? Helplessly, she shrugged.

His eyes narrowed. "Does your mother know you are here?"

"Of course not."

"Did you tell anyone of your plans? If, God forbid, something happened to you on your way here, would anyone have known you were on your way to see me?"

Of course she hadn't told anyone. Her parents would have forbidden her to see Sean, even with an escort. And if she'd told Juliet, her maid would have felt honor bound to tell someone. Otherwise she would be let go.

Unfortunately, her elusiveness was disturbing to him. His expression grew colder as he shook his head. "Miss Carstairs, I have to say that at the moment, you are not making any sense at all. It seems you are determined to traipse around the city in some twisted need for excitement."

Twisted? "Definitely not."

"Instead of helping me, you have only given me more to worry about." He glared. "On a silver platter."

"That isn't fair."

"By coming here unescorted, you have yourself in a precarious spot. A perilous situation."

"No one downstairs was anything but respectful, Lieutenant."

"Correction. They were respectful to your face, Eloisa. No doubt they had much to say behind your back."

She rolled her eyes. "You make it sound as if no other men and women do the same thing."

"Don't pretend to be so naïve. We both know you are governed by a different set of rules."

She thought they'd moved beyond such things. That they'd moved beyond merely thinking of each other in terms of their social standings.

What had happened? When he'd escorted her to Hope House he seemed to understand her need to be around other people, in a way very few people ever did. But now? Now it seemed they were once again strangers.

His dissension hurt. Stung. "Why are you so angry with me?"

"I'm sorry. I'm not angry, I am worried. I know it isn't my place to tell you this, but I wish you would take more precautions. You should be staying home where it is safe."

"Don't you understand, Sean? That is exactly how I have been passing the past few weeks. Living in fear, reliving what Douglass did to me."

He visibly flinched. "I would give most anything to have spared you that. But don't you understand that what happened should have made you even more aware of the dangers around you?"

"Living the way others want me to is how I've lived my entire life! I don't wish to do that anymore. If I have a question, I want to be able to ask it."

"There are different ways to go about that. You should have waited until I paid you a call."

"You want me to sit at home until you have a spare moment for me? To stare out the window waiting like a child?"

"If that is how you choose to characterize it, yes."

Stunned and hurt and more than a little confused by his tone, Eloisa sprang to her feet. "I thought you were different. I thought we were different. I thought we were friends."

He straightened. "We cannot be friends."

"Why not?"

"Because I'm Irish, Eloisa. Because I'm working class. Because my family built canals and railroads and worked in the stockyards while yours financed them. Because each of your evening gowns likely costs more than I earn in a month."

"Those things don't matter."

"They most certainly do." He held up his hands, as if they were stained beyond repair.

"Those things don't define you."

His head jerked. "Eloisa—"

"Just as my parents and their house do not define me, your family and home do not define everything you are. You are more than that." She bit her lip. "At least I thought you were."

"That is true. But their personalities and circumstances aren't more than a stone's throw away from who I am. We can't live in a narrow tunnel pretending things we don't like don't affect us." Quietly, he added, "If I've led you to believe I would welcome such familiarity from you, I am very sorry."

She stared at him in mortification. Not knowing what to say. No longer having any idea of what she should do.

Luckily, the sound of heavy footsteps and the rattle of the door opening broke the silence.

She turned to see Owen Howard striding forward. "Eloisa?" he asked, his eyes searching her out. When they connected, his voice softened. "Dear, you've given me such a fright. Why are you here?"

"Owen." Seeing his kind expression, tears pricked her eyes. "Owen, I'm so glad to see you."

He reached her side in an instant, and wrapped an arm around her shoulders. "Darling, what is it?" Darting a lethal glance Sean's way, he murmured, "You are overwrought." He pulled her into his arms, wrapping her in a reassuring hug.

Making her realize that had been the real reason she'd come to the police station. The real reason she'd wanted to see Sean Ryan. She'd needed the comfort of a warm embrace.

"Oh, Owen," she murmured as he pulled her closer. And his reassuring hand on the back of her neck, the feel of his arm around her shoulders, made the tears fall and all her fears no longer at bay.

After a few moments, he pulled away. Then he gently wiped away the tear tracks that stained her cheeks with a pressed handkerchief that smelled of cologne. "May I get you some tea?"

"No, thank you. I need to leave." Unable to stop herself, she glared at Sean. "I realize now that I never should have come."

"Please, let me escort you home."

Seeing Sean's face set in a careful, hard mask, she nodded and edged closer to Owen. "Would you mind?" she whispered. "I know you have a lot to do . . ." She'd tell him outside the station that she needed to return to Hope House instead.

"There is nothing more important than your safety, my dear." He winked. "Besides, I do believe walking by your side will make me the envy of every man here."

"Owen, even now you are a shameless flirt."

"It's not flirting if my feelings are genuine. I promise, I cannot think of a better use of my time than seeing you safely home."

She smiled at his words. Looked into his eyes, saw a delicious warmth in them. And a tenderness too. So different than the caustic, bossy, guarded Sean Ryan. "Thank you."

As she moved to the door, Owen turned to Sean. "Will you be here when I return?"

"If I'm not, I'll leave word where I am." His cool tone matched Owen's.

"Very well," Owen replied before placing a firm hand on the small of her back and guiding her out. "Let's go, dear."

Eloisa smiled at him gratefully as he led her through the stacks of papers on the floor, the mismatched chairs, and the rickety-looking side table stained an unfortunate shade of brown.

She exited the office and made sure she didn't look back once. She also knew she didn't really need to know what was happening between the two men. Both were policemen. One was of her social standing—one was definitely not. Both seemed concerned about her, but only one seemed to know how to communicate that without scaring her.

One she was comfortable with. The other? He was the last thing she thought about when she went to sleep at night and the first thing she thought about when she woke up in the morning.

One man was safe; the other was not. But she realized, too, that she'd only run to one of them when she was afraid.

She was very sure Sean Ryan was still standing motionless. Glaring at her. And making her wish she'd never, ever considered being alone with him.

Hopefully she wouldn't make that same mistake again.

CHAPTER 17

"You are certainly in a mood," Maeve declared as she bustled around his kitchen, making him a fresh pot of tea.

"Can't always be walking around with a grin plastered on my face," Sean replied, not even attempting to curb his sarcasm.

She was making tea and bread-and-butter sandwiches. Sitting on another chair, but looking far more thoughtful, was Katie. As he gazed at his youngest sibling, Sean again couldn't help but feel proud of her. Katie was the beauty of the Ryan family, and also had a more polished air about her than any of them. It was likely because by the time she was born his family had moved away from the rickety apartment and into a small house in a far nicer neighborhood. She'd also gotten the opportunity to get some schooling, so she had been reading at a young age. He hadn't learned until he was twelve or thirteen. Maeve still was basically illiterate.

But Katie? She was their light. Smart and lovely. His parents expected great things for her. As far as he could tell, however, she wasn't sure what she wanted.

Night and day from the way their Maeve looked at the world. Long ago she had made it her duty to tell everyone what she wanted, what she thought. At the moment he was in her sights. She stilled as she was slathering a thick piece of bread with butter. "Was work really as bad as all that?"

It really had been. His whole day had been filled with a million moments of regret for the callous way he'd behaved toward Eloisa. Coupled with everyone in the precinct's interest in Eloisa's appearance in their midst, their meeting behind closed doors, followed by Owen Howard's careful escort out of the building, Sean had gotten next to no momentary break from all things Eloisa.

To make matters worse, after Owen returned, the two of them found it necessary to return to Miss Redmond's house. The twelve hours following the notification of their daughter's death had, of course, not been kind to her family. Her father looked haggard, her mother pale and extremely fragile. And though Sean had informed dozens of family members about loved ones' deaths, there had been something worse about this family.

Added to the difficult situation was the unusual, new tension that had sprung up between him and Owen. Owen hadn't come right out and said anything, but Sean knew his partner was displeased about his treatment of Eloisa.

To top it off, there now seemed to be something new brewing between Owen and Eloisa. In the last year that they'd worked together, Sean couldn't remember Owen ever mentioning the beautiful Eloisa Carstairs, not even in passing.

But this afternoon, Owen had been intent on making sure he

reminded Sean that only he had been able to ease her fears, not Sean. That he had been the one to escort her home, not Sean.

And though it was exactly as it should be—after all, hadn't he very firmly reminded Eloisa that she should not be having anything to do with him?—he knew now that he and Eloisa could never even be friends. He was honest enough with himself to admit that seeing the way Owen had comforted her had been physically difficult to witness. Every nerve inside of him had felt about ready to snap in pain. It had taken everything he had to remain passive and distant and not glare when Owen had wiped the tears from Eloisa's cheeks.

The tears he knew he'd put there.

By the time he worked through the new stacks of paperwork Sergeant Fuller had placed there, the last bit of restraint he'd been holding was stretched perilously tight.

When he'd walked in the door of his small home, all he'd wanted to do was eat some leftover soup and attempt to forget about everything. But no less than fifteen minutes after he'd gotten home, Maeve and Katie appeared. Then Maeve began bustling in his kitchen like she owned the place, even though they lived a good ten blocks from each other.

Of course, that wouldn't be difficult to do. He barely knew how to do much more than make toast and tea.

"I'm only in a mood because I am not in the mood for company. You shouldn't come over here uninvited." Looking at Katherine Jean, who was staring at him with wide eyes, he murmured, "No offense to you, Katie."

"None taken," she said with a small grin. "Though Maeve is right. You do seem fairly disconcerted today."

"Disconcerted, hmm? That's a new word."

Maeve rolled her eyes. "She's doing that a lot these days, throwing out words we all have to guess the meaning of."

Katie tucked her chin. "I'm trying to improve my vocabulary. There is nothing wrong with that."

"Of course there isn't." He was proud of her. He even knew that, secretly, Maeve was too. "Any special reason you are working on your vocabulary?"

"Simply trying to improve myself."

"Ah."

"She went in the Women's Pavilion and started getting all sorts of ideas," Maeve explained with a sniff. "I told her all she needs to be doing is keeping herself out of trouble until the right man comes along."

"All anyone talks about anymore is my future husband."

"It is about that time. Most girls are getting married at your age," he murmured. As much as he wanted his sister to remain a young girl, he was enough of a pragmatist to realize that those days were long gone.

Katie met his gaze with a definite look of disdain. "Like that is all I've got to think about."

He wondered what else she was thinking of, but knew better than to ask her in front of Maeve.

Sean stood up and took his cup of tea from Maeve's hands. "Thanks for this." After taking a fortifying sip, he smiled. "You make a good cuppa, for sure, Maeve."

She sat down. "If it makes you feel any better, I'll be glad about that."

Her sweet words brought him what he was sure was his first smile of the day. "Maeve, you better be careful. If you keep talking like that, I'm going to have to tell Jack that you do have a fair share of sweet words in that thick head of yours."

"You'd better not even think about doing something like that. He'll walk all over me, he will."

Katie giggled. "Nah. He'd only call Sean a liar. You know your man doesn't think you're ever sweet, Maeve."

"I'm not that bad," Maeve retorted, though her lips twitched.

"Sure you are," Katie teased.

Sean bit back a bark of laughter, but only succeeded in half choking. "I wouldn't blame him, neither. I'd say anything I could to make sure Maeve didn't let loose her temper on me."

"Jack O'Connell knows I love him."

"And he also knows the wrath of your temper," he quipped just as an impatient rap sounded at his front door.

"You sit here, I'll get it, brother," Katie said as she trotted out of the kitchen.

Thinking it was his elderly neighbor, wanting to sit in front of the fire for a few minutes and chat, he called out, "Tell Jeremy I'm not up for company tonight."

"Sean, it isn't Jeremy," Katie called back. "It's Detective Howard."

There was enough worry in her voice that Sean leapt to his feet. "Owen, what's happened?" he asked as he ran into the front room and grabbed his jacket off the back of his couch.

"Nothing alarming."

Sean looked at him in surprise. "Aren't you here on business?"

Owen glanced at Katie, then shook his head. "No, but we can do this later. I didn't realize you had company." Glancing Katie's way again, he said, "Please forgive the interruption."

"It's nothing. Only my sisters."

"Thanks, Sean," Maeve said from the doorway leading into the kitchen.

"Owen, this is my sister Maeve, Maeve O'Connell."

He inclined his head. "Ma'am."

Sean continued. "And you know Katie, of course."

Katie smiled prettily. "It's nice to see you, Detective Howard."

Behind him, Maeve inhaled sharply, though whether she was finding fault with Katie being so forward with a gentleman or to a policeman, he wasn't sure.

And to Sean's further dismay, Owen bowed slightly. "It's a pleasure to see you again, Miss Ryan."

Maeve entered the room and raised her eyebrows. Sean felt like doing the same. He had no idea Katie even possessed such pretty manners. But then, as he noticed Owen doing everything he could to look anywhere but stare at his sister, Sean took things into his own hands.

"How about some tea? My sisters and I were just sitting in the kitchen."

"Actually, I think we'd best be leaving," Maeve said. "Katie, let's go."

"Oh. Yes, of course." After darting another shy look at Owen, Katie hugged Sean good-bye. "I love you, Sean."

Pressing his lips to her cheek, he murmured, "I love you too. Stay out of trouble."

After a quick, sidelong glance at Owen, Katie glared at him. "I'm not a child, Sean."

"I am discovering that, Katherine Jean. Thanks again for the tea and fresh bread and butter, Maeve," he added as she led Katie out the door.

"Get some sleep now." Looking at Owen, she added a cheeky smile. "I think both of you are going to need some."

Then they departed without another word.

Sean closed the door behind them, then immediately felt more self-conscious. He had never been to Owen's apartments, but he imagined Owen could probably fit three of Sean's house in his drawing room.

"Again, may I offer you a cup of tea, Owen?"

"No, thank you."

"Well, if you don't mind, let's go sit in the kitchen. It's a bit warmer in there."

"Wherever you would like is fine." Owen looked like he wasn't aware of the temperature in the room. But Sean noticed that some of the fire had gone out of his eyes, that he now looked more reflective.

He added a bit of hot water to his tea from the kettle on the stove, sat, and took another fortifying sip. His pleasures were few, and he didn't intend to miss this one because of good manners. "So you said this wasn't business. What is it? How may I help you?"

Owen shifted from one foot to the other, looking everywhere but directly at him. "I came over to talk to you about Eloisa."

"Oh?"

"I think we need to discuss what happened with her this morning." When Sean straightened, ready to kindly ask him to leave, Owen raised his hand. "This is important, Ryan."

"I did not invite her to come to the station. I may be more than a little rough around the edges, but even I wouldn't have done something like that. I hope you realize that."

"Of course I know." He shifted, glanced at the doorway to the front room in a curious way, then looked even a bit more uneasy. "I thought I should let you know that she was quite upset with you."

Regret filled him as some of the harsh things he said played in his head. "I'm sure she was."

"So much so, she discussed it at length, Sean. I don't believe anyone has spoken to her so sharply before."

"I imagine not." He hoped not. Barely stifling a sigh, he gestured to a chair on the opposite side of the table. "Have a seat. I'm feeling more and more awkward, looking up at you like I'm a child."

While Owen unbuttoned his jacket, then took the chair, Sean

prepared his explanation. He needed to be completely honest with his partner. Their relationship deserved that. And, well, as much as Sean hated to admit it to himself, Eloisa's relationship with Owen deserved it. It was obvious that there was something brewing between them.

When Owen leaned forward, resting his elbows on his thighs, Sean said, "Eloisa would be very correct in thinking that I spoke too harshly to her. She caught me off guard, and I hated the idea of her being looked at and remarked upon by the assortment of criminals and petty thieves who were lounging around the premises. However, instead of telling her any of this, I lashed out at her. It was wrong. I'll apologize to her the next time our paths cross."

"All right."

Sean had expected Owen to bounce to his feet and walk out now that he'd gotten his way very easily. But instead of darting out right then and there, his partner continued to stare. It seemed more needed to be said.

Perhaps, even, that the whole situation was not completely his fault. "It should be said, however, that while I did not behave as mannerly as I would have liked . . . I'd venture that you would agree that Miss Carstairs should have never come to the station, let alone unescorted. Any number of things could have happened to her."

"Ah, yes. She told me you told her that as well." Owen's voice had turned languid, almost as if he was finding Sean to be amusing. Almost as if he was finding the whole situation amusing.

Which, of course, irritated Sean to no end.

Eventually, Owen shifted, resting one foot on his opposite knee. It was a pose Sean had seen him strike dozens of times, usually when it was late and they were in their precinct office, discussing the intricacies of a particular case. "For the record, I don't disagree. At all. Eloisa made a serious error in judgment."

Sean relaxed. "Are we all right then?"

"Of course."

"Then, why . . . ?"

"Ryan, to be honest, the reason I came over was because I discovered Eloisa is entertaining thoughts about you." He paused, then blurted, "Of a romantic nature."

Sean felt his neck. "I'm afraid I don't understand." Though, of course, he did.

Owen stared at him a long moment, then shrugged. "I think you do. I think we both do." He shook his head. "Sean, I was practicing my speech to you the whole way here. Believe it or not, I was searching for the ideal words to attempt to describe Eloisa's spotless reputation."

"I am well aware of her flawless character."

"I was going to remind you of her place in society."

"I don't need any reminder, Howard." In the eyes of most of the elite, Sean Ryan was little more than an Irish laborer. Little more than a drunk, a vagabond. An unskilled, illiterate, uncouth man who very likely carried disease. "She and I are as far apart as the stars in the sky and the soles of my feet." She was also as bright and beautiful as one of those stars. And just as unobtainable.

Owen shifted, looking uncomfortable. "But, well, now I'm wondering if I was wrong."

Sean was taken aback, which said a lot since he was still coming to terms with the fact that Owen had shown up at his modest home uninvited. "Pardon me?"

Still staring at him, Owen murmured, "The fact of the matter is that she is not only beautiful, she has a lot of integrity. She is also smart and knows her mind."

"And?"

"And for whatever reason, I do believe she has set her sights on you."

Looking increasingly contemplative, Owen murmured, "Perhaps the heart doesn't have as much control over love as I had once imagined."

It was all Sean could do not to roll his eyes. "Owen, we've been partners for a year now."

"I know that."

"I know you are as aware as I am that there are not two men who could be farther apart in the realm of society. Fact is, most people wondered when you were going to run from this job. Go to something more suited to your station—or at least search for a partner who was at least a little closer to being your equal."

"I like this job. I also might remind you that you outrank me."

Sean ignored the reference, knowing his rank was not what was under discussion. "Once more, I would be lying if I said I didn't appreciate how you've treated me as your equal."

"You are my superior, Lieutenant."

Sean knew why Owen threw out his rank. It had been hard-earned, and receiving the promotion had been one of Sean's greatest achievements.

For Owen to reference it said a lot about the type of man he was.

Which, ironically, reminded Sean of how different they were. "While it is true that I'm your superior in the department, in every other way I'm far beneath you. That's no secret."

Owen kept his eyes averted. "Times are changing. Social rank doesn't matter as much as in our fathers' time."

"God willing, they will continue to change. But they haven't changed completely yet." Sean shrugged. "I've long since come to terms with who I am. I will also not lie to you. I am attracted to Eloisa. I'm drawn to her in a way I can never remember being to anyone else. When she's near me, I can't even imagine another woman meaning so much to me. But we both know I could only hurt her."

"Not like she's been hurt before."

Sean stared at him. Something blazed in his partner's eyes, an anger mixed with a flicker of pain. It made him realize Owen had guessed Eloisa was the lady Douglass Sloane raped.

Sean suspected he shouldn't have been surprised. When he heard Reid Armstrong describe the woman who'd been assaulted as a well-known, beautiful young lady of unquestionable reputation and great wealth, Sean realized there were very few women fitting that description.

Owen, of course, knew all the women in that circle.

"If she feels safe with you, well, that is something to hold onto. She needs to feel safe.

"I know that."

"Especially these days. Women are being stabbed and garroted—killed. I know Eloisa is struggling to regain her independence, but I am beginning to realize she also needs to feel safe, safe with men like you and me."

Owen was right. She'd come to him at the precinct because she needed his immediate assurance. However, instead of promising her he would do everything he possibly could to keep her safe, he chastised her for coming to see him at all.

"Point taken," he said dryly.

Owen stared hard before leaning back in his chair with a soft exhale. "If I ask you something about your sister, will you promise not to clock me?"

"I assume you are referring to Katie?"

When Owen nodded, a strange, new prickling slid up Sean's spine. "What would you like to know?"

"How old is she? Is she affianced?"

"Katherine is nineteen." When he noticed Owen's shoulders relax, Sean added grudgingly, "She is not affianced."

"I see."

"I don't know if you do." Staring hard at Owen, Sean added, "To my knowledge Katie has never even dated."

Owen blinked. "Truly? She's beautiful."

"She is. She is beautiful and trusting. Innocent." She was also the youngest sister of a police detective. Most men who would normally be sniffing around her were too afraid of jail to get very close.

Personally, Sean had never thought there was anything wrong with that.

Inserting a thick note of censure in his voice, he said, "Perhaps I should remind you that she might be Irish but she's a good girl. An extremely sheltered good girl."

Owen's eyebrows rose. "Of course you don't need to say such a thing. I would never suspect anything less. My questions spur from nothing but respect. And sincere appreciation."

Now it was Sean's turn to reposition himself. "You only just met her. Is there a reason you are asking about Katherine Jean?"

"If I were to ask you if I could see her again, what would you say?"

Sean wasn't one for extreme exaggerations, but he had a feeling if Owen had knocked him out with a right fist, he couldn't have been more surprised.

He looked away, wanting to kick Owen out of his house. But there was also a part of him that knew his sister could never do better than to catch the eye of a man like Owen Howard. He was a good man. He was also rich.

And only someone who had been hungry and cold in the depths of a long Chicago winter could truly appreciate that. Only someone who had heard stories about his father working in every menial job possible for next to nothing would want something far better for his sister.

Because of that, he weighed his words. "I'd say you would have to be careful."

"And if I told you that I've already been thinking about this, that I've been thinking about it ever since she showed up at the station looking for you, just long enough to get up the nerve to come here to talk to you about it?"

"Then I would hasten to remind you that a man like you would be putting your life in your hands if you trotted down to the street where she lives. A gent like Owen Howard would be as out of place there as a girl like Katie Ryan would be on Prairie Avenue."

"That is fair. Would you consider escorting her to where the three of us could have tea?"

"Tea?"

His lips twisted. "Or something?"

Sean still wanted to jump to his feet, kick a chair, yell at Owen, remind him of their places. But once again, he reminded himself of the truth: never could Katie do any better than the man in front of him. But then, insidiously, he was reminded of his feelings for Eloisa. Like Owen, he knew what it was like to think about someone he shouldn't.

"I only want to get to know Katie better," Owen said quietly. "I want to do this right. I want to spend some time with her to see if it would be possible for her to return my regard. I'm asking for your permission, Sean."

To return his regard. "Are you sure that's all?" he asked sarcastically. They both knew it was a very tall order.

Looking mildly uncomfortable, Owen shrugged. "That's all."

"We both know my sister Katie is as unsuitable for you as a lady like Eloisa Carstairs is for a bloke like me."

"I do know that. You are exactly correct. But I'd still like to get to know her."

"We haven't even talked about your family. Can you imagine what they would say if you brought her by?" Sean didn't want to think about the humiliation they would put Katie through, humiliation a man like Owen, a man who'd had most everything he'd ever wanted, wouldn't even realize he was putting her through. "Owen, would your parents even allow you to see her?"

"I'm of age, Sean. And if you think it was easy informing them that I was becoming a policeman working for an Irishman like Sean Ryan, you are wrong."

"Understood." And maybe he really was understanding a bit more. Maybe Owen was more aware of the obstacles than he was aware.

"Sean, would you be willing to ask your sister if she would be amenable to such a meeting?"

"Yeah." He held up a hand. "And I will apologize to Miss Carstairs."

Owen got to his feet. "I'm glad that's settled," he murmured. "I'll be seeing you."

"Hey, how are you getting home? It's sometimes hard finding a hack this time of night."

"No worries there. My driver's out front."

"Oh. Yes, of course." How could he have forgotten even for a moment how different their lives were? "Good evening, then. Listen, I'm going to pay a call on Eloisa in the morning, so I'll see you some-time after." If they weren't called out for an emergency before that, of course.

"Good evening, Ryan. And God willing, I won't be seeing you until tomorrow afternoon."

"I hope not. I'm very tired of standing next to you gazing at victims' bodies."

Owen tipped his hat. "Sir," he murmured, then darted out of the kitchen and out the door.

Leaving Sean to think about tea and his sister and their families and Eloisa.

But most of all he thought about the glow of happiness he'd see on his sister's face on her wedding day. And the sense of pride and relief he would feel knowing that she was truly cared for.

CHAPTER 18

Another day, another visit to the mansion at the top of Sable Hill.

As Sean stood hat in hand in the foyer, Worthy having already greeted him with a faint smile on his face, Sean reflected on his conversation with Owen and how much of what he'd said was true.

Perhaps life really was worth grasping and taking chances. Perhaps life really was for living by what a person wanted instead of how others would view their having it.

And maybe, too, Eloisa already had done enough. It was time for him to take some chances.

"Lieutenant," Eloisa murmured as she descended the stairs. "I must say this is a surprise." Her step faltered. "Or has there been another incident?"

"No. I was hoping to speak with you."

Something new crossed her features. "Yes, of course. Uh, let's go to the back terrace. It's an unusually warm day for this time of year."

"Thank you." He followed her silently, practicing his speech, wondering how he was going to be able to share everything he wanted to say. Was there even such a way?

She led him into a solarium of some sort. Like the rest of the house, it was spacious. However, because of the openness and many windows, it felt warm and inviting instead of serving as a reminder of the many differences between her life and his.

He paused for a moment to take in its splendor, wishing for the first time that Maeve could be with him. She would enjoy everything about this room. The white wicker seating arrangement was surrounded by a grouping of exotic-looking plants and flowers. The window-filled walls brought in the warmth of the sun. And the rays of that sunlight filtered through onto Eloisa's face.

And that is when his attention skittered from the beauty of their surroundings to concern for her. Because she looked far different than she had twenty-four hours ago.

Lines had formed around her eyes and lips. Her eyes were faintly puffy and red. But overriding both was the way they were filled with pain.

Immediately he pushed aside his prepared speech, filled with trite explanations and excuses. He also stepped past the chair he'd intended to sit on, preferring to be as close to her as possible.

When he sat next to her on the sofa, he reached for her hand. "Eloisa, are you all right?"

Her bottom lip trembled. "No."

"What is wrong? Did someone hurt you?" Immediately he began inspecting her for signs of bruising. It took everything he had not to clasp her other hand and inspect her arms and wrists. "Did something happen last night?"

"No, Sean. Nothing happened. I mean, nothing like that."

"Then like what?" Sharp terror slid through him. "What did happen?"

With the shaking hand that was free, she brushed back a strand of hair from her temple. "Nothing out of the ordinary. I just can't seem to stop thinking about what happened with Danica and Millicent, and now June. Every time I close my eyes, I imagine them covered in blood. Hurt. It haunts my dreams."

He respected her too much to push aside her comments. He, too, had been haunted by the sight of the well-dressed, well-to-do women marred by the Slasher.

"I know you are frightened. And it would be wrong of me to pretend there isn't any reason for you to be. You know the victims. You've seen how injured Danica was. The madman is targeting women of your station. It would be intolerable of me to make light of such things."

"If you think such words make me feel better, you are wrong."

"I don't expect anything will make you feel better until I come to inform you that the Slasher has been apprehended."

One perfect eyebrow arched. "And that is not why you've come to see me today?"

"I'm afraid not." He drew a breath. "Eloisa, I want to apologize for my behavior yesterday. I was beyond rude, and for that I am very sorry."

"Sean, there is nothing to apologize for. You were right. I shouldn't have gone to your precinct. I shouldn't have gone anywhere without an escort."

"You shouldn't have. But I shouldn't have been so angry with you. It wasn't fair or very kind."

"You were working. I interfered." She bit her bottom lip. "If my parents knew, they would have been terribly frightened."

"I was frightened for you. But I also should admit that I wasn't only thinking about your safety yesterday."

"Oh?"

"I . . . I was thinking about myself." Before he could prevaricate again, he plunged ahead. "The thing is, I cannot stop thinking about you, Eloisa."

"I see."

But she didn't. And no small wonder, either. At the moment he couldn't seem to form a decent sentence. Brutally, he forced himself to continue. "What I'm trying to say is that I have come to care for you."

"You have?"

She didn't look as pleased as he'd secretly hoped. Instead, her lips were slightly parted. She seemed at a loss for words and was staring at him in confusion.

And that, of course, made him fumble a bit. "Yes. Um, Miss Carstairs . . . I know who I am. I know what I am. But I haven't been able to help myself."

"Why did you want to help yourself?"

"You know why."

"Sean, the reason I wanted to go to Hope House with you did have a lot to do with my need to see more of the city. To get out of my bubble. I want to do something worthwhile with my time. I want to make a difference." She paused, then added, "However, I also wanted to spend more time with you. Not for protection, but because I have come to care about you too."

His heart eased. Actually, everything in his body started to relax, just as his heart began to pound. "I don't have the words to express how much that means to me."

"You don't need to find the words, Sean." Treating him to a beautiful smile, she added, "I do believe you've already found them just fine."

CHAPTER 19

It had been awhile since he'd spent any time on Haversham Street. Most of the time, when he saw his mother at Maeve's or at church on Sundays, he would politely push aside her offers of lunch or an early supper at home.

Connor derided Sean for this, saying he'd been putting on airs above himself.

Privately, Sean worried his brother was right. His life on Haversham didn't bring him any warm memories or feelings of nostalgia. Life had been hard when he'd been growing up there, and now his reluctance to visit there was a constant source of tension between him and their mother.

In part because he wanted to see Katie, he'd given in to his mother's pleas and relented enough to join her for lunch today. But already he was counting the minutes until he could leave again. Time hadn't been kind to the old house.

The kitchen looked smaller, the floor more scratched, the walls more pocked with holes and uneven plaster. Even the smells of his old home seemed more pungent, staler. Worse.

As Sean dipped his spoon into the bowl of thin cabbage soup his mother had just served him, he wondered if she would notice if he didn't eat every last drop.

The idea didn't make him proud.

The fact was, now that he was living somewhere cleaner, nicer, he never wanted to go back. To his shame he was even starting to realize how much he was becoming comfortable in the Carstairs' home.

It seemed that Mr. Pullman, the wealthy businessman who'd designed the sleeper train car, had been right. Everyone, no matter what their background or circumstances, liked and hoped to deserve nice things.

"Whatcha doing, Sean?" his mother asked over her shoulder. "Waiting on a fancy footman to put a silver spoon to yer lips?"

"Not at all. I was merely waiting on you before I began."

"Why on earth would you do that?"

No way would he tell her that he'd adopted company manners now. He'd watched and learned from Owen over the last year, knowing that the man's good manners and charm were a product of years of training and practice.

He lifted the spoon, sipped the broth, and was immediately scorched by heat and spices. His mother believed in her food creating an impression.

To his bemusement, once he pushed aside the memories attached to the simple fare, he found it tasted good. Like the best of his memories. He took another sip. And another.

Seeing that he was now eating and no longer simply staring at his bowl, his mother relaxed. "Glad you still like it."

With a start, he realized that he'd embarrassed her. It was as if they both knew he didn't belong here any longer. He was like a new couch in an old room. He looked out of place and didn't quite fit in. "Soup's good, Ma."

She smiled. "Glad to hear it. It's bracing on a cold day." She sniffed the air. "These are the days I always forget about, when winter is just around the corner."

"Yes." Knowing it would make her smile, he shuddered like he used to when he was getting ready for school. "One day I'm going to move somewhere warm."

She chuckled, as he hoped. "You've been sayin' the same thing since you learned about Florida."

"One day I'm going to get there, at least for a visit."

"I imagine you will." Her smile grew soft, almost wistful. "So far, you've done pretty well for yourself. I can't think of too many wishes that haven't come true for you."

After he finished his soup, he stood up and carried the bowl to the sink, his mother on his heels. "Thank you again, Ma."

"Anytime." After taking the bowl from his hands, she cleared her throat. "Now, what brings you here? We both know you didn't come for soup."

"I want to talk to Katie. Will she be here soon?"

"She will. Why have you come looking for her?"

"No real reason. Just thought I'd check on her."

"Check on her?"

"Well, I haven't seen her in a while."

"Is that right? I could have sworn she recently paid you a visit."

"Ma—"

"Here I am," Katie announced as she joined them in the kitchen.

With a happy smile, she crossed the floor and threw her arms around his neck. "I love it when you stop by, Sean."

"And I love seeing you." After giving her a squeeze, he held her off at an arm's distance. "Look at you! You're looking as pretty as a picture. New dress?"

"Kind of. It's one of June's old ones that Maeve helped me alter."

"It's a fetching shade of green."

"Thank you, Sean. It's called moss green."

Their mother looked from one of them to the other, narrowed her eyes, then braced her hands on her hips and glared. "Sean and Katie, it's been quite awhile since anyone's tried to pull the wool over my eyes like you two are trying to do."

"I'm not doing anything, Mom," Katie retorted.

"Don't start adding lying to your sins, child."

"Sean." Katie gave him a pleading look.

He agreed that their mother was getting a little riled up. "Ma, Katie isn't lying. There's no need to get on your high horse, now."

Katie's giggle only seemed to solidify their mother's suspicion.

"I'll get on my high horse whenever I feel like it, Sean."

"No reason to glare at me like that."

"I think different." Still glaring at him, she pressed her lips together. "Now, you two can stop your protestations because we know that's a ruse."

"Oh, brother."

She wagged a finger. "Don't try me, Boy-o. We both know you don't come over here on any old day, and especially not to see Katie on a whim. What do you need to speak to her about?"

This conversation was not only disintegrating by the second, it was actually becoming uncomfortable, and why, he didn't know.

Honestly, he could wring Owen's neck for placing him in such a position.

"Mother, you are embarrassing me," Katie murmured.

"Embarrassing you? Since when did you care about that?"

She lifted her chin. "Since I grew up. I'm not a child any longer."

"Pshaw. You're barely nineteen."

"That's old enough."

"To do what?"

"Everything. Lots of girls my age are already married and have a babe on the way."

"At least that isn't you." She narrowed her eyes. "Is it?"

"No. Ma, stop." Katie turned to Sean, all blue eyes and hurt. "Do something."

"Let's go for a walk, shall we?" Before their mother could interfere again, he leaned close and kissed her cheek. "Thank you for the soup, Ma. It was as good as I remembered. Now, let's go, Katie. I have to get back to the station soon."

As he expected, she grabbed her cloak and followed him out the door. Her eyes full of anticipation and light.

Once they were outside, he pointed toward the end of the street, where there was an alley and the train tracks. All the kids in the area had walked along them for years, some even trying their best to hitch a ride in an empty car.

"Okay if we go down this way?" he asked.

"Sure."

As they walked along, they talked with all the people out on the stoops and filling the street. Everyone from children to gossiping mothers to tired men to drunk men filled the area. The air smelled of lunches cooking and trash littering the streets. It was everything that was familiar and, in a strange way, comforting. He knew these people. He knew how they behaved and what pleased them, and what set them off.

He also had come to terms with the fact that he really wasn't a part of their group now. Being on Haversham Street reminded him of everything he'd been so eager to escape. As with his old home, time had done no favors. Buildings that had once seemed ramshackle now appeared to be on the verge of falling down. People who were once down on their luck were now long gone or even looked to be worse off than before.

Underlying it all was the real knowledge that life here was a struggle. It had been when he was little, it had been after the fire in '71, and it had been when his parents first moved into their home. There was also the knowledge that tomorrow wasn't likely to be better.

And that was at the heart of why he'd been so eager to escape. It had been hard, living in a place where feeling hope and optimism for the future was as foreign as valets and evening gowns.

And in the midst of it was his sister Katie. Somehow she had remained untouched by the dirt and grime, the despair and the disease. She was everything bright and shiny.

It was no wonder Owen had taken one look at her and decided he wanted to know her better. And after mulling over all Owen had said, though still not completely enthused about the idea of his partner seeing his sister socially, he knew he had indeed recognized the truth. Katie could do far, far worse than have a man like Owen Howard by her side.

If he refused to let Owen call on her, assuming that was what Katie wanted, Sean feared it was only a matter of time before the other men in the area would press their advances. And no matter how good their intentions, if they didn't leave the area, if they didn't try to better themselves, they would slowly ruin both Katie's inner and outer beauty.

"Do you feel safe here, Kate?" he blurted.

She looked around her warily. Her steps faltered. "Out here in the alley?"

"You know what I mean. Here. On the street. At home. In Chicago."

"I feel as safe as any girl my age."

That wasn't an answer, and they both knew it. Or, maybe it was.

"Detective Howard talked to me about you after you left."

"He . . . he did? What did he say?"

"He asked for my permission to call on you."

Her expression showed she was aghast. Gripping his arm, she shook her head. "He can't."

"Why not?" He was surprised. He could have sworn he'd seen her giving him moony glances.

"I don't want him to see where I live, Sean." Right away, heat suffused her cheeks. "I mean, where you used to live too. I mean, it's fine for me. But I think he would be shocked."

"Do you truly think so? He is a policeman, dear."

"I don't want him thinking of me like this." Looking down at her feet, she bit her bottom lip. "I'm sorry. I know that sounds bad."

It didn't sound bad to him. For better or worse, he felt much the same. Not only would it be beyond awkward for Katie to have a wealthy man like Owen come calling in front of the whole of Haversham, Sean also wasn't in any hurry for his partner to begin assuming things about Katie's life. Because of that, he had no intention of bringing Owen anywhere near the area.

But he wasn't ready to share that yet. "I think I know your reasons, but I'd appreciate it if you'd share them with me too."

"You know why. He's a gentleman."

"He's also a policeman."

"But—"

"He started at the bottom, just like I did, Katie. He's tougher than you might think." The moment he said the words, he realized that toughness was also why he had even considered giving permission. Owen was several steps above anyone the family had hoped for her. But there was also a steel core to him, proving there was more to him than charm and charisma.

"I don't want him looking at me here. If he sees where we live, he won't ever forget it."

"I told him most of the neighborhood only puts up with a copper in their midst because they know my family. He would do you no favors showing up at your doorstep."

She shuddered dramatically. "Oh, can you see it? I'd be run out of here on a rail."

He knew she wasn't exaggerating.

"I told him he may take you to tea, chaperoned by me," he said at last.

Her eyes turned as big as saucers. "You would do that?"

"Of course I would. You're my sister. Plus, it's only proper for you to be chaperoned."

"I bet he didn't count on you being there. What did he say?"

He wrapped an arm around her shoulders and gave her a tiny squeeze. "About what you would expect a prospective suitor to say," he said softly. "First he said that would be fine with him. Then he asked if I would see if you would consent to such a thing."

"Really?"

"Really." He smiled. "His interest in you is why I came over. I wanted to ask you what you think about him. And to reassure you that he is definitely asking you out. I am not telling you that you have to say yes. If you would rather not see him again, you don't have to."

"But you are giving your permission?" She stared at him intently. "Is he who you would like me to be with?"

"So far, we're only talking about tea."

"I know. But, Sean, if I were to end up liking a man like Detective Howard and he ended up liking me . . . would you support such an alliance?"

"How can I not, Katherine Jean? He's one of the finest men I know. And though I don't want to start putting the cart before the horse, I think it goes without saying that a future by his side would set my mind at ease."

"I don't know how to be a lady."

"I think you know enough."

"But—"

"Katie, it's just tea. But I'll tell you what. If you do enjoy tea and do want to see more of him, I'll ask Miss Carstairs to visit with you and give you some advice." Thinking of how everything she did was graceful but that she could also see the humor in the myriad of social graces, he said, "I imagine she would be more than happy to give you some tips."

Katie rolled her eyes. "Tips."

"Yes. You know, pointers."

"I know what you meant, Sean. However, a lady like her would never consent to spending any amount of time tutoring a girl like me."

"I've gotten to know her fairly well. I think she would be more than happy to visit with you about anything that might concern you."

She bit her lip. "What should I tell Ma?" She winced. "Maeve? Or what about Connor?"

It was on the tip of his tongue to suggest she avoid telling Connor about Owen at any cost. But that wouldn't be fair to any of them. For better or worse, having everything out in the open was the right decision. "All that matters is if you're happy, Katie. That's all any of us care about."

"Ma won't care about that."

"I'll talk to Ma. And I'll ask Maeve to step in too."

"She won't—"

"She will. Because she, like me, knows what it feels like to move away from here."

Glancing sideways at him, she blurted, "Connor says you and Maeve try too hard to forget where you came from. That you think others are going to forget who we are, but no one ever will."

Though he would have thought he'd be used to such sentiments by now, the statement still hurt. It also bit into his insides that Connor would share his opinions so freely with their little sister. He would have thought Connor wanted to protect Katie's sweet hope and optimism as much as he did.

"I love our brother," he said slowly, weighing each word carefully. "I respect him because he's our eldest and he's always been fair and a hard worker."

She exhaled, whether it was from relief to hear him speak so carefully about Connor or something else, he didn't know. But even though he didn't want to hurt her glowing belief in their brother, he couldn't withhold his opinion. "Katie, Conner is a good man. But I don't agree with his views. He never wanted anything different, Katie. I do. I always did."

"He says being a cop doesn't make you better."

"I don't want to be better than him. However, I did want a life different from the one I had here. God gave me a good mind and the ability to deduce things. He gave me the skills to walk the streets of our city and apprehend criminals. To bring down folks whose only purpose in life is to hurt others. In return, I am compensated for it. And, in some small circles, it's given me a measure of respect."

"Respect," she echoed softly.

"There's nothing wrong with that, Katie. Nothing wrong with believing in yourself, nothing wrong with believing you are as good, as worthy as the richest lady living on Prairie Avenue or shopping at Field & Leiter." Looking at her, he willed her to believe him, realizing that he believed it too. "There's not a thing wrong with that. Not a thing."

"I want more too."

"Good. We're at the turn of the century. The fair is filled with all kinds of things that remind us everything is changing. The world is changing, and though there are still many injustices and many hardships, everything ain't all that way. That's something to believe in."

"Connor doesn't want to see that. Billy doesn't either."

Sean carefully schooled his expression. He didn't want Katie to see how much his brothers' disappointment in him affected him. "Maybe they do. Maybe they don't. I can't control what they think."

"But we can try to convince them, Sean."

He almost smiled at her earnest expression. Almost. "We can't, pet. And I don't blame their views, either. I'm almost eight years younger than Connor, six years younger than Billy."

"So?"

"So they remember seeing our dad being treated worse than a dog. They remember better than me how almost every stitch of pride in his body was taken away when he was forced to work on the canals, with everyone dying around him."

"But they should be proud of you. You've made something of yourself, Sean."

"But they are still surviving, doing what our father did. There's no shame in that."

"But still . . ."

He shrugged. "Katie, I haven't spent much time with Connor

and Billy in years. You know that. All I can do is follow my path, and that's what I want to do. For better or worse, it's my path."

Lifting her chin a bit, she said, "Please tell Mr. Howard I'd be delighted to join you both for tea."

He yearned to grin foolishly but was afraid she'd take it the wrong way. He wasn't necessarily glad his partner had his eye on her. He wasn't so much of a fool to think one afternoon of tea really meant anything.

But he was so very happy that she was making her own decision. "Shall we try to set this up, for say, in three days' time? This Sunday afternoon?"

"Yes, Sean. I would like that very much."

He couldn't hide his satisfaction. "Then smile. It's something to look forward to, yes?"

As her dimples appeared, she tilted her chin coquettishly. "Let's hope Mr. Howard feels the same way."

CHAPTER 20

Eloisa, it seems as if you are turning up everywhere now," Philippa Watson cooed over her half-opened fan as their group of friends made their way down the tree-lined pathway toward the Japanese Gardens at the fair.

"I suppose I am," Eloisa replied, deftly matching Philippa's icy sarcasm with every syllable. Unfortunately, she'd had plenty of practice partaking in their verbal battles.

After looking at the three other women surrounding them, Philippa smirked. "Is your mother as desperate for you to make a match as we've heard?"

"I'm sure I have no idea." Privately, Eloisa knew no words could ever come close to describing her mother's frenzied attempts at matchmaking. She scanned the social sections of the newspaper with the fervency of the most devout and could easily spend hours complaining to Eloisa every time another woman of their acquaintance announced her engagement.

Glancing around at the other girls—most of whom used to look at Eloisa with something approaching awe but now glanced at her with a vague disdain—Philippa cleared her throat. "It is a shame, I think, that your star doesn't shine quite as brightly as it used to." She frowned, her lips curving into a delicate pout. "It is a shame, too, about Douglass Sloane."

Eloisa inhaled. What did Philippa suspect? "Douglass drowned."

"Yes, but everyone knew his eye was on you." She chuckled low. "As was Mr. Armstrong's—until he got a wild hair and became engaged to that maid."

"I've met Mr. Armstrong's fiancée. Rosalind is a lovely girl."

"Yes, I imagine she is . . . if one needed some coal delivered."

"Be careful, Philippa."

"It's no matter. Perhaps Mr. Howard will take pity on you after all. He might be a detective now, but he is still as handsome as ever."

Eloisa said nothing. She was trying her best to push the awful reminder of Douglass's attack from her mind.

While Philippa prattled some more, she tried to think of excuses she could implement next time she was asked to attend a party with this group of girls. She'd never liked Philippa, and time had only cemented those feelings.

"I do believe Detective Howard is planning to attend the party tonight. I hope so." She hoped that she would see him sometime over the next few hours.

"Don't mind Philippa," Avery said from her side. "Her mother is pressing her to accept suit by a gentleman from Milwaukee."

"Milwaukee?" she repeated, intrigued by the idea of Philippa being far, far away. And doomed to live somewhere that was reputed to have even worse winters than Chicago.

"His money is in breweries," Avery whispered.

"In alcohol?" Eloisa wasn't as shocked by the idea of marrying into spirits as much as the rumors that seemed to fill the air about the new, very strong temperance movement. Her practical side would worry about marrying a man whose business seemed doomed.

"To make matters worse, he is a burly man," Avery added. "And not cowed by Philippa's looks or demeanor in the slightest."

"Then heaven help her."

"My sentiments exactly," Avery agreed just as they approached a large tent that had been set up and festooned with twinkling lights. "Oh!" she exclaimed as the lilting strains of a string quartet drifted toward them. "This is lovely, don't you think?"

"Very lovely." For the first time that night, Eloisa felt her lips tilt upward as she followed her friend to the receiving line. Avery had never met an occasion or party that didn't entrance and intrigue her. Her fiancé was a lucky man, indeed.

Eager for a calming breath, she stood to the side of the receiving line, hoping to get her bearings. But then a strange prickling crept up her spine, creating chill bumps on her arms.

And making her feel like she was being watched. Again.

After being announced and greeting the hosts, most of whom seemed to have something to do with manufacturing, Eloisa glanced around the room. She was amazed to see not only Owen but Sean Ryan approaching her.

Automatically, she braced herself, wondering what else on earth could have happened with the Slasher, when she realized Sean wasn't dressed in his usual ill-fitting suit or tuxedo.

Instead, his suit was of much higher quality and fit him like a glove. He was also freshly shaved and his hair trimmed. Though she suspected he would always look slightly rough around the edges, at this moment, he looked dashing, strong, and confident.

Owen caught her reaction first and grinned when they reached her side. "I see you notice my afternoon's project. And I take it you approve?"

Sean grimaced. "Please. Don't hesitate to make me feel more foolish than I already do, Howard." Turning to her, he reached for her hand, seemed to worry that it wasn't proper form, and dropped his gloved grasp just as quickly. And even though the light was dim, she was almost positive she spied a faint sheen of blush on his cheeks.

"Lieutenant Ryan, good evening," she said, and meeting his gaze, she raised her hand. Leaving him no choice but to grasp it and slowly bow.

After he released her fingers, his hazel eyes met her own. "You look beautiful, Eloisa."

"Thank you."

Owen nodded in her direction. "Very fetching," he said, before whispering under his breath, "A bit too enthusiastic, Ryan, to utter in public."

Eloisa braced herself, ready to hear Sean's retort. But instead, he nodded and seemed to pocket that bit of advice to memory. "What are you gentlemen doing here? Are things really so dangerous? I already saw a lot of police officers standing guard around the area."

"We were asked to come and observe," Sean said. "But that isn't the only reason."

"Ryan wanted to see you. And I told him that perhaps it was time to begin to attain a bit of polish."

"Your suit is very nice."

"It cost a pretty penny." Looking at Owen, Sean fairly bristled. "At least it would have been if I had been given the option of paying for its entirety."

"I'm afraid I don't understand."

"Good," Sean bit out.

Howard smiled. "I told you it was a token of my thanks. Let's leave it at that." Clasping his hands behind his back, Owen winked. "I've been attempting to give Sean some pointers about social niceties. Perhaps you might consider taking over the job for a few moments?"

"Of course."

Sean raised his head. "Something wrong?" he asked his partner.

"No. It's just that I noticed the captain is in the crowd. I'm going to make sure nothing is amiss."

"The captain is here?" Sean glanced around. "Perhaps I should go with you."

"No. Stay here with Eloisa, will you?" Owen asked. "No reason for both of us to go."

As Owen walked off, Sean appeared a bit bewildered. Seeking to make him smile, Eloisa glanced his way. "Was Owen serious about your lesson? I'd be happy to help, but I don't want to run the risk of offending you."

"You would never do that. And yes, I'm afraid he was serious."

"Then perhaps you'd like to escort me around the room?"

"Doesn't that mean visit your acquaintances?"

"Yes. With my arm on yours."

"But—"

"Not to worry."

"I apologize. I think I'm a little on edge."

"Because?"

"Because while nothing would make me happier than to get to know you better, I know I risk embarrassing you."

She was shocked. "Never."

He continued as if she hadn't spoken. "The truth is, though I can never measure up to your reputation . . . well, I am hoping to not bring it down too far."

She placed her hand on his sleeve. "I don't think that will be a worry, Lieutenant." Scanning the area, she smiled brightly. "Let's go give this a try, shall we?"

━━━

He'd never thought he would be the type of man to be struck dumb by a hesitant smile, a crowd of people, or the opportunity to be in the middle of an awkward situation. He came to this conclusion as a result of thirty years of life experiences. Once he realized if he didn't attempt to drastically change his situation he would be resigned to living a life much like his father's—every penny earned from muscles in his back merely to survive—he'd made plans.

Plans that, for a poor Irish boy from some of the worst parts of Chicago, were pretty outlandish. But he persevered.

He'd gone to school long after his brothers had quit. And after his brief period of wondering if he should ever attempt to reform himself, he directed his goal toward becoming a member of the police force.

Once there, he was just as determined to rise through the ranks. He'd worked long hours, faced off drunks, dealt with thugs, and been up close and personal with too many people he'd like to forget.

But none of that gave him the feeling of nervousness he was feeling with Eloisa on his arm. As they approached a small cluster of people—three women, two men—all five of them turned their way. Appreciative gazes settled on Eloisa. And gazed at him with a sharp interest he couldn't shy away from.

He looked directly back, praying to the Lord to help him not make a complete fool of himself.

"Eloisa," a young girl with dark-brown hair and clad in a fussy emerald-green gown said. "We were hoping you would join us."

"Oh?" Eloisa glanced at him quickly before smiling. "I'm sorry to keep you waiting, then. It took a bit of convincing to get Mr. Ryan to spend any time with me."

"Martin Upton," one of the men said, holding out his hand.

"Sean Ryan." During the rest of the introductions, he shook hands with the other man and inclined his head at the three women.

"Have we met before?" the brunette, whom he'd just learned was named Cassandra, asked.

"I don't believe so."

"Why not?"

"Excuse me?" Sean blurted.

"I simply meant that I haven't seen you in our circle." She looked at the others and shrugged. "And it seems we all see each other only at these functions."

Sean was rendered momentarily speechless. Just as he was about to explain who he was and to share that, of course, there was no reason their paths would have ever crossed, he glanced at Eloisa. She looked pensive and more than a little reticent.

And that expression made him keep his silence. This was Eloisa's circle. And would never be his. When the Slasher was caught and the investigation was all over, all of them would go back to their regular lives.

Beyond that, when Eloisa was no longer afraid, she would realize they had nothing in common. She'd turn her attentions to one of the gentlemen in her life who was worthy of her. And he would merely become a reminder of everything violent in her life. When this was all over, the only place he would probably ever see her again was in the society pages.

Which meant if she was determined to keep his identity a secret, then he would allow that. His purpose was to keep her safe, not make her a social pariah.

Just as he was nodding to everyone, intending to step away and disappear back into the crowd, Eloisa placed a gloved hand on his sleeve. "Forgive me. Mr. Ryan is actually *Lieutenant Detective* Sean Ryan. Of the Chicago Police Department. Until recently, he hadn't much occasion to attend our functions."

The men looked intently at Sean while the women tried unsuccessfully to pretend they weren't shocked.

"I'm afraid I don't understand why you are here," Martin Upton said. "Unless you are Eloisa's new beau?"

Sean glanced her way, again unsure how to explain their relationship. But when he caught a glimpse of warmth in her eyes, he decided to be frank. Well, as frank as he thought Eloisa's reputation could handle.

"I am concerned about her safety, of course," he replied. "But I would be lying if I didn't say that I feel like the luckiest man in the city right now."

He knew he'd done the right thing when her grip on his arm tightened and a new, sweet softness appeared in her expression.

Eloisa's lips curved. "You know, I actually believe you mean that."

"I do."

While the other women sighed, Martin Upton frowned. "Eloisa, out of all the men in the world, you've chosen to be by this policeman's side? Truly?"

Sean lifted his chin, fueled by every instinct he'd learned growing up on his block to defend both his reputation and Eloisa's honor.

He must have looked fearsome, because Upton raised his hands in mock surrender. "Easy now, Ryan. I didn't mean disrespect."

"Of course you did," the other man, Jack Collingsworth, said. "Don't mind him," he continued. "He doesn't know any better."

"Watch it, Collingsworth," Martin cautioned.

Collingsworth ignored him. "See, Lieutenant Ryan, Martin here was raised to have a healthy distrust for anyone who works for a living." He shrugged. "That means, of course, that he looks down on the majority of the population."

Martin flushed. "That's putting things a bit harshly."

"You used to give Reid Armstrong the cold shoulder because his family made a fortune in silver."

Sean blinked, hoping his recognition of the name wasn't apparent.

As the tension between the men grew, and Eloisa tensed, obviously at a loss for how to ease things, her friend Avery smiled brightly. "This is simply so exciting. Now, before you whisk Eloisa away, tell us how you two met."

"Mr. Ryan escorted me home after the tragedy at the Gardners' ball," Eloisa said. "We started talking." Smiling his way, she added, "Then, when he stopped by my house to check on me the next day, we found even more to talk about. We've seen each other quite a bit ever since."

Sean was about to ask Eloisa if she'd like something from the refreshment table when Owen appeared in his vision. Noticing the expression on Owen's face, his body tensed.

Eloisa noticed. Leaning close, she murmured into his ear. "Is everything all right?"

"I am not sure, but I think I had better go find out."

She worried her bottom lip. "Could I come with—"

"No." Softening his voice, he gently pulled her hand from his arm. "You need to stay here, please."

"All right."

He gazed into her blue eyes a second longer, aching to reassure her that everything would be okay, but he knew that would be an empty promise. He had no idea what had just happened to Owen. He was also learning that things were happening over which he had no control.

Gathering his wits, he turned to her friends. "Please excuse me. I believe I am needed."

Collingsworth nodded. "Let me know if I can help in any way."

Sean realized the man meant what he said. "If you could make sure none of the women go anywhere unescorted, I would be in your debt." Without waiting for a response, he strode toward Owen's side, noticing as he closed the distance that his partner looked pale. "What happened?"

"I believe I've been injured."

Sean thought his partner's voice seemed unnaturally strained. "Are you all right, man?"

Owen pointed to his side, where blood stained his shirt. "I'll be fine. It's not life-threatening, but I fear I might need stitches," he said in a halting way as they walked to the edge of the tent away from the crowd.

"I cannot believe this. You were gone mere minutes. What happened?" he asked again. "Was it a robber?"

Owen shook his head.

As they walked farther, across the lawns, Sean began to put the pieces together. He knew his guess was correct when Owen led him to a darkened path. Just off to the side Captain Keaton was kneeling next to a young lady clad in a white gown. She looked shaken and her coiffure was mussed, but otherwise seemed unharmed.

After taking a fortifying breath, Owen continued. "The captain told me he had everything in hand, but he needed me to walk the perimeter. That's when I saw Miss Berkley, Caroline Berkley, standing alone. Just as I was walking toward her to tell her not to be anywhere by herself, someone knocked into me and got me with his stiletto knife."

"You didn't catch a glimpse of who stabbed you?"

"All I noticed was a dark suit. It could have been any of the gentlemen here."

Just then, Captain Keaton approached them. "Ryan! Go ask your fancy heiress to help you locate this girl's family."

"All right. But, Owen here—"

Owen shook his head. "I'll be all right. Go."

"When I get back, we're getting you help."

"Thanks."

Sean stared at him a moment longer. It was evident Owen had something else on his mind but wasn't in any hurry to share it.

As he stepped back into the party, all of Eloisa's group immediately stopped chatting and turned to stare at him.

"Lieutenant Ryan, is everything all right?" Eloisa asked.

"I'm afraid there's been an incident. Detective Howard needs medical attention."

Eloisa's eyes grew wide. "Where is he? Can I help?"

She really was the kindest woman he'd ever met. "I'll take care of him, but I am asking for the rest of you to help me find Miss Caroline Berkley's family. Do any of you know them?"

"Why?" Cassandra asked. "Is she hurt? Did something happen?"

On another evening, in a different situation, Sean might have tried harder to keep what had happened quiet. But he was too tired of this cat-and-mouse game they were all playing with the Slasher. "She has been accosted. I don't believe she's injured, merely shaken up. But she needs her family. Owen and my captain are with her now."

Collingsworth nodded. "I believe she's here with her parents and older sister. They're over near the quartet."

"Please ask them to follow you outside, toward the wooded paths." He paused. "I might mention that it would be best for everyone if you attempted to keep their daughter's situation private. Not only will it stir everyone up, but it could harm her reputation."

"I'll go with you, Jack," one of the women said.

"And Avery and I will go with you and stay with her until they get to her side," Eloisa spoke up.

Every protective bone in his body wanted her to stay where she was, stay safe. "Eloisa, I'd rather you didn't."

"Please, Sean. Don't put me in a crystal box. I have no desire to be treated as if I am about to break."

"No, no, I suppose you are not. Come with me, then."

Minutes later Avery and Eloisa were at Miss Berkley's side, offering her comfort. And as soon as Jack and another concerned-looking gentleman arrived and Sean ascertained they would not leave Eloisa's side, Sean motioned for Owen to follow him.

It was now evident that Owen was no longer going to be able to hide his discomfort.

Or hide the blood seeping from his wound, for his handkerchief was now stained red.

CHAPTER 21

The pounding on the door was accompanied by a harsh voice. "Maeve. Maeve, open up."

Just as Katie was debating whether to leave her makeshift bed on the couch and answer the summons, both Maeve and Jack raced down the stairs.

As Jack unlocked the deadbolt, Maeve cast a harried eye in her direction. "Put on your robe, Kate. Be quick about it."

"Maeve. Now!" the voice called out.

With more than a few inappropriate words under his breath, Katie's brother-in-law pulled open the door. "Get in, then," he said with a glare. "But you'd better have a good reason for waking up half the street."

Now with her robe fastened securely about her waist, Katie stood motionless as Sean burst in, Owen Howard at his side. Owen looked rattled and pale—the complete opposite of his usual self. Katie gasped.

That, unfortunately, directed Owen to glance her way. Straight away a look of shame filled his gaze.

"It's near on eleven, Sean," Maeve said.

"I know that, but we need your help," Sean replied. "Owen is hurt. I need you to sew him up."

Jack groaned. "Really, Sean? You couldn't think of anyone else to involve besides my wife?"

Still grasping Owen firmly, Sean said, "I'll explain everything in a minute. But for now, we really need to get him to a chair."

"Bring him in the kitchen, then." Maeve looked her way. "Kate, go upstairs and get my kit."

Katie did as she was bid. On her way back downstairs, she passed her brother-in-law. "Is everything all right, Jack?"

"I think so. You can go on into the kitchen. I'm going back to bed. I've got an early shift in the morning."

Katie nodded, then hurried to the kitchen. "Here you go, Maeve."

Her sister was washing her hands at the sink. "Thanks, dear. Go set it over by Mr. Howard, please."

"Kathcrinc Jean, seeing you here is a surprise," Sean stated.

"I'm visiting with Maeve for a few days."

"Because?" Automatically, he thought of a dozen scenarios where Katie could have gotten into trouble with Conner.

"Because nothing," Maeve said impatiently. "Sean, now isn't the time to be fussing with our Katie."

"So something did happen."

Neatly sidestepping the statement, Maeve shook her head. "No, I'd say it looks as if something happened to our guest."

Edging closer, Katie held her breath as her brother helped Mr. Howard out of his dinner jacket, revealing a dark stain of red on his side. "Oh, Detective Howard. Look at you."

Detective Howard pointedly ignored her outburst. "Do you think you can sew me up, Mrs. O'Connell?"

"What happened?" Katie asked.

"Nothing you two ladies should be worrying about," he murmured.

"You have lost a lot of blood," Katie cried, feeling slightly queasy.

"Oh, stuff," Maeve bit out. "He's gotten stabbed, Katie." Her gaze hardened. "Don't you turn into a crying baby on my watch. If you can't be of use, you need to leave this kitchen—and be quick about it."

Katie flinched at her sister's criticism. "That's hardly fair, Maeve. I don't go around acting like a baby. Ever." It took everything she had not to glance Detective Howard's way. The last thing she wanted to see was him, too, looking at her like she was too silly to be of use.

Or worse, that she had a terrible crush on him, something he was no doubt used to happening. A man as handsome and charming as he was probably had scores of admirers, each one far prettier and more accomplished than a girl like her.

"Just remember that you asked to be here," Maeve muttered as the kettle started whistling. "Sean, get his shirt off."

"I believe I can do that myself," Mr. Howard said as he unfastened the buttons.

"I imagine you could. I believe you could also manage to do more damage by twisting this way and that," Maeve added, her voice as sharp as a tack. "Let us help you, please."

Immediately Mr. Howard's hands fell to his sides, the new position revealing a sliver of his bare chest. "Of course."

Katie bit her lip so she wouldn't smile. "Don't mind my sister, Mr. Howard. She's gruff with everyone."

He glanced up at her, winked, then sat up as Sean began to pull off his shirt from behind him. "Good to know," he quipped before stifling a wince as his side started to bleed once again.

Katie suddenly felt light-headed. She'd seen blood before. Of course she had. She'd also seen a man's bare chest. After all, she was one of eight children.

But there was something about seeing Mr. Howard's bare chest while he was sitting in her sister's kitchen bleeding that made her heart ache and her insides twist and knot. He was in need and she had no earthly idea how to help him.

Holding the soiled shirt, Sean darted a glance at her. "Buck up, Katherine."

"Or as I said before, leave," Maeve ordered with another harried glance at her. Then her voice turned sweet. "We'll clean your wound, Mr. Howard, then I'll stitch you up. I'll try not to hurt you too much."

"Don't worry about that. I'll be fine."

Katie found herself holding her breath often over the next thirty minutes as her sister carefully cleansed Mr. Howard's side with clean rags and hot water, then sewed seven stitches into his side.

Through it all, their guest—such as he was—sat silent and still. Only the muscles straining in his face gave any indication that he was in pain.

When her brother knelt down to help Maeve, he tossed Mr. Howard's soiled shirt into her hands. Katie found herself gripping the cloth tightly, practically wringing it into a hopeless mass of wrinkles.

Then Maeve stood up and smiled tiredly. "That'll do it, I think. If you wash it every morning with soap and keep clean, you should heal in no time."

"I'm obliged, Mrs. O'Connell. Please forgive my intrusion into your home so late in the evening."

Again, something gentle crossed her sister's features. "Think nothing of it. Between my siblings, my husband, and my own two children, I've done more than my share of patching up scrapes and cuts over the years."

"Maeve has become something of our savior," Sean said, irony lacing his voice. "Our mother has never been particularly skilled in any situation involving blood."

"Faints at the sight of it, she does," Maeve blurted. "It's still a mystery to us all how she birthed eight children."

Seeing Mr. Howard's blink, Katie was mortified. "Maeve!"

Maeve looked at their gentleman guest. "Sorry for my plain speaking, sir. I hope I didn't offend your sensibilities," she added with a wry look at Katie.

Detective Howard's lips twitched. "Think nothing of it."

"Well, now. I'm going to go find you one of my husband's shirts so you can be on your way."

"Thanks, Maeve," Sean said. After she left the room, he looked at Katie. "You're looking pale, dear. I have a feeling you might have inherited some of our mother's squeamishness."

"I am fine. Though I'm still not understanding why you came here, Sean. I would have thought you policemen would have access to a physician. Or that you would have your own, Mr. Howard."

Mr. Howard smiled weakly. "Either of those options would have taken far more time. It would have also necessitated me answering more questions than I would be inclined to answer. This is police business, not a physician's."

"Why?"

"That is none of your concern, dear," Sean said. His tone was gentle, always far more gentle with her than Maeve ever had been. But in its own way, it was just as firm and made it known that he would brook no arguments.

She was prevented from questioning that remark with her sister's return. "This cloth and tailoring won't be what you are used to, Mr. Howard, but it should get you home all right."

"I'm sure it will be fine, Mrs. O'Connell."

Sean snapped it out of Maeve's hand and held it out to assist him. "Easy now."

Detective Howard glared at him. "Give me my shirt, Ryan."

"I can play valet with the best of them, sir. Deal with it. The last thing you want is to pull a stitch and have my sister redo her handiwork, fine as it may be."

Looking put upon, Detective Howard stood up and let Sean help him on with the shirt. "I will have this laundered and returned to you tomorrow, ma'am."

"Thank you, Mr. Howard," Maeve said as she cleaned up the last signs that any of them had been in the kitchen at all.

After helping Owen on with his dinner jacket and overcoat, Sean smiled again at his sister. "Thanks again, Maeve. Tell Jack I'm sorry for disturbing his house, but I didn't feel like I had a choice. I owe you."

Reaching out, Maeve gently pressed a hand to Sean's cheek. In that moment Katie realized that Maeve was giving thanks that it had not been Sean who'd been stabbed. "You don't owe me a thing. I was glad I could help."

Sean glanced Katie's way, at Owen, then seemed to come to a decision. "Katie, walk out with Owen and me, if you please."

Maeve stiffened. "What are you about, Sean?"

"None of your concern. Katie, if you will come with us?"

Katie's hands trembled. Obviously, she was now going to get questions about being at Maeve's instead of at home. About whether or not she'd fought again with Conner. About staying in the kitchen instead of retreating back to the couch. About asking Detective Howard cheeky questions instead of remembering her place and being more respectful.

Once more, this would all take place in front of Detective Howard, and he would again witness her embarrassment.

"Katie?" Sean's speech was clipped. "Now, if you please."

"Yes, Sean." Leaving Maeve alone in the kitchen, she joined her brother and Mr. Howard next to the front door. Steeling herself, she faced him. "Yes?"

Then, to her surprise, the corners of her brother's lips turned up. And then he took hold of her hand. "Dear, Owen asked if he could speak with you privately for a moment. Would you be willing to do that on the front stoop?"

As she gazed at Detective Howard, she felt a myriad of emotions that could only be described as a mixture of shock and joy. "Of course."

"Thank you."

And with that, he opened the door and gestured for her to precede him out the door. Then, to her surprise, Detective Howard closed the door and shared that top cement step with her. He was standing very close to her. So close she could feel his body heat. So close, she was able to see the lines of strain around his eyes and mouth.

Close enough that, if her imagination took hold, she could imagine leaning against him as he circled his arms around her waist. Close enough to let herself imagine what it must feel like to have a man like him as a beau.

She tilted her head back, stared into his dark-brown eyes. Felt her own lips part.

He noticed. After the slightest hesitation, he stepped down. Allowing more air to flow between them, but maybe it wasn't really that at all? Maybe it was more a matter of him recognizing that they needed to keep a respectable distance from each other.

It was the right thing to do, but she felt the loss like it was a tangible thing. Like she'd had her opportunity to be in his world, and now that moment was gone. It made her sad, but she wasn't surprised. Not really.

"Miss Ryan, thank you for your assistance this evening."

She looked down at her feet. "We both know I didn't do anything." Actually, they both knew that she almost fainted right in front of him.

"You and your brother and sister did *everything*. You saved me a lot of questions and a lot of bother as well."

Something in his voice sent up a red flag. Did he not see his worth? Or were there not enough people in his life who did? Hesitantly, she said, "Detective Howard, are you sure you're going to be all right?"

"I'm better now, I believe."

"I fear you're going to be hurting something awful in the morning."

"I'll be all right. I've overcome worse," he added, as if he were sharing a secret joke that she had no hope of understanding. "Miss Ryan, I asked you to speak to me out here for a reason."

"Yes?" Worry claimed her. Was he going to take her to task again for walking around the city streets by herself?

He straightened. "I would still like to have tea with you."

"You would?"

A hint of a smile played across his lips. "Would you still care to join me? I'll ask your brother to join us as well, of course, so there will be no hint of impropriety."

She was tempted to tell him the boys in their neighborhood didn't worry so much about impropriety. In her world, couples dating simply went for a walk or for a stroll in the neighborhood. But, of course, here most of the neighborhood watched them every step of the way.

"Mr. Howard, are you sure you're still wanting to? I don't want you to feel obligated."

"Obligation is not what I am thinking of."

His words meant everything. "Then, yes. Yes, I still want to. Thank you."

"On Sunday afternoon, perhaps? I should be right as rain by then. Sean said he is going to be accompanying Miss Carstairs to Hope House. Perhaps you could go, too, and then I could meet you?"

"I would like that." She ached to ask him a hundred questions about his wishes. About why he was seeking her out. Wanted to ask what she'd done to ignite his interest. She yearned to ask him questions about himself, to discover why a man like him would ever lower himself to even contemplate seeing a girl like her.

But when he looked at her like that, when she was standing so close to him and no one else was around to say a word, not a single word of her own came to mind. Instead, all she seemed to be able to do was smile at him.

But perhaps that was enough, because he smiled right back. "Thank you, Miss Ryan. You have just made a difficult night far better."

He stepped next to her again, paused for a moment, then opened the door and gestured her inside. "You'd best go in now. You'll catch a chill otherwise."

Obediently, she stepped through the doorway.

Then she looked back his way. "Good night, Detective Howard."

"Good night, Miss Ryan," he said before turning toward an awaiting coach.

As she watched it start forward, Katie let herself smile. Even though he'd been bleeding and in pain, he'd still been thinking of her.

"Is he gone?"

Startled, she glanced at her brother, who was standing against a wall, his arms crossed over his chest.

"Yes." Sean had already agreed to her having tea with Owen, and he must have known that was what Owen wanted to talk to her about.

Still, she braced herself for a dozen questions, followed by another lengthy lecture about proper dating. She might be Sean's favorite sister, but she had no doubt that his fondness for her would in any way prevent him from sharing his thoughts.

She was also, unfortunately, just as sure that she would have no words to answer his questions. Her emotions were too raw, her feelings too muddled and strong to put into some type of coherent order.

All she did know was that she was now definitely old enough not to live in fear of what Sean had to say. She would honor his opinion, but in the end she knew she would be accepting every invitation Owen Howard extended.

The silence between them lengthened. Tension rose inside her. She really did wish he would simply lecture her now and be done with it.

"So, is everything all right?"

Everything was better than she could have ever imagined. What could she say? "Yes." And because he looked to be waiting for a report about what happened, she added, "He asked if I'd still like to join him for tea on Sunday afternoon. He said you could be there, and perhaps even Miss Carstairs."

"Yes." The word hung there between them as he stared at her. "What did you say?"

"I said I would be happy to join him. I mean, everyone."

After gazing at her for another long moment, he nodded. "Good. Good night, then," he said over his shoulder as he opened the door and headed back outside into the darkness.

More confused than ever before, Katie sat back down on her makeshift bed on the couch.

She'd barely pulled the sheet and quilt over her when Maeve stood in front of her. "What did Detective Howard want to talk to you about?"

"He wanted to thank me for my help and asked me to join him for tea on Sunday afternoon."

"Just the two of you?"

"No. It seems that Miss Carstairs is going to be visiting Hope House with Sean again on Sunday. Detective Howard suggested I tag along, then the four of us take tea together."

"You, Detective Howard, Sean, and Miss Carstairs."

Katie nodded, practically bracing herself for Maeve's temper to erupt.

But instead of bursting into a tirade, Maeve looked flummoxed. "Really?"

Katie nodded. "Really." She bit her lip, then continued. "I know what you must be thinking, and I have to admit that I can see your point. I mean, what would a handsome, wealthy gentleman like Owen Howard want with a girl like me?"

"I wasn't thinking that at all." Maeve's voice was, for once, quiet. Carefully gentle.

"No?"

"No, I was thinking maybe that Detective Howard is smarter than Sean had first thought."

"Really?"

"Really. You . . . you are a lovely young lady, Katherine Jean. As long as Detective Howard treats you with respect, I don't think there is a thing wrong with you accepting his invitation."

"Thank you, Maeve."

Maeve walked to the front door, locked it securely, then walked to the foot of the stairs. "This has been the strangest evening in memory. You'd best get to sleep now, pet. It's been quite a night."

"Yes, Maeve."

Then, to Katie's further surprise, Maeve paused on the steps.

"Tomorrow, we'll think about a dress for you to wear. June or Mary Patricia might have one we can alter. Or I think we can even find some fabric and fashion one by Sunday."

"Really? You would do that?"

"You might be just a poor Irish girl, but you're the bonniest thing I've ever seen. Obviously, that Mr. Howard is no fool and knows you are just as lovely on the inside. That says something for him, I think."

"Thank you, Maeve."

"Mind you, there's no telling what the Lord has to say about our future. Maybe things will work out with Mr. Howard, maybe they won't."

"I understand." Katie agreed with Maeve. Though she might be a bit astonished when it came to thinking about actually having a future with him, she'd seen enough on Haversham Street to have been reminded that all sorts of things can happen without a person ever planning for them.

Maeve's voice gentled. "No matter what happens, love, we need to make sure we do you proud."

Once the light from Maeve's candle flickered away as she went upstairs, Katie wrapped herself up in the quilt on the couch. Thought about her brother. About Mr. Howard sitting stoically while her sister stitched him up.

About Maeve's compliment and offer to discuss dresses.

And Katie was sure she would never sleep again.

But then, of course, she did.

CHAPTER 22

The dream had come again. So had the night sweats. And the necessary change of nightgowns. As well as yet another few hours spent on her window seat, watching the approaching dawn, all the while wondering if her life was ever going to be the same.

Juliet's arrival with her breakfast tray couldn't have been more gratefully received. Eloisa needed coffee and sustenance for the full day ahead of her. First she was going to head over to Hope House. Though she was still nervous about fitting in, she knew the only way she could prove herself to the women and children there was to continue to show up. Today she even planned to take some storybooks to the house. Maybe some of the children would even let her read to them.

After she returned home, she was going to have to spend the remainder of the day preparing for yet another evening of entertainment.

"Thank you, Juliet," she said from her spot at the window seat. "I'll pour my coffee this morning."

Juliet set the tray on her dressing table, eyed her carefully, then walked to her wardrobe and snatched up the previous night's soiled nightgown. "Looks like you had another bad night."

"I'm afraid so."

Her lovely maid looked her over for one long moment, seemed to come to a decision, then, ignoring what Eloisa had said, poured coffee into Eloisa's favorite china cup and handed it to her. "Miss Carstairs, I think we need to talk."

"All right. Is there something wrong?" She stilled the cup in her hand, ready to listen. "What might I help you with?"

"It's not me we need to talk about. It's you."

Eloisa felt every muscle in her back and shoulders tense. "Pardon me?"

"Not only have I noticed that you have trouble sleeping, but I think you've changed too."

"I have no idea what you might be referring to."

But to Eloisa's surprise, Juliet brushed aside her haughty response, walked to her desk chair, pulled it close to Eloisa, and sat down. "I think you do."

"Juliet, I'm sorry, but you are forgetting yourself."

"Oh, don't act so high and mighty. Or offended."

"Now you are most certainly forgetting yourself."

"And you are forgetting that we've known each other for a long time now, miss."

After taking a fortifying sip, Eloisa nodded. "I have not forgotten our long relationship." She wanted to say friendship, but of course that wasn't exactly what they had.

"What happened to you?"

"It is nothing I can talk about."

"Have you talked about it with anyone?"

Eloisa didn't want to say. She didn't want to say a word or even pretend that she was willing to have a conversation about this. But Juliet's gaze was warm. And it reminded her that she had a lot to be thankful for in her life, most especially Juliet. She'd been her prime ally in the fight to foil her mother's intent to see her married off well—but not to someone she could love.

"I've talked to Lieutenant Ryan about it." Feeling her cheeks heat, she said, "Though I don't know him all that well, I feel I can trust him." She shrugged. "Maybe it is because he's seen so much through his work? I never worry that I am going to shock him."

"Did having him listen help?"

"I think so. I mean, I felt better right away, but when I'm alone in bed and it's the middle of the night, the same dreams and nightmares return."

"I'm glad you spoke to somebody. From what I can tell, those kinds of nights seem to be lessening. Are they?"

Eloisa hesitated, debating about how much to share.

Juliet gazed at her for what seemed to be an eternity. Then she looked down at her hands. "I remember when everything changed, Miss Carstairs. I remember how pale you were for days. How you were bruised."

"You never said a word."

"Just because you don't give me permission doesn't mean I don't notice things. Are you sure you don't want to confide in me?"

"Juliet, there's nothing you can do." And though she'd promised herself she wouldn't say another word, suddenly she found herself speaking. "I was violated," she blurted. "I was at yet another one of those ridiculous parties, the ones we spend almost as much time dressing for as the time I'm actually there." She breathed in, gasping inwardly, her breath coming out faintly like a hiccup. "My escort took me to a quiet area."

Eloisa stopped, trying to find the words. Trying to gain her composure, but suddenly the tears started flowing and there wasn't anything she could do to stop them.

She felt her body tremble. "I–I . . . c-couldn't stop . . ."

And then, the dam burst. With shaking hands, she covered her eyes, unable to face her maid.

Oh, who was she kidding? She was unable to face herself. Unable to face what had happened. Unable to face a future where she wasn't the person she wanted to be. As the tears continued, she bent her head, moving her body inward. Anything to bear the brunt of what she was feeling in silence.

"Sorry," she said around a hiccup. "I'm sorry—"

"No, Miss Carstairs," Juliet whispered as she wrapped her arms around her. "No, Miss Carstairs, don't stop. Don't stop crying. You cry as long as you want. And whatever you do? Do not, under any circumstances, apologize for those tears."

Eloisa stilled. Part of her wanted to say that continuing to cry would be exactly the wrong thing for her to do. She needed to stay strong. She needed to put it behind her. Unfortunately, she couldn't seem to calm herself enough to say any of that.

"It's okay to be upset," Juliet murmured. "I promise, it is. You can cry all day long if you want. If anyone deserves a crying spell, it is you."

"B–but—"

"It's okay," Juliet murmured. "It's okay. Because you're not alone anymore, dear." Leaning back, Juliet raised a hand and pressed two fingers under Eloisa's chin.

When Eloisa was able to at last meet her gaze, Juliet stared hard at her, seeming to force Eloisa to listen to her, as if what she said was the absolute truth and nothing else mattered. "You are no longer alone,

Miss Carstairs. You have me. And Lieutenant Ryan. And, miss, don't forget . . . the Lord has been with you too."

Eloisa blinked. Saw the strength in Juliet's gaze. Felt the reassurance flowing through her. Felt the gentle reminder of God's love. And at last believed those words to be true.

She was not alone. Not anymore.

CHAPTER 23

It had been two days since Eloisa had given in and cried in her maid's arms. Two days since she'd finally allowed herself to admit she was still hurting, even still angry about what Douglass had done.

Two days since Juliet had reminded Eloisa that she didn't need to carry all her burdens alone. Instead, she could reach out to others and seek solace in prayer.

Now that she'd allowed herself to break free from her pain, something miraculous had happened. Instead of wallowing in grief or being further depressed, her life seemed to have gotten easier.

By letting down her barriers and finally admitting to herself once and for all that she had been traumatized by Douglass's attack, she'd been able to put it behind her.

She breathed easier now. Smiled easier. Felt far lighter, almost like her old self.

Something wonderful had also happened. Now that she wasn't

as worried about keeping up a wall around her emotions, she and Juliet had become friends. There was a trust between them that hadn't been there before. Now, it wasn't just that she and Juliet were kind to each other. It was that she could trust Juliet with her deepest secrets.

And Eloisa now felt she could be herself. She wasn't biting her tongue or worrying about how something she said might be construed.

After Eloisa's crying jag, Juliet had poured her another cup of coffee, heated some water, then carefully moistened some cloths and pressed them to Eloisa's swollen eyes.

After reviewing Eloisa's schedule, Juliet pulled out a dress, helped Eloisa into it, did her coiffure, chose a bonnet, and shooed her out the door, with only an encouraging nod and a brief wink.

Yesterday their ease together was just as apparent when they'd convulsed in laughter as Eloisa relayed her mother's latest hope for her matrimonial bliss—some visiting Austrian who had a fondness for lace and jeweled stick pins. He also possessed an unfortunate lisp.

She'd whispered to Juliet about how peculiar he'd been and how she'd even caught him staring at her décolleté far longer than was seemly. And that her father had witnessed him doing so and had promptly pulled her away from the Austrian's company. Her mother had not been pleased at all.

"He sounds like the worst one yet."

"He was."

"Your mother is a smart lady, but she sure isn't putting those smarts to use when it comes to you."

"That's because she's only thinking about his title and his bank account."

"Those things aren't everything."

"They are to my mother. Well, unless my father doesn't want

anything to do with him," Eloisa said, around another burst of laughter. "My father's will trumps everything and everyone."

"Except handsome, burly police lieutenants."

Eloisa had felt her cheeks heat. "Yes, except for them."

Today she was another ball of energy. After getting home from church just an hour ago, she was now changing clothes in preparation for another visit to Hope House, this time with Sean and his little sister, Katie. They were coming to her house to pick her up, even though Eloisa had assured Sean in her brief note she'd had delivered to his precinct station that she would be perfectly fine getting to Hope House without his assistance. She'd even promised to take a maid.

But he would have none of that. Then, to her surprise, he sent over a note, asking if she would mind terribly if he brought his sister by to meet her.

There's a reason I'd like her to make your acquaintance, Miss Carstairs, he'd written. *I hate to be cryptic, but I'll explain more when I see you.*

She was instantly curious by his words as well as interested to meet another member of his family. She'd written him back quickly, saying she would be honored to make Miss Katie Ryan's acquaintance.

"They're going to be here in fifteen minutes time, Miss Carstairs," Juliet said as she artfully arranged her smart-looking gray and violet bonnet on her head.

"It looks like I'll be ready then." Standing up, Eloisa looked at the small box filled with the sweaters, gloves, mittens, and scarves she'd collected from both her things and from several of her friends. "I hope the women will be able to put some of these things to good use."

"I think that's the least of your worries."

"Oh?"

"They're going to start wondering how they ever got along without you, miss."

Eloisa smiled at that thought. "If they do, that will make me happy indeed. I've been thinking the same thing about them."

She'd just gotten downstairs, Juliet having snagged one of the footmen to carry the box for her, when the doorbell chimed.

She'd already sent word to Worthy about Sean and Katie arriving, and had even gone so far as to ask Juliet to ask the rest of the staff to be especially nice to Lieutenant Ryan and his sister today.

But Juliet said Eloisa didn't need to worry about that. It seemed much of the staff had become fans of the policeman.

Still thinking about that, she stood to one side as Worthy greeted Sean and guided both him and his sister inside.

"Lieutenant Ryan and Miss Ryan to see you, Miss Carstairs."

"Thank you, Worthy." Striding forward, she allowed herself to follow her wants and held out her hands to Sean. "Good morning, Lieutenant."

"Miss Carstairs, may I present my sister, Katherine Jean?"

"Katie, this is Miss Eloisa Carstairs."

"Miss Ryan, it's a pleasure," Eloisa said when Katie turned wide eyes to her.

"Yes, miss. I mean, I am pleased to meet you." Craning her neck, she noticed Worthy standing in the distance, obviously awaiting instructions for where to seat them. "And you too, sir."

Worthy's eyes widened for an instant before bowing his head. "Yes, miss."

"I know we have to go, but perhaps you'd like to refresh yourselves before we head to the train station? May I offer you some coffee or tea?"

Katie pressed her hand on his arm. "Can we, Sean?"

If Sean had his way, he wouldn't stay a minute longer on Sable Hill than he had to. Though Eloisa had been nothing but gracious, he'd been well aware of the way her mother had perceived him. In his darker moments, he didn't blame her mother's lack of enthusiasm about his attentions to Eloisa.

Actually, in his darker moments, he was sure he should do nothing but keep his distance from Eloisa.

But as he thought about Owen's interest in Katie and how he was trying to show her that she was just as important as any well-born lady, he knew he needed to give this moment to Katie. "If we do indeed have time, Miss Carstairs, I think we would appreciate your hospitality very much."

She looked delighted. "Let's go to the sunroom then." She led the way through the drawing room where he'd first met her and her parents, beyond the conservatory until they came to the small, warm room where she'd met with him the day after her visit to the station.

Katie looked around her in awe. "This is beautiful, Miss Carstairs. I thought the white buildings Sean took me to at the fair were special, but your home on Sable Hill surpasses even those places."

Eloisa chuckled. "That's a true compliment. Like you, I have found the White City to be breathtaking. But of course, I must admit to being partial to my home because it is actually habitable."

"What do you mean?"

"Most of the buildings of the fair are only plaster designs molded over cheap lumber. They had to be assembled quickly." Looking winsome, Eloisa shrugged. "Years from now the elements will no doubt have gotten the best of those buildings. They'll be nothing more than distant memories."

"That's too bad."

"I think so too. But someone told me that it is better to experience life than to merely live on its sidelines. I'd like to think that is the case with Chicago and our World's Fair. At least all of us are getting the opportunity to experience such an event. By all accounts it's a very successful fair as well, and it's placed Chicago on the world's stage. If the construction workers hadn't been able to put that city together so quickly, why, nothing would have happened."

Sean smiled, liking her point. "We should have you talk to one and all about our fair, Miss Carstairs. You make some lovely points."

As he'd hoped, she blushed. "Forgive me. Sometimes I get a bit exuberant." Pure relief entered her eyes when one of their servants entered the room. "Ah, Mrs. Anderson has coffee and tea for us. And just in the nick of time."

Sean leaned back as he watched Eloisa gracefully serve them warm beverages and small tea cakes. Through it all, Katie watched her closely, as closely as Sean used to watch his senior officers in the department when he'd first started at the police department. He assumed there was a bit of similarity there. It was becoming apparent that Katie would like nothing better than to have a bit of Eloisa's polish.

His heart warmed as he noticed how patient Eloisa was with his sister. As was Katie's way, the more she got comfortable, the more questions she asked. Soon, Katie was asking Eloisa all about her dress, her hairpins, the parties she went to, and if she truly did know how to waltz.

Eloisa answered each question without a touch of impatience. He also noticed that she was valiantly glossing over the things he knew she had grown weary of. Her answers to Katie implied that her life was just what his sister no doubt imagined it to be—a life of privilege punctuated by numerous events and glittering affairs.

"You are so lucky," Katie whispered.

"I know I am. I've been blessed beyond measure," Eloisa replied.

"All I really have to do is spend my days in ladylike pursuits and hope-fully try to make a difference in others' lives."

"And marry well?" Katie asked.

Eloisa blinked before nodding. "Yes, that is all I have to do." Hating the new thread of vulnerability he saw in her expression, Sean got to his feet. "I hate to be rude, but we need to catch the train if we are going to get to Hope House at the time we planned."

"Of course you are right," Eloisa agreed. They didn't want to miss the train. She also had a feeling Sean was quickly losing patience with all the talk of fashion and hairstyles. "Let's head to Hope House."

Their journey on the grip car to the train station was uneventful, as was their short trip to the stop for Hope House. Sean took care to seat himself between Katie and Eloisa, holding the box of donations Eloisa had wanted to bring along. Katie seemed determined for there to be no moments of silence, and Sean didn't want her to tire out Eloisa with her continuous questions.

Though he ached to visit with her, to ask how she was really feeling, he knew the train wasn't the appropriate place to ask such questions. He was in no hurry to have such a private conversation within twenty feet of his sister, either. Therefore, he kept his tongue and concentrated on assisting her to her feet.

But then, just as they were stepping out of the train, everything fell apart.

Katie had just stepped off when she turned abruptly.

"Katie, what is wrong?"

"I forgot my satchel. I'll be right back."

"Katie—"

"I'll go fetch it," Katie blurted, and then darted off before he could order her to stay by his side. Everything inside of him ached to tell her no, but there was nothing he could do. Literally scores of people were bustling both in and out of the train car and stepping onto the platform.

He moved to the side, still holding Eloisa's box, and glared at Katie's backside as she snaked her way through the throng to get back on the train. "Come now, Kate," he called out, though that was a useless endeavor. The crowd's noise had risen as people around them were scurrying to either exit or enter. He turned to look at Eloisa, but he couldn't see her in the crowd.

"It was just where I'd left it!" Katie called out only moments later, a happy smile lighting her features.

"That's both a surprise and a blessing," he replied as he tucked the box under one arm and reached for her hand. "We've got to find Eloisa."

Then, just as the train's whistle blew again, they heard a shrill cry on the platform behind them, followed by a mixture of exclamations.

And right then, he knew who had just cried out. Grabbing Katie's hand, he pulled her with him, frantically scanning the crowd for Eloisa.

But nowhere did he see her golden hair or smart-looking, dove-gray dress.

He drew to a stop, his heart beating so hard he was surprised he was able to still function.

"Sean?" Katie asked. "Sean, you're hurting my hand."

He ignored her protests as he continued to skim through the crowd, looking on benches, against the walls, on the stairs, down the platform.

And then as the train whistled again and the doors slid shut, the mass of people transformed from chaos to more focused groups of people.

Some talking. Some pointing.

With at least twelve surrounding a woman lying on the platform. "Eloisa," he breathed as he rushed forward.

"Miss Carstairs!" Katie cried as she at last jerked her hand away from his grip and ran to the group.

"Do you know her, miss?" a gentleman wearing a gray top hat, a morning suit, and sporting a goatee and silver hair asked.

"Yes. She is . . . she is my brother's friend."

Sean pushed his way through, dropped the box, and knelt by Eloisa's side, tears pricking his eyes as he saw the long, thin lines of blood marring her neck, shoulder, and upper chest.

With what he was sure was too much force, he pressed his fingers to her throat, hoping and praying to find a pulse.

When he felt her faint pulse beating steadily against his fingers, his eyes filled with tears.

She wasn't dead. She wasn't dead, not yet.

Not wanting her head to be resting on the filthy cement for a second more, he pulled out his handkerchief, pressed it to the worst of the bleeding, then eased her upper body onto his lap.

"Hey now," the gentleman sputtered. "You should leave her alone. Wait for the police to arrive."

"I am the police," he bit out. Looking at the sea of faces peering down on him, he ordered, "One of you go call for a doctor. Now."

After two men who looked to be in their twenties ran off to do his bidding, he said, "Someone else go find me a uniformed officer."

"Lieutenant Ryan, is that you?"

The voice was familiar. Looking up, he was shocked to see Quentin Gardner standing over him, his expression looking pained. Sean jerked a nod. "Mr. Gardner."

"I just got off the train when I heard the commotion. Is that Eloisa?"

"Yes."

"What can I do to help?"

"Find me a constable. They're supposed to patrol these stations. Keep looking until you find one. Please."

Only when Mr. Gardner ran off did Sean start to breathe easier. Help would come. Help was on its way.

He just had to keep her alive.

Looking up at the many concerned expressions leaning his way, he said, "I need a clean cloth for her wounds. Someone hand me a handkerchief." Immediately another three handkerchiefs were thrust toward him. As gently as he could, he pressed the fresh cloths to her wounds.

She cried out.

And though her cry was brought from pain, he was sure nothing had ever sounded so sweet. She was alive.

"Is this the Slasher, then?" another man asked. Obviously not caring that Eloisa was nearly unconscious and bleeding.

"Sean? Sean, what should I do?" Katie clenched her hands over and over. "I need to help. Please let me."

He wanted his sister close to him. But he also knew he was going to need Owen Howard and a physician. And he wasn't sure if he could trust the men who had run off for help to return. Even if they did, twice the help would be far better than not enough—especially with the crowd increasing as it was.

"Katie, we're four blocks west and two blocks north of my precinct." He held her eyes with his own. "When you get to the stairs, look around you. Get your bearings."

"Yes?"

"Then go right away to my station and ask for Howard. He should still be there. He wasn't going to meet us at Hope House for another few hours."

"If he's not there?"

"If he's not there, you tell Fuller what happened. And don't you leave that station without either Sergeant Fuller or Detective Howard by your side."

"I won't."

"Can you do this? Are you sure?"

"Of course I can," she said through trembling lips. "Will she be okay?"

He couldn't bear to tell her he didn't know. "Go now," he answered instead.

When he saw her disappear into the crowd, he pressed his fingers to Eloisa's pulse again, not caring that his fingers were getting stained with blood. Not caring that he was showing his true feelings for all the world to see.

Not caring that he wasn't looking for witnesses and attempting to find whoever hurt her.

All that mattered was that her heart was still beating.

He leaned in closer, wrapping his arms more tightly around her chest so he could whisper into her ear. "Don't you leave me, Eloisa," he ordered. "I don't care what you have to do, do it. You are going to stay alive for me. For me," he whispered fiercely into her ear.

She moaned.

"Sir!" the silver-haired gentleman cried. "Have a care. You are hurting her."

Immediately he pulled back, just as a pair of uniformed officers trotted to his side.

"All right, everyone. Make room now," the taller of the two said. "If you have nothing to offer here, you'd best get on your way."

Then one of them knelt down next to Sean. "This your lady, sir?"

"This is Miss Eloisa Carstairs and I am Lieutenant Detective Sean Ryan of the 16th district."

The officer's blue eyes widened. "You're the detective on the Slasher case."

Sean glared at him. "Comb the area for witnesses. I've already called for a physician and my partner."

"Right you are, sir," the officer said amiably as Sergeant Fuller approached.

"Fuller? Someone found you already?"

"I was on break when I saw a pair of young gents running like their feet were on fire. I ran over here as soon as I got the gist of what happened."

Sean closed his eyes in relief. Sergeant Fuller could gain order out of a field of mice. "I sent Katie for Owen. Someone else went for a physician."

"Right, sir. I'll take care of things for now." Turning around, Fuller let out a shrill whistle that stopped everyone in the vicinity in their tracks. "Listen up, now. I need some answers and I need them now. Which of you saw what happened?"

Silence met the question.

Sean glared at the men and women surrounding him, now looking at each person more completely. Wondering if any of them had knifed Eloisa and then had decided to stay in the area, just to watch her suffer—and watch Sean squirm, desperately looking for leads.

However, now that most of the excitement was over, easily two-thirds of the people who had surrounded them were long gone. Though he wasn't surprised, disappointment struck him deep. Yet again another well-to-do young lady had been struck. And yet again he was nearby but had no idea who had wielded the knife.

He was failing everyone. He had failed her.

"I'm so sorry, Eloisa," he murmured. "So sorry."

She opened her eyes for a split second, obviously trying to get her bearings. "Sean?"

"I'm here," he said as she closed her eyes again. "I'm here and I will never leave you," he vowed. From now on, he was going to do everything he possibly could to keep her safe.

Everything and anything, even if it meant ruining her reputation by being seen with the likes of him.

Even that.

CHAPTER 24

Miss Ryan!"

Katie jumped to her feet and rushed to Detective Howard's side. The minute she was close enough, she clasped both of his biceps. "Thank goodness you are still here."

He looked startled by her touch, but the expression in his eyes surprised her. It was a true combination of worry and determination. "What are you doing here? And are you alone?"

"Yes, but—"

His lips pursed. "I thought your brother was going to talk to you about the dangers of touring this city by yourself."

"He did, but—"

"I don't know where he is, but I have to warn you that I will be telling him about your visit—"

"For all the saints above," Constable Barnaby called out impatiently. "Stop talking and listen, Detective Howard!"

Owen turned to the constable. "What?"

"Lieutenant Ryan sent for you!"

At long last he looked at Katie, this time really seeing her. She felt his gaze skitter across her face, suddenly noticing her rumpled dress, her tear-streaked face. "What happened?"

"Miss Carstairs was attacked at the train station! My brother wants to see you right now! Please, Owen."

He closed his eyes. "Eloisa," he murmured. When he opened his eyes again, a new, steely determination had settled in. "Let me grab my overcoat and we'll go."

"Just sent Peabody for it," Barnaby said as he tossed the expensive overcoat to Owen. "Do you want me to get backup?"

"Yes. I don't know what we'll find. Which train station, Katie?"

"Union."

Barnaby nodded. "I'll get the word out."

Owen barely nodded before clutching Katie's elbow in a firm grip and guiding her out the door. "Tell me everything," he said as they stepped onto the crowded street.

"We were on our way to Hope House," she said as she struggled to keep up his pace while at the same time avoiding running into the people Detective Howard was dodging.

When they stopped at an intersection, barely avoiding getting run over by a milk cart, he glanced her way. "Already? We weren't going to meet for several hours."

She rushed on while they were still stopped. "We wanted to spend some time at Hope House before you came. Sean and I went to Sable Hill, picked up Miss Carstairs, and took the grip car to the station uptown, then got on the train. When we got to Union Station and got off, I realized I'd left my purse on the train."

"And?"

She hated this part, because it showed how everything that had happened was all her fault. "And then I pulled away and got back on the train and Sean stayed with me," she said as the street cleared and Owen pulled her forward, continuing at a breakneck pace.

"Next?" he barked, not looking at her, looking only straight ahead with what could only be described as a murderous expression on his face.

"Well, Miss Carstairs had gotten out of the train ahead of us on the platform and it was crowded . . . we heard a scream. We looked all over the platform and then saw Miss Carstairs lying there, bleeding."

His hand tightened on her arm, likely bruising. Katie didn't protest his iron clasp, though. She deserved every bit of his anger, and every bit of his frustration with her. She was the one at fault.

"Is she alive?" he asked after they walked another twenty feet.

"I-I think so. Sean kept reaching for her pulse. But he had me run for you right away. I hope she's still alive."

Glancing her way, he bit out, "She better be."

Katie flinched at the dark look on his face. He was such a handsome man, so elegant with his lean body, blond hair, and dark eyes. She'd fallen asleep night after night thinking about him, imagining him gazing at her in a tender way.

Imagining him thinking she was worth his time.

Then, when he'd asked Sean about tea, she'd let her pride get the best of her, and she'd begun to think she was worth his time. That she could be his equal.

In her more fanciful moments, she'd even imagined asking Eloisa to help her become more ladylike. She'd wanted to do everything she could to fit into his world.

But now, seeing that dangerous look in his eyes, she knew without a doubt that she'd lost her opportunity. Sean had told her Detective

Howard and Miss Carstairs were good friends. He'd escorted her to several society events. They were comfortable with each other.

They understood each other.

And because she'd been so busy thinking about one day being as elegant as Miss Carstairs, she'd gone and left her purse on the train. That mistake could have very well cost Eloisa her life.

They were only two blocks away from the station now. Two blocks from discovering if her worst fears were realized. Two blocks away from being separated. She knew enough from being around Sean that Owen would be all business, barking orders, asking questions, taking care of things. There would be no time for her to tell him what had to be said.

Which meant, unfortunately, that she had to say the words right then and there.

"I'm very sorry, Detective Howard. I know this is my fault, and though it probably means nothing to you, I am very, very sorry."

He abruptly stopped at another intersection. Then turned his head and stared. "What?"

Tears were now running down her cheeks. Again. And though she was blubbering like the child he no doubt thought she was, she forced herself to continue. "If I hadn't forgotten . . . Eloisa would have stayed by Sean and she wouldn't . . . wouldn't have been hurt. I am sorry."

They started walking again, but to her amazement, instead of picking up their already frenetic pace, he slowed. Pulled her to a quiet spot next to the red brick side of an older apartment building.

And then, very slowly, he released his firm grip on her arm and pressed both of his palms on her cheeks.

Forcing her to gaze at him.

Her stomach in knots, she raised her chin and met his gaze. This was her penance, she realized. She had to face him and take his anger. It was only right.

But to her amazement, the hard, cold, calculating look she'd spied mere moments ago was replaced with something far different. "Katie," he rasped, his voice so filled with emotion it sounded painful. "Listen to me closely. What happened to Eloisa is not your fault."

She appreciated his lie. She did! And another time—maybe when she was a little bit younger—she would have grasped that excuse and held onto it as tightly as she could.

But she'd learned recently that with maturity came responsibility. And with that responsibility came the knowledge that she'd made an error, and that error might very well have cost someone her life. "Oh, but it is, Detective Howard. If I hadn't—"

With a shake of his head, he cut her off. "No. Katie, men and women ride the trains all the time without police protection. It wasn't your fault for being human or Eloisa's fault for stepping into the crowd without an escort on her arm. All the blame goes to the man who did this."

"I know, but Sean told me—"

"Katie, the Slasher attacked Eloisa. For some reason, he sought her out and wanted to do harm. He is at fault. Not you."

"But—"

He pressed his palms to her cheeks for a second before wiping off her tears with his thumbs. "Not you, Katherine. Sweetheart, no one is blaming you."

For a split second, she wondered if he even realized that he had called her by her Christian name. That he called her sweetheart. She thought not. It was obvious he was too upset to even realize he was being so free with her.

But she realized it. And more importantly—at least to her—she cherished his familiarity. Welcomed it.

And with that in mind, she gazed up at him. And for the first time, didn't even try to hide everything she was feeling. For the first time, she let everything in her heart, all her daydreams, all her wishes, shine through for him to see. "Not even you?" she whispered.

Something flickered in his eyes. "Especially not me."

She had no words to respond to that. Instead, she allowed herself to smile. Even though they needed to hurry to Sean and Eloisa.

And even though, very, very soon, Owen would likely not want another thing to do with her because she'd already caused so much harm.

But then, to her surprise, he enfolded her into his arms and briefly hugged her tight.

She pressed her face into his shoulder, breathed in his clean scent, and felt better.

When he released her, he grabbed for her hand and started walking. When they reached the train station, he walked straight ahead, his gaze alert and focused. "Which direction?" he barked.

When they got to the platform area, Katie pointed to their left. "She's over there."

Immediately he dropped her hand and started forward. Three police officers standing off to the side saw him and nodded deferentially. "Sir," one said.

"Watch over Miss Ryan," he said, vaguely pointing behind him in her direction. Not even looking her way.

"Miss?" the first one asked. She immediately recognized Sergeant Fuller. "Stand over here for a moment, if you please. Out of the way."

She stood. Stood in the shadows, trying not to cause any more trouble. Trying to do what they asked because she now knew it didn't matter what she might want to do. The fact was, she was only someone everyone wished wasn't there at the moment. She was a responsibility, a hindrance no one there wanted to have.

"Move a little closer to me, Miss Ryan," Sergeant Fuller repeated as another train pulled into the station and another crowd departed.

Eager to obey, she stepped closer. Not saying a word as both she and the policemen watched Owen stride forward and then kneel down next to Sean and another man who looked to be a physician.

Then, suddenly, it was as if they were all in a wind tunnel and nothing mattered twenty feet beyond them. The other people in the area might have been rendered mute for as much as she heard them.

Every sense was completely focused on Sean, Owen, and Eloisa. To her, nothing else mattered but Eloisa's survival. It was almost as if she knew deep in her heart that if Eloisa didn't survive, she wouldn't either. And that Sean and Detective Howard would always feel as if they'd failed her.

Heart in her throat, she watched the doctor lean back, allowing Owen to edge in. Katie was just close enough to see Owen move closer, hover over Eloisa's beautiful face. To his right, her brother looked ten years older. Blood soaked his shirt, his coat jacket, and traces of it smudged his cheek.

But it was the expression on his face that she couldn't look away from. Devastation, but also hope. And love shone in his eyes.

Katie gasped as she realized just how much Eloisa had come to mean to him.

"Careful, Howard," Sean ordered as Owen leaned over Eloisa, cradling her head in his hands.

"Eloisa?" Owen called to her. "Eloisa? Dear?"

Sean reached out. Grasped his shoulder. "She's lost a lot of blood. She will most likely always be scarred from this. But she is alive."

Owen popped his chin up. Looked at Sean directly in the eyes.

"She is going to survive, sir," the physician said.

"Thank God," Owen said. "Thank you, Jesus. Thank you, Lord."

As the tears she couldn't seem to help continued to fall, Katie echoed the very same sentiments to herself.

If Eloisa was still alive, then everything was going to be okay. And she owed it all to God.

CHAPTER 25

The physician—Stone was his name—had ebbed the flow of blood enough to move Eloisa. "I'll stitch her up properly when she's off the ground," he murmured. "Do you wish her to go to the hospital or my clinic?"

Sean had seen enough of the clinics in the area to have a healthy aversion to them. Many were dirty and filled with people he wanted Eloisa to avoid at all costs. "No." Thinking quickly, he realized Maeve's house was no more than five blocks away. "We'll take her to my sister's house. She can rest there for a few hours before we risk taking her home."

Just as he signaled two uniforms, Owen got in his space. "Sean, she needs to go home. Her parents will be frantic when they hear what has happened."

"Yes, but they don't know anything yet."

"Which is my point exactly."

"And my point is that she needs to be moved and resituated quickly." Seeing the two men standing at their side, waiting, he started barking orders. "One of you take charge of this area. Finish taking statements, clearing the space. You, go to my sister's house and let her know that I'll be arriving with Eloisa and a physician presently." After scribbling Maeve's address on a page in his notebook, he tore it off and handed it to another uniformed officer. "Quickly, now."

Owen's face hardened. "Sean, think about this."

Sean ignored Owen as he knelt and carefully lifted Eloisa into his arms. Her limp body should have felt awkward. In fact, nothing could have been further from the truth. She felt light and supple in his arms. And even after lying on the platform for far too long, she still smelled as fresh and sweet as he'd always imagined she would in his dreams.

"Sean, we need to think about what is best for Eloisa."

"I am. We need a hack."

"I sent Fuller to summon one," Owen said, his speech clipped.

"Very good. We'll take that to my sister's, if you don't mind." He started walking toward the exit, glaring at anyone who was either staring at Eloisa or too slow about getting out of his way.

By his side, Owen was glaring at him. "Sir, what would you like me to do?"

He paused. "Go inform Mr. and Mrs. Carstairs about what happened. And please, keep Katie with you."

"Why?"

"I don't have time to explain, but something was off about this. After you and Katie inform Eloisa's parents, come to my sister's house." He raised an eyebrow. "You remember how to get to Maeve's, I presume?"

"I do."

"By that time, Stone will have finished his handiwork and

hopefully Eloisa will have come around a bit. Then when she's ready, you can escort her home."

"Me?" he asked as they walked through the set of double doors.

When the doctor trotted ahead toward a rather fine-looking buggy and team of two horses, Sean followed, Owen right beside him. "It will be better if you escort her home," Sean said. "We both know that."

"Better for whom?"

"Eloisa," he said as Dr. Stone opened his buggy's door.

"Let me have her while you get in," Owen said.

Sean was reluctant to give her up even for that small amount of time, but he knew his partner's actions were in the right. After carefully easing Eloisa into Owen's arms, he got into the buggy, then held out his arms again for Owen to place her in his lap.

It wasn't easy, maneuvering a young lady around the way they were. And though they did their best to keep the manhandling to a minimum, he had no doubt that they were causing her discomfort. His suppositions were confirmed when she moaned softly.

Both he and Owen froze, but it was Stone who saved the day. "If she's moaning, that means she's coming out of it. That's good." Staring at her neck, he frowned. "Unfortunately, she's bleeding again."

Quickly, Sean rattled off Maeve's address before glancing at Owen. "Take care of Katie. See you soon."

Owen gave a mock salute and was turning away when the driver motioned the horses forward.

In the silence of the buggy, Sean thought about fights he'd been involved in when he was young. The hazing he'd endured being a new recruit. The things he'd seen on his beats, the things he'd done, all in the name of supposedly protecting the city's fine citizens.

He'd gotten knifed, been hit, thrown himself on men attempting to flee, and had once even had the misfortune to be on the wrong side of an escaped pig from the stockyards.

But none of it, none of it had ever given him the feeling of terror he'd experienced today.

"This Slasher's a bad one," Stone said after silence had settled on them. "I hope you catch him soon."

"No one hopes that more than me," Sean said. Absolutely meaning every word.

"I'm sorry you are forced to babysit me," Katie said to Detective Howard when they at last made their way from the train station.

"Babysitting is a bit harsh, Miss Ryan."

"You are being forced to watch over me. I don't know what else you would call it."

He winked as they walked out into the broad sunlight. "An honor."

Her cheeks heated at the flattery. And it was very kind, if rather too effusive. She decided to ignore it. "Do you understand why Sean is making me stay with you? I would have thought it would be better for everyone if I simply went on home."

"He has his reasons," he said evasively. "Now, please stop dwelling on it. We have more important things to do besides debate whether or not you should be by my side."

"What do we need to do?"

"You and I need to go over to Sable Hill and inform Mr. and Mrs. Carstairs about Eloisa's attack."

"My brother isn't going to talk to them when he takes her home?"

"Your brother is taking Miss Carstairs to your sister's home."

"To Maeve's?"

"Her house is closer than Sable Hill, I believe."

"Well, it is that." They were walking down the street, walking on the makeshift sidewalk, really just a long strip of lumber that was just elevated enough so women's hems would be saved from the worst of the dirt.

To her surprise, Owen was keeping their pace at an even, almost leisurely pace. She was grateful for that. She wondered if it was for her benefit or if he wasn't in much of a hurry to talk to Miss Carstairs's parents.

"Do you know them very well?" she asked after they crossed another block.

"Eloisa's parents?"

"Yes."

He shrugged, then at last nodded. "Well enough. Eloisa and I frequent the same circles."

She wasn't exactly sure what he meant. Oh, she understood the gist of it, but the way he phrased things made it sound as if there were more between them than she'd guessed.

Or maybe, perhaps, even less?

"Are we going to walk all the way to Sable Hill?"

He chuckled under his breath, just as he stepped a bit closer to her and took her arm. "No, Miss Ryan. Walking there would take most of the day and we don't have time for that. I just, uh, wanted to give us both a few minutes of peace before we grabbed a grip car."

His lengthy reply embarrassed her. It sounded as if he were taking care to explain things to her, as one would a child. "Sorry."

There were more people around them now, which made sense since they were nearing the financial district. Detective Howard's expression became harder, giving off a further hint of an aura that stated firmly to one and all that no one should mess with him.

"No, I'm the one who should be apologizing. I sounded short with you, didn't I? That certainly wasn't my intention."

Katie knew she should point out that she was nothing to him, merely another obligation bearing down on him on top of an already difficult day.

And because every other topic of conversation she could think of seemed to be a minefield, she asked something that would hopefully give her more information about him but not create another crease of worry around his eyes. "Detective Howard, why would someone like you become a policeman?"

They crossed an intersection before he replied. "I'm surprised your brother didn't already tell you my life story."

"Sean's not one for divulging private information."

He glanced her way. "No, I suppose he is not. Well, the short of it is that I am not the oldest son in my family. Or even the second. I'm number three." His lips thinned. "My father owns a manufacturing facility. It does rather well. There was plenty of expectation for my eldest brother to take after him. And he did."

"What about your next brother?"

He shook his head. "Sam isn't one for business, but he has a good head on his shoulders." She gazed up at him in time to see him frown. "No, that isn't fair. He's bloody brilliant. Smartest man I know. He became a lawyer."

"I see," she said. Though she still really didn't. Running a company and being a fancy lawyer were both respected professions. Being a policeman was definitely not. Even she knew his job was a far cry from where his father no doubt had expected him to go. To make matters worse, he wasn't even in charge. He was a detective, which was a matter of honor for someone of her family, but it had to grate on a man like Owen to be paired with Sean Ryan.

And to make matters even worse, her brother was technically his superior.

He grinned. "If you see, then you are definitely ahead of the rest of my family. They don't see what I'm doing at all. And as a matter of fact, I don't blame them."

"So what did happen?"

He glanced at her, his handsome face looking apprehensive. "The fact of the matter is that the Lord blessed me with good looks—best in the family," he added with a grin. "My mother said she used to tell everyone she met that the Lord had blessed her with her own angel."

"I bet you did look angelic as a baby," she murmured without thinking.

He grinned. "I did. But, uh, what I wasn't all that blessed with was a brain."

"What?"

"I'm smart enough, of course. It's not like I was born with a defect of some sort." He shook his head. "But schooling was hard for me. Especially hard. I had a difficult time learning to read. I still don't read all that well, and sometimes when I write, the letters get turned around." His voice lowered, deepened. "My dad used to say I got all the beauty and none of the smarts."

"That's horrible."

"It was true." He shrugged. "However, it turned out that I might not be able to write things all that well but I can figure things out with the best of them."

"And so you decided to become a policeman?"

"And so I decided to work for a friend of my father's in his store."

"You were a shop worker?"

"Briefly. On the third evening I was working, a pair of hooligans came in and stole some of the merchandise. My boss summoned the police—which I thought was a waste of time."

"Why?"

"Because even five years ago much of Chicago believed that the police weren't all that capable of keeping order. Worse, they were considered to be mostly crooked. Anyway, what did happen was that your brother was one of the men who showed up at the shop."

"I had no idea that was how you met!" Their conversation was certainly a revelation.

"We didn't hit it off real well at the beginning, but your brother did recover the merchandise. And I suddenly realized that I didn't want to have my day's goal to be about selling lots of things to people who didn't need them. About a month after the incident, I asked your brother to meet me for coffee."

"I'm surprised he met you. Sean isn't one to meet anyone for coffee. He's usually all about work."

"I was surprised too. Surprised but relieved. And to this day, no matter what happens, I'll always be grateful to him for doing that. Otherwise I would have really made a fool of myself when I went into that precinct office and asked to be hired."

"What does your family think of your decision? Are they proud of you?"

"No. But my father is a hard worker and he has appreciated my work ethic. He took me out to dinner when I made detective last year." He shrugged. "They also know that I haven't given up my place. I still help out the family by representing them on boards. I still go to gatherings and social events too."

"Which is what you meant by you and Miss Carstairs being in the same circles."

"Yes. She's a friend to me. A kindred spirit, if you will. We are both hoping to be more than pretty faces. More even than what our relatives expect from us."

"I'm glad for you then." And she was, but now she felt even more at sea about him. He was far above her on the social scale than she'd ever imagined. He'd also beaten odds to do what he thought was important.

She, on the other hand, had barely started living. So far all she'd done was study as much as she could in the hopes of having a better life.

He glanced at her, his gaze slowly warming. "Do you have a better understanding now of why I asked your brother if I could spend more time with you?"

His voice was gentle and kind. Tender. Everything she'd ever wanted. But she was still reeling from his story.

And reeling more from her own insecurities. "No, sir. Now I have even less of an idea of why a gentleman like you would ever look twice at a girl like me." The moment the words left her mouth, she steeled herself for his rejection.

He said nothing for a full minute, then pulled her to the side of the street. Away from the majority of the people.

This was now the second time he'd done this. "Detective Owen, forgive me, but we have things to do."

"Miss Ryan, forgive me, but there is something you need to explain to me before we go another step farther."

Only with great effort did she keep from gaping. "What is that?"

"What have I done that makes you think I am a liar?"

A liar? "Nothing," she blurted. "Of course you've done nothing."

"Then why, when I tell you my whole story, reveal to you that I am really nothing more than the third son born into a wealthy family, did you not realize that you are exactly worthy of me?"

He didn't see himself, she realized. He didn't see his worth, his value, his looks, his demeanor, his kindness. He didn't see everything that made him so much more than simply the product of his birth.

"You must know you are more than those things."

He looked around, seemed to notice that they were drawing more than one curious look, and exhaled. "Forgive me. Eloisa has been injured, your brother is beside himself, you've witnessed some terrible things, and we are on the way to tell two people their daughter has been brutally attacked. And here I am, trying to have such a conversation with you in the middle of the street."

Katie didn't know where this was going. She had no idea what would happen between the two of them, what would even happen between the two of them the following day. But she did know that whatever was happening between them was more real than she'd originally imagined.

"Perhaps when this is over, you might consider taking me out for that tea?"

His brown eyes warmed. "I would like that above all things, Miss Ryan. Thank you."

And with that, he guided her back into the fray, signaled for a hack, and helped her inside. "Take us to Sable Hill," he told the driver.

The driver raised an eyebrow. "Quite an address you're going to."

Owen shared a smile with her. "You don't know the half of it."

CHAPTER 26

The first thing Eloisa became aware of was that she was comfortable. More comfortable than she could remember being in weeks. So much so, she was reluctant to let go of the curious daze she'd cloaked around herself. She was sure waking up out of the stupor would mean the return to her reality. The one where her evenings were accompanied by an increasing feeling of uneasiness, her sleep was littered by nightmares, and her mornings were an exercise in an attempt to pretend she'd actually slept.

But as she stretched her toes, she knew returning to reality was inevitable. As inevitable as the air turning colder or the White City eventually becoming a distant memory.

As she gradually opened her eyes, Eloisa focused on the bright sunlight shining through the sheer draperies, fluttering through an open window.

The breeze felt soothing on her skin. Giving in to temptation, she stretched, wiggling her toes against the smooth sheets. Enjoying the feel of freedom.

She smiled. Stretched her neck. And then winced as a sharp, burning pain sliced through her awareness.

Confusion settled in as she tried to remember when she'd last hurt so badly.

Of course, that had been the morning after Douglass had forced himself on her.

No matter how much she enjoyed the feeling of luxuriousness, she gasped. Attempted to focus on where she was, which unfortunately wasn't her bedroom at home.

"Eloisa?" a sweet voice called out.

She didn't recognize it.

With effort she moved her head toward the voice. Stared at the young girl with the pretty blue eyes and the brush of thick bangs over her dark eyebrows. "Katie?" she murmured, trying to place the girl in her life. "Miss Ryan, is that you?"

"It is." Smiling brightly, Katie jumped to her feet, then scurried to her side. "I'm so glad you remember me. I was worried for a moment that you wouldn't."

Eloisa's cheeks hurt too much to smile. But even so, she couldn't help but be charmed. "Of course I remember you."

Looking around the room again, she continued, "Forgive me, but I don't know where I am." Taking a guess, she said, "Is this your room?"

A blush suffused her cheeks. "Goodness no. You're at my sister Maeve's house. Owen and Sean weren't too eager to take you right home until you got your bearings."

Little by little, she began to recall some of the day's events. She had a vague recollection of a doctor stitching her, then she remembered riding in a coach with Sean.

"I see." Though she didn't at all. She would have thought Sean would want her resting in her own house and therefore out of his hair. However, she couldn't help being very grateful that she hadn't woken up in her own bed. At home her mother would have been too shocked by what had happened to Eloisa to do anything but retreat to her room. She would have been alone, with only Juliet in attendance. She and her maid were closer than ever, but . . .

Instead, she had Katie for company, and perhaps, her brother. She certainly hoped so! Though it might be improper, there was only one person she wanted to see at the moment. One person whom she knew she could completely trust.

"Is Mr. Ryan here, by any chance?"

Katie brightened. "Sean is. He went downstairs only about an hour ago. Until then, he was keeping watch by your side."

"Is that right?"

"Oh, yes. After you were attacked, Sean wouldn't leave your side. When the physician came, he patched you up enough to move you, then Sean and he brought you here while Detective Howard and I went to tell your parents what happened."

Her head was spinning. "You went with Owen to my house?"

Katie nodded, looking unsure for the first time. "Yes. I hope you don't mind," she said hurriedly. "Sean didn't want me to be alone and he thought Detective Howard would be the best person to talk to your parents."

So her parents knew she'd been attacked at the train station. While in the company of Sean and his sister.

And they knew that she hadn't been taken directly home.

What they had to say about all of it, she really couldn't begin to fathom.

Somewhat in a less exuberant fashion, Katie said, "Well, um, as

I was saying, while we went to Sable Hill, Sean brought you and Dr. Stone here. After Dr. Stone cleaned your cuts and stitched you up, my sister Maeve put you in one of her old house dresses."

Well, that answered another question. She fingered one of the soft fabric sleeves. "I see."

Katie cleared her throat. "I know this garment isn't quite what you're used to, but your beautiful dress was stained."

"Ah." There was so much she wanted to say, but Eloisa still felt too fuzzy to respond correctly. At the moment, she thought there was a very good chance she would say the wrong thing and hurt Katie's feelings.

"You were really bleeding, you see."

Eloisa felt her cheeks heat. It seemed she was still managing to say the wrong thing. "This is fine," she said quietly.

But still Katie looked like she was worried that Eloisa was about to start complaining about the quality of the cotton.

"I'm obliged to your sister," Eloisa added.

After biting her lip, Katie nodded. "Anyway, um, after Dr. Stone left and Maeve changed your dress, Sean came in here and sat with you."

"In here?"

"Uh-huh. He sat here for a full two hours. Like I said, he was here until Detective Howard and I showed up."

"Would you bring him here? Please?"

Katie gazed at her worriedly. "Of course. I'll be right back. Do you need anything else?"

"Some water, if it's not too much trouble?"

The wrinkle in Katie's brow eased. "Of course I can bring you water. It's not too much trouble at all, Miss Carstairs."

Only when Katie left the room did Eloisa close her eyes again. Only then did she let all the ramifications of the afternoon settle in. She'd been attacked. Her parents had been informed. A man who was not a relative had kept her company while she was lying in a bed that was not her own.

Her mother was going to have a fit, and that was putting it mildly.

Mere moments later, Sean entered holding a glass in his hand. "I thought I heard you two talking."

Katie smiled. "She just woke up."

After returning his sister's smile, Sean strode to Eloisa's side. "I brought you a glass of water. Here, dear. Try to take a sip." Before she could even think about it, he seated himself next to her on the mattress, curved an arm around her shoulders, and helped her hold the glass and take a few fortifying sips.

The first few sips stung like her throat was on fire, but then she was able to appreciate their soothing effects. "Thank you."

He set down the glass, then carefully took her hand in between the two of his.

She knew she should yank her hand from his and remind him that never was it appropriate for him to be so familiar with her.

But for the life of her she couldn't do what was right. His presence was too comforting for her to push him aside.

He scanned her hair, her face, the area of her neck and shoulders that was bandaged. As each second passed, his expression became more and more distressed.

And, if she wasn't mistaken, ravaged by guilt.

At last he spoke. "Eloisa, I am so very sorry."

"This wasn't your fault."

"I should have never taken you to a train station."

"The train is perfectly safe. Hundreds of people—if not thousands—take it every day."

He continued just as if she hadn't spoken. "I should have never allowed you onto the platform without you firmly by my side."

"I am a grown woman, Sean."

"We both know that makes no difference."

No, she knew it made all the difference in the world. She knew she'd been injured, but exactly what had happened was a blur. Now that she was getting her bearings back, she needed to know exactly what had occurred at the train station. "Sean, tell me what happened."

He blinked. Obviously her confusion surprised him. Exhaling, he said, "The Slasher attacked you."

"The Slasher." It wasn't that she didn't believe him, she was having a difficult time understanding exactly how it could have happened. She'd only heard of the Slasher attacking women at parties or at events given by the upper crust of Chicago. In a train station? Dressed as she had been, in a simple day dress, looking much like every other woman in the area?

It sounded rather far-fetched.

"Are you sure about that, Sean?"

"Unfortunately, yes. Though other women have been victims of knife attacks before, no one else that we know of wields a knife so skillfully."

That seemed an odd descriptor. "Skillfully?"

Though it seemed as if every word were being forced out of him, he murmured, "He cut your cheek, neck, and the area around your collarbone." The muscle in his cheek jumped, letting her know just how difficult it was for him to keep his voice even and sure. "He did a lot of damage to your beautiful skin, Eloisa, but he didn't thrust his weapon hard enough to sever an artery. It's like he merely wanted to mark you."

She wasn't sure how his statement made her feel. She supposed she should be grateful to be alive. And she was, of course.

"Why did you bring me to your sister's house?"

For the first time, he looked vaguely uncomfortable. "My sister doesn't live far from the station. We needed to take you someplace close by, somewhere where you could be afforded some privacy. I didn't want to take you to the hospital, and we didn't have time to take you all the way to Sable Hill."

His lips thinned, as if he were struggling with whether or not to give her any more information. "To be perfectly honest, I was so worried about you—I am so worried about you—that I didn't want you to go home just yet. I will take you home presently. Forgive me, but I wanted to focus my attentions on you, not answering your parents' questions."

He might be surprised, but she didn't blame him in the slightest.

———

Two days had passed and still Sean was no closer to the identity of the Slasher. Actually, the only thing he and Owen were fairly sure about was that the man had to be either someone in Eloisa's close circle . . . or someone involved in the investigation.

Over and over he and Owen reviewed the different crime scenes, examining the lists of people present, even going over which police officers responded. The only thing they could agree on was that the Slasher had to have known Eloisa was going to be at that train station. Otherwise it simply made no sense for her to have been singled out. Her attack felt like a personal thing.

Unfortunately, that realization didn't narrow their list of suspects all that much. Not only had he and Owen discussed their Sunday afternoon plans at the station where anyone might have heard them, but they'd also discovered Eloisa's maid had told some of her friends at the park about Eloisa's plans for the day. Any one of those maids could have passed on this information.

The case and his paranoia were starting to take their toll on him. So much so, he'd asked Owen to meet him in one of the back storage rooms of the Illinois building. It was easy to get to, one of the few places where it was relatively easy for them to talk without being interrupted, and they could be reasonably sure no one who was involved in the case would think to look for them there.

When Owen closed the door, he shook his head. "This is now the fourth time we've met here, Ryan. I spent less time at my desk when I was in boarding school than I've spent here."

"Not even to visit? Not that I've been a frequent visitor here either."

"Your sister has."

"Katie?"

"Of course I'm referring to her." Owen held up a hand. "And if you are gathering your wits to start lecturing me about being a proper gentleman around your sister, I'd caution you to wait. I'm in no mood to be talked down to."

Sean fought off his smile. "I wish your desire to court my sister was all I had to worry about. No, I think we need to make a move and soon."

Owen pulled open a leather-covered folder. After scanning a list of at least twenty-five names, he pushed it across the table toward Sean. "Here's everyone we considered."

Sean read over the names, then came upon one he didn't expect. "Your name is here, Howard. Is there something you want to confess?"

"Of course not."

"Then, why is your name listed?"

Looking a bit sheepish, Owen said, "I wanted to be as thorough as possible. When we decided to catalog men who were at most of the crime scenes, I decided it would be wrong not to list myself."

"I wonder if that's significant."

"It would be if I was going around stabbing people," Owen replied, looking affronted. "However, I am not."

"You weren't anywhere near the train station when Eloisa was attacked."

"You're right. And I was too far away to even run back to the precinct before Katie got there."

"You are calling my sister Katie now?"

"Fine. Miss Ryan," he said impatiently before continuing. "My point is, we can't think of anyone we can place at every scene. After the first two attacks, we started searching the surrounding areas for commonalities. We quickly determined that the sheer amount of people at every scene makes it virtually impossible to gather the names of every possible suspect or witness."

Sean knew what direction he was heading. "Millicent Bond's attack was too vicious for her attacker not to have clothes stained with her blood afterward. Whoever did that would have had to become hidden."

"I agree." Picking up a pencil, Owen said, "So may I cross off my name without any qualms from you?"

"Yes." After Owen did the honors, Sean glanced down at the list again. "What makes it hard is that so many men in the force have been doing extra duty around the city. Too many of us have been too many places at the same time."

"I think we need to focus on the officers who could mix in with a crowd unobtrusively. And men who are active in the social circles."

"That's a good point. A rough fellow like Barnaby would make most of the ladies nervous. Too nervous for them to allow him anywhere near them. At least not in a private alcove."

Owen dutifully crossed off a few more names. "That leaves just Captain Keaton, Sergeant Fuller, and Officer Craig."

"Do you really think the captain could be our culprit?"

After a long pause, Owen shrugged. "I'm not saying he is, but I also have to say that I've noticed him in the vicinity but never right when one of the victims has been found."

"But he was there when Danica was knifed at the Gardner home."

"After the fact."

Sean nodded. He kept his name on the list reluctantly. "Now, what about the gentlemen?"

Owen's lips twitched. "Obviously I don't know all of these men extremely well, but some just don't seem the type to bother with knifing a woman."

"Bother?" That seemed like an odd choice of word.

"Whoever planned these attacks took a lot of time and effort. Some of these men barely feed themselves."

Sean chuckled. "Anything else you notice?"

Owen tapped on one name, Martin Upton. "Maybe him, though I can't really see him doing something like this. I don't know if he'd have the nerve . . ."

"That's not a good enough reason. It could be a ruse."

"Point taken." He pointed to another name. "And as for Quentin Gardner?"

"Yes?" Sean vividly remembered watching Quentin waltzing at the gala at his home. He remembered how he'd held Eloisa a little too closely and how he hadn't wanted to release her when Sean had approached. "He is not wimpy."

Owen's mouth flattened. "No, he is not. He's also known to have a rather volatile temper. And to be unreliable."

"What do you mean by unreliable?" He thought that a curious turn of phrase.

"Quentin is the type of man to organize an outing, then cancel at the last minute."

Sean met his gaze. "Which would go against everything we know about the Slasher's methods. Most of the victims were right where everyone knew they would be."

"Except for Eloisa."

"You're right."

"Quentin told me at his family's party that he was intrigued by Eloisa, especially given the rumors swirling about her."

"Rumors? I don't think Eloisa is aware there have been rumors about her, nor was I. Was Quentin actually interested because some suspected she'd been violated?" Sean didn't even attempt to keep the contempt from his voice.

"I don't know that the rumors went that far. But he saw her as a conquest. A lot of men and women are secretly jealous of Eloisa, though they'd rather be stabbed themselves than admit such a thing out loud. Eloisa, with her stunning looks, spotless reputation, and extreme wealth, seems almost untouchable."

"But she isn't untouchable."

Owen looked away. "When rumors started circling that she might not be quite as pure and perfect as she used to be, many people celebrated that. I am thinking now that perhaps Quentin had thought that was a good thing. He could take advantage of Eloisa and no one would be the wiser."

Sean bit back a few choice words about that. Instead of giving in to the fierce emotions surging through him, he put down his pencil and looked at Owen directly in the eye. "He sounds like our most viable suspect."

Owen jerked a nod. "Perhaps."

"Perhaps?"

"Yes. I mean, no." Pain filled his gaze. "Quentin has never been one I would call a true friend, but I truly can't imagine him committing these crimes."

"I think you should watch him carefully from now on. Most especially whenever Eloisa is at the same event."

"I will keep my eye on him, of course. But most likely you'll be escorting her from now on?"

"I don't know if I will be seeing her again."

"Why?"

Sean cleared his throat. "Her parents are justifiably anxious about her forming any sort of relationship with me."

"I thought you've both already come to terms with that."

"That was before . . ." He couldn't even bear to finish his sentence.

"Before what? Before she fell victim to a madman with a knife?"

"You're being overly dramatic."

"If I am, it is by the narrowest of margins." Owen glared at him, then slammed his hand on the table.

"Calm yourself. You're going to get us thrown out of here."

"Hardly that. You listen to me, Lieutenant. You cannot give up on Eloisa."

"I'm not giving up on her. I'm merely recognizing my place. I am no good for her, and everyone knows it. I have brought her down in every way possible."

"No, you are abandoning her in every way possible."

"That is easy for you to say. You have no idea what it is like to fall in love with someone you shouldn't."

"No, I'm only attempting to see your sister, a woman who is over a decade younger."

"Who is beautiful."

"Who has just as many worries about her background as her brother does."

"Katie is a sweet girl. And she'll do anything she's capable of to make you happy."

"Do you actually think my family cares about that?" Owen asked, his voice incredulous.

"You've told them about Katie?" Sean respected Owen and his intentions toward Katie. But that said, Owen was a grown man who had already gone against his family's wishes. Sean guessed that they'd been hoping he would at least marry well.

"Of course I have! I would never have approached you about her if I wasn't serious about my feelings for her. But perhaps you never had those types of feelings for Eloisa."

"Of course I did."

"Sean, in the last weeks, she has been raped and attacked in a train station. She'll be scarred from both events for the rest of her life. All while this has been happening, she's had to keep Douglass's violation a secret and listen to her mother berate her on an almost daily basis about not having yet made an exceptional match."

"Which is why she doesn't need a man like me."

"Which is *exactly* why she needs a man like you. She needs someone strong enough to bear her pain and stand up to her parents." Owen lowered his voice. "She thought she found someone strong enough. To make matters worse, I told her I believed in you. I promised her you would walk through fire to get to her."

"I would walk through fire."

"But yet, you won't knock on her door?"

Now Sean felt like banging his hand on the table. Owen was right. He'd really made a crucial mistake. He stood up. "I need to go to her, don't I?"

"As soon as possible."

"If Keaton asks, tell him I'm asking more questions."

Owen grinned. "Just be sure you ask the right ones. And also see if she plans to attend the Meyers' closing World's Fair gala at the New York State building in a couple of weeks. If so, come to my home directly after you talk to her."

"So you can be there too?"

"So you can get fitted into one of my tuxedos."

Sean grinned as he walked out the door. A year ago he would have let foolish pride and ignorance stop him from accepting such an offer.

Now he realized how the offer had been given out of friendship. It was an offer for the use of a suit. One of many Owen Howard owned, but one that, if Sean wore it, would make all the difference when accompanying Eloisa.

And that made all the difference in the world.

CHAPTER 27

"Lieutenant Ryan has returned," Worthy announced when he entered Eloisa's private sitting room, where she was working with Juliet to sew a couple of dresses for Gretta. "Are you receiving, miss?"

"She is," Juliet said before Eloisa could formulate a lie. "Please tell Lieutenant Ryan that she'll join him in a few minutes."

To Eloisa's dismay, Worthy smiled—smiled!—at Juliet before leaving to do her bidding.

"I can't believe you just answered for me," Eloisa said. "And I really can't believe that Worthy didn't even question it."

"The reason you can't believe these things are happening is the reason all of us servants have to take matters into our own hands," Juliet said practically. "Otherwise you would continue to refuse to see anyone who has come to call."

"Those women only came to look at my face." Still, Eloisa could barely look in the mirror. She'd never thought of herself as particularly vain, but having her face, neck, and chest marred like it was for the rest of her life made her realize how much she'd taken her looks for granted.

"I know that. But we both know that not every one of those women is catty. Some are truly concerned. You should have let them see you."

"I'm just not ready."

"It's been two weeks, Miss Carstairs. Your stitches are out and the swelling is gone."

It took everything Eloisa had not to lift her hand to her face and attempt to cover the red mark on her jaw and neck. "Two weeks is not long enough for them to fade."

Juliet pursed her lips together before speaking. "Forgive me for being blunt, miss, but those marks aren't going to fade anytime soon. They'll still be there next month and next year."

"That gives me no comfort." What she was afraid to admit was that no amount of time would be long enough to get used to them.

"You don't need any more comfort. You need to be reminded that you are still living." After placing the half-sewn dress on a side table, Juliet stood up. "Now, let's have you put on something more presentable."

Eloisa glanced at the dress she was wearing. It was one of her older ones, a little loose, given the weight she'd recently lost. Because of that, though, it was rather comfortable. "I don't think Lieutenant Ryan will care about my dress."

"He won't care because he cares about you, miss. But in two seconds he's going to know you aren't doing all right if you walk out there looking like you do. You're going to scare him half to death, you are."

Eloisa let Juliet coax her to her feet and start guiding her to her wardrobe, but she still felt obliged to protest her maid's heavy-handedness. "You heard what my parents said."

"I did. I think even the scullery maids down in the kitchens heard your mother's tirade. As well as the way your mother refused to let Lieutenant Ryan see you."

Her mother had been especially harsh, practically laying all the blame for her attack at Sean's feet. Eloisa had been horrified. But upon further reflection, she'd started to wonder if perhaps severing any ties with Sean was the best thing for both of them. She was damaged goods. An upstanding man like Sean should have a woman worthy of him.

"Juliet, there mustn't be anything between us."

"If you don't care for him, you don't. But we both know you do," she said as she motioned Eloisa to her dressing room, pulled out her new periwinkle dress, and motioned for her to turn around.

Eloisa turned, though she wasn't exactly sure why she was being so compliant. "Even if I do care for him, my parents . . ."

"May I continue to speak plainly?"

"It's too late to stop you."

"All of us servants love your parents. They are nice people and treat their help very decently. But your mother has never let up on you, miss. Not once."

"What?"

"You know what I'm saying. Even when the society papers declared you to be the season's diamond, that was never enough for your mother. She pushed you to always look perfect, then she pushed you to make not just a good match, or a great match, but a *brilliant* one."

"She was only hoping the best for me . . ."

"She had such high expectations, no one could meet them. Not even Eloisa Carstairs."

After helping Eloisa step out of the day gown, she helped her step into the new one. "But worse than that, your mother never even noticed when you were hurting."

Eloisa couldn't bear to think about that.

"We all knew you couldn't sleep. We heard the cries from your nightmares. We saw the circles under your eyes and the way you retreated into yourself. Everyone knew something terrible had happened. But your mother refused to let you be imperfect."

"You're right."

"And now, here you've been attacked again! Scarred. It's obvious that the Society Slasher sought you out. But instead of finally thinking about something other than your reputation, your mother has fixated on your looks. And she is mourning your looks, Eloisa."

"She has every right. My face is forever ruined."

"Miss Carstairs, you are still exquisite! If anything, those red marks only serve to accentuate just how pretty you are," she said as she guided Eloisa to her dressing table and began quickly combing her hair.

"Through it all, Lieutenant Ryan has liked you. He's tried to protect you. He looks at you like you are the world to him. Let him love you."

"But my parents—"

"Will survive," Juliet said as she put the finishing touches on her hair. "And when your brother, George, arrives home from his trip to Europe, he'll say the same thing. Now, go see Mr. Ryan before he grows tired of waiting for you."

Eloisa knew she was right. And so she started walking toward the one man who had claimed her heart. One who knew what happened to her at Douglass's hands and still thought she was worthy. One who'd held her when she'd been lying on that platform bleeding.

He was quite possibly the only man who also didn't seem to care at all that she was no longer perfection personified.

Only from years of experience at keeping his emotions close to his vest was Sean able to keep his expression neutral and composed when he stood up to greet Eloisa.

"Miss Carstairs, thank you so much for seeing me," he said graciously as he crossed the room to meet her halfway. He held out his hand, ready to take hers.

She kept her own hands firmly by her side. "Would you be upset with me if I admitted that I almost sent you on your way?" she asked lightly.

He knew she expected him to be everything proper. But he was only a common man, and no matter how much he might want to be a gentleman, Sean knew enough about himself to know he was never going to be very good at anything other than being the man he was. "I would be upset," he said baldly. "Very much so."

She blinked. Then, to his pleasure, a faint sheen of happiness floated into her expression. "You are teasing me."

Unable to refrain from touching her a second longer, he stepped closer, reached for her hand, and pressed his lips to her bare knuckles. "I can't help but tease you."

"Sean."

He continued. "However, I must admit that if you had refused to see me I would have been crushed."

She was still letting him hold her hand. "Is that right?"

"Oh, yes," he murmured as he pressed his lips to her knuckles again. "I would have been sorely disappointed to not show off my new skill at kissing ladies' hands."

"You are certainly gallant today."

"Since it has made you smile, that makes me happy." Unable to help himself, he carefully wrapped the hand he still held around his arm. "Would you care for a turn outside in your gardens?"

She looked doubtful. "I'm afraid they aren't much to see now. The sudden cold snap put an end to that."

"I don't care what the gardens look like, Eloisa. You know I came to see you."

"I know. Thank you." She glanced out the window, then with a shake of her head, said, "Would you mind if we chatted in the solarium instead? I'm finding myself not ready to venture out in the cold today."

"Wherever you'd like to be is fine."

Just as they turned, her mother descended the staircase. Fastening a glacial stare on him, she murmured, "Eloisa, I didn't know you were expecting company."

"I wasn't. Lieutenant Ryan's appearance is a surprise."

Only out of respect for Eloisa did Sean stand quietly while her mother eyed him with distaste.

"Was there a reason you needed to see Eloisa yet again?"

"Yes."

"Oh? Is there a new development in the case?"

"My interest this afternoon is of a personal nature."

"Personal?"

"You must have known how worried I have been about Eloisa. Since this is now the third time I've come calling."

Eloisa stared at him. "I thought you only came one other time."

"The first time, Worthy met me at the door and regretfully refused me entrance at your parents' orders. Yesterday your mother was kind enough to do the honors herself."

"Mother?"

"You are being impertinent. I must ask you to leave. Immediately."

"I think not."

"Eloisa—"

With not a bit of trepidation, Sean watched the muscles work in

Eloisa's throat. He hated that he was bringing her so much tension, but until she actually told him she didn't want to see him, he wasn't going to go anywhere. She mattered too much to him.

"Mother, please excuse us."

"If you continue to press your attentions on my daughter, Mr. Ryan, I will be forced to notify your superiors."

"I'll let them know to expect your call," he said before turning to Eloisa. "You are looking a bit pale. Perhaps we should go sit down?"

"Yes. Thank you."

Her mother stepped forward. "Eloisa, think about what you are doing."

"For the first time in my life, I do believe I am." With a shudder, she leaned closer to him. "Please, Sean. Let's go sit down."

"Of course," he murmured. As he guided her through the grand rooms, he kept his pace slow and steady. When they arrived at the solarium, he helped her sit down on one of the wicker sofas, then took a place right next to her.

"Eloisa, the truth now. Are you all right?"

"Sean, you know I am not."

There was so much trepidation in her face, so much fear in her eyes, he made a decision. Pulling off his gloves, he reached up and ran his thumb along the red scars on her cheek and jaw. When she flinched, he paused. "Do they hurt you? Or is it my calluses? Is my touch too rough?"

"Your touch isn't rough at all."

He was glad because he had no intention of removing his hand. At least not yet. Giving in to temptation, he brushed two fingertips along her jaw, tracing the line of the red scar. "In time, the marks will fade. And the wounds will become less sensitive."

"You sound like you have experience with a knife's blade."

He dropped his hand. "I'm afraid a boy growing up in the streets like I did has little choice about that. Knife fights aren't uncommon."

"So you are scarred too?"

"I am. They're hardly visible now. But I do remember their sting. Eventually, they won't feel so foreign. And they'll fade in time."

She nodded. "Did you come to give me an update on the investigation?"

He shook his head. "I told your mother the truth. Right now we are following a couple of leads, but there is nothing new to report. I came to see you. I needed to see you, Eloisa."

"I'm sorry you were refused entry before."

"I am too. I thought I was going to have to start climbing trees and sneaking in through your window."

As he hoped, his statement made her smile. "Now wouldn't that be something? You'd scare me half to death, sneaking into my room like a thief."

"Then your mother would really have to call my superiors."

She chuckled. "How is Katie?"

"She is doing better. She's been worried about you."

"She is a dear."

"I'm afraid she is a bit too full of herself right now. My mother has her hands full with her."

"Such is a mother's lot, I suppose."

"Eloisa, Owen told me there is a closing gala at the fair."

"Yes. Is Mr. Howard going?"

"He's planning on it."

"Ah."

"I'm asking because I'd like to be your escort."

"I hadn't planned to attend."

"I think it might be the right thing to do. That way you can show everyone that you are all right."

"People won't be looking out for my welfare, Sean. They'll be looking to see how bad I look."

"Which is why it might be best if you show them you are still as beautiful as ever."

"But I'm not."

"I promise, you are still the loveliest woman I've ever seen."

Panic filled her eyes. "Thank you, but I will not be attending."

"Is it me? If so, Owen promised he could escort you if you'd rather not be seen by my side."

"It is not you." Leaning forward, she gripped his hands. "Sean, you must know that I think you are a wonderful man. I would never be ashamed to be seen on your arm."

"Then let me do this for you. Let me help you put this episode behind you."

"No other woman who has been attacked has ventured out into public—none that I've heard of anyway."

"I don't see why that matters."

"I'll be a source for gossip."

"I'm afraid you already are." Even when she looked at him sharply, he didn't dare retreat. "You can either stay here on Sable Hill and wonder what others are saying or make the choice to hear the words yourself."

"You have no idea what you are asking of me."

"You're right," he agreed. "I'll never know what it is like to be Eloisa Carstairs. I don't know what it's like to be born to so much. To live in a home like this, with dozens of people hoping to keep their jobs by making you happy."

DECEPTION ON SABLE HILL

"That isn't fair. You know there's more to me than that."

"I do know. But do you, Eloisa?"

His question was jarring. Especially since it forced her to realize that she'd been hiding behind so much of what she'd claimed didn't matter to her. Taking a deep breath, she said, "I am more than those things."

"Are you sure?" After a pause, she jerked her head up to look at him but said nothing. "Then prove it. Say you'll go with me. Say you'll let me come to your door, be your escort, and help you get through the evening."

"But the Slasher—"

"This time I won't let you out of my sight."

"You're not going to give up, are you?"

"I have no choice," he said quietly. "I care about you too much." Lowering his voice, he added, "I care about you enough to risk your hurt and scorn, Eloisa. I care that much about you."

"What are you saying?"

He knew what she meant. And he knew what he wanted too. He wanted her bound to him. Forever. He wanted to cherish her and love her. He wanted to spend the rest of his life making sure she knew all he cared about was her. What happened to her at Douglass Sloane's hand didn't matter to him. Whether the scars completely faded from her skin didn't matter to him either.

She was far more than the worst things that had happened to her. Far more.

"I want to go anywhere and everywhere with you, Eloisa," he at last admitted. "To me the possibilities are limitless."

Eloisa studied him. Then at last sighed. "If you believe in me so much, I don't know how I am going to be able to disappoint you."

"So you will go to the gala at the fair?"

"Yes, Lieutenant Ryan, I will go with you to the gala at the fair."

Her lips were trembling. Her eyes were glistening. And before he knew what he was about, he leaned closer and brushed his lips against her cheek.

"You've made me very happy, Miss Carstairs. Thank you," he said before standing up and walking out.

CHAPTER 28

Does your mother know you are back at the fair, Miss Ryan?" Detective Howard asked as he and Katie took another turn around the Women's Pavilion.

"Of course not. She thinks I am helping my brother Billy and his wife with their new baby."

"They won't let on that you weren't there?"

"Not until it will be too late to do anything about it."

When she noticed how shocked he looked, Katie regretted her impetuousness. "I am not usually so disrespectful. But they are closing most of the buildings this week." Pointing to some of the wooden crates already nailed shut, she said, "If I waited until I finally got permission, it would be too late."

"I suppose I don't need to tell you your excuse doesn't hold much weight. Or that your brother wanted you to be chaperoned."

Katie was beginning to realize that a man like him was always going to be surprised by the willfulness in a girl like her. "I figured Sean would trust us together now. But if you'd rather not be alone with me, we can leave, of course. I don't want to make you do something you'd rather not, especially not on your day off."

He looked nonplussed for a moment. "You continue to surprise me, Miss Ryan. Every time I think I have the upper hand, you throw me off-kilter."

"I don't know whether you are glad about that or not."

"To be honest, I'm not sure about that either," he commented. "Now let's move on."

She inclined her head, then settled in to following his lead. They circled the rooms again. Over the next hour, Owen stayed by her side, listened carefully when she pointed out things that interested her. Smiled softly when she finally revealed that she would like to write for a newspaper or ladies' publication one day.

As she revealed more about herself and he patiently listened to every word she said—even some of the not-so-smart things—Katie began to relax. It really did seem that he was with her by choice, and that for some reason known only to him he was pleased to be by her side. Once she even saw him coolly eye a young man about her age who was watching them closely.

Another time Owen carefully placed a hand on the small of her back when a group of several men and women passed them. The gesture was full of not only his manners but also possession. And in that moment, she realized he was staking a claim on her.

She found herself smiling when they exited the building.

"What has you looking like the Cheshire cat?" he asked.

"Nothing." There was no way she was actually going to admit she was feeling like one of the luckiest girls in the world.

"Sure it's nothing?"

"It's nothing I'd like to share."

"Now you have me very curious."

She tucked her chin in embarrassment, then decided she had nothing to lose by being honest. "I was only thinking that I am happy to be by your side. When I think of how different we are, I get nervous."

"Because?"

"Because we have very little in common. But then, when I spend time with you, whether it is here or at my sister's house, I forget about my doubts and I start thinking that perhaps we have more in common than I'd originally thought."

He was walking with his hands clasped behind his back. His pace was slow, his focus solely on her, which was how she knew her words pleased him.

"There's no hurry, Katie," he said. "We are on no timetable. We can take all the time you want to get to know each other better."

She exhaled. "I'm glad about that."

He'd just smiled at her when his posture stiffened. Then, almost imperceptibly, he changed positions. His hands dropped to his sides and he stepped closer to her. "Quentin. Hello."

"Howard." His friend eyed Owen in a sardonic way before directing his attention to Katie. Then he tipped his hat. "Miss." And stopped directly in front of them.

They had no choice but to stop as well, though Katie could tell Owen wasn't happy about it. He raised his chin, and she noticed his expression was set like granite. "Did you need something?"

"Only to be introduced." Smiling at Katie, he said, "I don't believe we've met."

After the briefest of pauses, Owen said, "Katie, may I present Quentin Gardner. Quentin, may I present Miss Ryan."

"Ryan?" His eyes narrowed. "Irish, yes?"

Katie nodded. There was something peculiar about the man's interest.

Suddenly he grinned. "Wait a minute. Ryan . . . Ryan. Are you the illustrious Lieutenant Ryan's sister?"

"Yes." Though she could practically feel Owen's hostility next to her, she wasn't about to deny the relationship. She was proud of her brother, and she couldn't ignore her birth. She was Irish and there was nothing she could do about that. "Sean is one of my brothers."

Something dark entered Mr. Gardner's face, and his eyes turned back to Owen. "I thought you were seeing Eloisa?"

"I believe that is none of your business."

"Ah, yes. I suppose it is not. After all, we all know you are far more concerned with catching the Slasher." Flicking a piece of lint off his sleeve, he murmured, "Pity you haven't made much headway."

"We are closing in."

"I seem to have heard that before." After another long look at Katie, he said, "Will you be accompanying Owen to the closing gala tonight?"

"Good day, Quentin," Owen said, then firmly put his hand on the small of her back and guided her away.

Katie let him move her away because she didn't trust Quentin and she knew Owen was fighting to hold his tongue. Only after they had walked a good fifty feet did Owen stop. "I'm sorry about that. Quentin can be, uh, somewhat of a challenge."

"Yes, sir."

"There's no need to be so formal, dear." He sighed. "Actually, Quentin reminded me that I need to check the location for the gala tonight. Do you mind if we walk over to the lagoon? The party is going to be in the New York State building. I need to make sure everything is in order."

"Of course we can walk over there." She attempted to smile, but inside she was calling herself ten times the fool. They really were too different, and the leering way Owen's friend had regarded her cemented that notion firmly inside her.

They walked to the New York State building. After they went inside, Owen suggested she walk around for a moment while he conferred with the men and women who were already working like busy bees in the various rooms to prepare for a string quartet and servants, adding small tables and chairs for people to enjoy their libations and hors d'oeuvres.

In addition, several policemen were inspecting the rooms. She had just moved to what was essentially a gallery of sorts, displaying artwork by illustrious New Yorkers, when she noticed a familiar face.

When she caught his eye, Sergeant Fuller started, then walked her way. "Hello, Miss Ryan. I don't know how you got inside, but I'm afraid the building is closed for the day. Some swells are going to be having a party here this evening, you see."

"Oh, I'm not alone. I'm here with Detective Howard."

Fuller blinked. "Why on earth would you be with him?" Before she could even think of a reply, he stepped a little closer and grabbed her arm. "What's wrong with Sean?"

"Sean?" She wasn't sure why he would have even imagined anything was amiss with him.

He grimaced. "I mean your brother, Lieutenant Ryan."

"Nothing is wrong with him. He was perfectly fine when I saw him yesterday."

"Then why would you be keeping our gentleman detective company?"

Now that was a phrase she hadn't heard in a while. She remembered Sean calling Owen that quite a bit when he was first assigned to work with him. But that had been almost a year ago. Since then the two had developed a firm friendship.

She attempted to laugh, though she was feeling more awkward by the second. But she wasn't in any hurry to lie, either. "Detective Howard offered to accompany me to the fair today."

"He is here as your escort?"

"Well, yes. I, um, wanted to see the Women's Pavilion one last time before the fair closes."

"But you ain't there. And he isn't by your side."

"He wanted to check something here," she said meekly, feeling more and more awkward. Though Sergeant Fuller was a member of the police force, she didn't really know him. Furthermore, Sean always warned her not to gossip about his job. "He'll be right back, though."

"I'll stay with you until he returns, then."

She smiled weakly. She didn't want his company. Not only was she far too old to be watched over like a wayward school girl, she couldn't escape the notion that Sergeant Fuller was being far too familiar with her.

She flinched when he wrapped his hand around her wrist.

"What's wrong? Do you not take the arms of sergeants?"

"I simply need to stay here. Like I promised Owen."

"Owen? You are that familiar with him?"

"I mean, Detective Howard," she said somewhat breathlessly.

"You don't know what you want or what you mean, I think. But you should. After all, you're a pretty thing, but in the end, you are just poor Irish trash—"

"Miss Ryan?" Detective Howard called out. "Fuller? Sergeant, what are you doing here?"

"I'm here for the same reasons you are, I suppose, Detective. Checking things out for the high and mighty."

"The captain sent you?"

Fuller ignored the question, merely looked toward Katie. "Now that your escort is here, Miss Ryan, I'll be on my way."

She nodded, barely. But otherwise didn't do a thing until he was out the door. When they were alone, Owen looked around at the other visitors. When it was obvious that no one was paying them any mind, he leaned closer to her. "What was that about, Katie?"

"I don't know. He took hold of my wrist. He . . . he was asking why I was here."

"Was he?" he asked in his gentle way. "What did you tell him?"

"The truth. That I came here with you." She raised her chin and looked into his eyes, struggling to understand what had just happened. "Was that wrong?"

Owen slipped a reassuring hand at the middle of her back. "Not at all, Katherine Jean. Nothing you are doing is wrong or improper."

"He acted like I was acting above myself."

"What does that even mean?" he asked lightly. "You are a lovely young lady and you have allowed me to spend some time with you. That doesn't sound like you're acting above yourself at all."

"You did ask me to be with you, didn't you?"

"Of course I did. And even though I'm past thirty years of age, I even asked your brother's permission to do it." He flashed a wry grin. "Now I think we had best be going." He paused. "Plus, I have a favor to ask of you."

"What is it?"

"Would you care to go to the gala tonight?"

The invitation was lightly asked, but the weight of the importance in her life couldn't be measured. "Why are you asking . . . me?"

"Because I want to spend more time with you. I promise, my motives are above board. Your brother will be here and you may arrive with Eloisa."

It sounded like a dream come true. "I don't know how to waltz or anything."

"You won't have to waltz. Just stand with us and enjoy yourself."

"I . . . I don't have anything appropriate to wear." And she couldn't even begin to imagine how she or her sister could ever afford anything even remotely suitable—even if there were time to shop. Even June didn't have a dress fine enough for a social event like this.

"That is why I asked Eloisa if she might lend you a hand."

"You've already asked her?"

"I did. She wanted to repay your kindness. Well, the kindness of your family. Sean mentioned that you would probably like to attend one of the social events. And so she offered. If you'd like to go, dear, all I have to do is take you to Eloisa's house. We can send word to your family so they won't worry about you."

He was making it seem so simple, when it wasn't at all.

He was giving her choices about attending functions she never thought she'd ever even hear about except when June read the society papers out loud.

And though she was nervous to say yes, she realized that was from a great many things that didn't have anything to do with Mr. Owen Howard, society gentleman, police detective, and no doubt the object of more than one lady's affections.

"I'm only afraid of embarrassing you. Not of being with you," she admitted. "Is that wrong?"

For the first time, something bright and unhidden shone in his eyes. "Katie, I promise, what you just said could never be more right. I feel the same way about you. So may I escort you to Miss Carstairs's home?"

"Yes, Mr. Howard. I would like that very much."

He held out his arm for her to take. She took it, thinking of how right it felt to be by his side.

Only as they left the building and she caught sight of Sergeant Fuller watching them did she flush. Perhaps Fuller had been right. There was a very good chance that any sort of relationship between her and Owen was going to be perceived by most as very wrong.

CHAPTER 29

The New York State building, located to the west of the Palace of Fine Arts, was glorious. It was large, a brilliant white, and looked as if the architects had dubiously combined a large mansion with an Italian villa. It was sumptuously decorated, boasted two towers, and had a second-story banquet room that was decorated in shades of cream and gold.

Eloisa had visited the building more than once, of course, but this was the first time she'd been invited to attend a party there.

Her parents had declined the invitation, as did some of the most high in the instep sticklers of Chicago society. Many felt that the denizens of New York had built the awe-inspiring edifice as a deliberate snub to the people of Illinois, showing that while the World's Columbian Exposition might have its home in Chicago, it would have been much better for everyone if the site of the fair had been in New York City, like most had wanted in the first place.

As for Eloisa, she had far more important things on her mind at the moment than whether or not she should be seen mixing with the high steppers from New York society.

Actually, at the moment, she was far more concerned about making sure Katie Ryan was enjoying herself. And then there was the small matter of feeling just about everyone's eyes on her face wherever she went.

She'd chosen to wear ivory, hoping that her gown, practically glowing in the sea of dark gowns and black tuxedos, would both complement the also-glowing White City buildings as well as detract a good bit of attention from the marks on her cheek and jaw.

She'd been wrong.

No matter to whom she talked or smiled, the other person's attention was first drawn to the angry red marks on her cheek. An uncomfortable silence usually followed, accompanied by a few probing questions.

Only then could conversation about the fair and the party and trivial gossip ensue. Usually it was stilted and strained. Eloisa supposed she couldn't blame them. Her marks served as a reminder that the public areas of Chicago were not safe. But hitting even more close to home was the fact that Eloisa was a symbol of all of them.

The privileged, the blessed few. The select gentlemen and ladies who were supposed to be insulated from the rough-and-tumble life so often reported in the *Chicago Tribune*. They were supposed to be immune to such things.

And they had been . . . until the Society Slasher had begun to terrorize them all.

The only silver lining in her appearance was that it was so remarked upon that very few people were concerned about the identity of her escort, Lieutenant Detective Sean Ryan. Those men and women who knew he was a policeman acted as if they were glad he was staying by Eloisa's side.

Others only took note of his appearance, saw that he was handsome and wore a well-cut suit, and kept conversation geared toward trivialities.

Still others were more intrigued by the youthful beauty of Katie. She was wearing one of Eloisa's gowns, and the blue in the fabric accentuated her bright-blue eyes, dark hair, and winsome smile. She looked adorable, and was comporting herself well. No one there had any idea Katie was from a part of Chicago most of them didn't even know existed.

After they'd been there for an hour, Sean, who had been checking in with the uniformed officers standing watch at the entrance, smiled at her. "How are you faring, Miss Carstairs? I'm sorry I had to leave you. I know I promised not to leave your side, but it seems even here I have to be a lieutenant."

"Think nothing of it. I've been having a wonderful time watching your sister create quite a stir."

"Truly?"

Eloisa hid a smile. Sean looked as if he wasn't sure what to think about his sister creating such an impression on the crowd. "Very much so. I have a feeling she's having an evening she won't forget anytime soon."

Eloisa watched him scan the crowd and locate his sister, who was standing prettily next to Owen while they were talking to Reid Armstrong and his fiancée, Rosalind. "I'm glad Owen is staying by her side."

"Sean, I think it's more of a matter of him not wanting to leave her side." She lowered her voice. "He's smitten. I'm sure of it."

"I'm afraid he is."

"She's a wonderful young lady."

Something passed in his eyes before he seemed to gather himself and look her way. "What about you?"

"What about me what?" she teased.

"Are you regretting your decision to come here with me?"

"Actually, I am not. Before you returned, I was just reflecting on how glad I am that you encouraged me to come. It has been awkward, seeing as how my scars seem to be about three steps ahead of me. But now, at least, people are talking about what they see and not merely sharing stories about what they think happened to me."

"Yes, the truth is always better, I think."

"I'm slowly learning that—though I fear I've gotten used to not only practicing deception with others but deceiving myself."

"How so?"

"Deception can be so very dark. So much so, it's often a struggle to enjoy the light of bare truth. So I've been hiding in the dark."

She had been thinking about how she had thought no one would see her pain if she stayed hidden on Sable Hill, about her evasion with Juliet, about the way she'd been afraid to even tell her mother about Douglass's attack. And she realized she'd been deceiving herself. She'd taken to pretending she was fine, especially when she'd finally made the practically heroic effort to leave her house. But she hadn't been fine, and now she saw her actions for what they were.

Sean looked at her intently before he responded.

"Deception can feel like a comfortable cloak at times, I imagine." He looked around the room. "It's like this place, I suppose. It's beautiful and pure white and grand."

"It says a lot about the people who built it."

"And for the people who paid for it too, I imagine."

"Always."

He grimaced. "However, many of the surrounding buildings are already almost empty. Soon these white buildings will only serve as memories of another time."

Unable to help herself, she felt the raised lines on her jaw with her fingers. "As will my scars. Perhaps one day I'll forget they're even on my face. Only a look in the mirror will remind me of being attacked."

"Or perhaps you won't view them as unsightly reminders."

"What else would I ever think of them as?"

"As part of yourself. As a mark of bravery. As a sign that you became more than you ever thought you would be."

"More than I ever thought I would be," she murmured. "That sounds an awful lot like something you said when we first met."

"I guess it's a sentiment that I've adopted over time. I had to, you know. My origins were not conducive to attaining big dreams."

"Yet you are on your way. You are a lieutenant, after all."

"That, I could imagine." His gaze warmed. "Standing here with you? Going to your home and offering my escort to a gala such as this? It is all beyond my wildest dreams."

"Being in the company of a man such as you is that way for me."

"Is being so close to an Irish detective more than you ever imagined, Eloisa?"

"No. Being so close to a man who cares so much for me is."

All humor fled his eyes. "Once again, you render me speechless."

"And once again, you make me wish I was simpler."

"Because?"

"Because I want you to want to be near me again."

"That is not something you ever have to doubt." He took a breath, visibly steeling himself to say his next words.

She leaned closer, rested her hand on his forearm, knowing that their intimate conversation was no doubt causing more than a few raised eyebrows. But not caring about that at all.

Not caring at all.

"Eloisa," he murmured.

"Yes?"

━━

"Lieutenant Ryan!" a voice called out, piercing the low murmur of conversations. "Detective Howard, I'm going to need you too."

Sean pulled away, turning to the entrance of the banquet room. And there was Sergeant Fuller, looking pale and out of breath. And sooty?

"Report. What happened?" Sean barked as he strode across the room, Owen meeting him.

"Fire!" Fuller called out. "There's a fire in one of the buildings two away."

Aware of the women crying out behind them, Sean glared. "You know better than to set a panic like this. Watch yourself, man."

"It's a bad one, sir," he said contemptuously.

Owen inhaled in frustration. "Where do you want me, Ryan? Here or at the fire?"

"Here. We can't do anything to stop a fire, but we're going to need to get everyone away from this area. You start directing everyone down these stairs. I'll take care of getting them out of the building as safely and quickly as possible."

"Fuller, where are the other uniforms?"

"Two are here. I sent two others to get close to the burning building, to make sure we keep everyone away."

"Good thinking. The two here can help Howard. Let's go," Sean ordered as he ran down the stairs, knowing he would report the sergeant to the captain when all was said and done. The man's cheekiness was bordering on true insubordination.

The moment he reached the bottom, he felt as though the wall of people was flowing down the stairs in an unstoppable crest. There was no way he could have even slowed them down—especially since Fuller had also not followed him as Sean had expected. The most he could do was attempt to get everyone to use caution so no one would get hurt.

Stepping to one side, he motioned for everyone to leave. "Exit and follow the directions of the officers outside," he called.

"What is happening?"

"What are we going to do?"

"What about the party?"

"Are we in true danger?"

The questions were aimed at him with the force of verbal spears. Each one pointed and painful.

"Your questions will be answered later. For now, please don't hold up," he said again and again.

Only his training and experience helped him keep focused on his job and not search through the crowd for Katie and Eloisa.

And with that, he realized he had to put his trust in Owen to make sure they exited the second floor. He had to trust Eloisa and Katie to look out for each other.

And more than ever, he was going to have to trust the Lord to look out for the both of them. He couldn't leave, and he couldn't search for them. He couldn't protect them like he ached to do.

As one elderly lady tripped and he reached out to break her fall, Sean realized the Lord already was looking out for them. He already had drawn them into his comforting embrace. He'd given them each other, and he'd given Fuller the foresight to run to them and warn them about the fire.

The Lord was already watching out for them. Now Sean dared to hope that, at this moment, it would be enough.

CHAPTER 30

This way!" a uniformed policeman called out from the back of the room. "There's another exit. Some of you head this way."

Eloisa, swept in between two panicked women and their somewhat alarmed escort who happened to be walking with a cane, couldn't have switched directions even if she'd wanted to.

But that didn't stop her from looking around for Katie. At first she didn't see her slight figure, but then the bright-blue dress caught her eye.

She cried out in relief. "Katie!" she called, hoping her voice would carry over everyone else's frantic calls. When Katie looked in her direction, Eloisa hoped and prayed she'd turned her way in response to her call.

With a touch of hopefulness in her voice, she added, "Katie! Go down the back stairwell and I'll meet you outside. Yes?"

Katie stared at her blankly, but then was directed to go toward the uniformed policeman by Quentin Gardner.

Eloisa breathed a sigh of relief. Now, at the very least, she could tell Sean that she did see his sister leave the banquet room.

"You're blocking our way," a rather rotund lady yelled in her ear. She started, then realized it was now time to find her own way downstairs to safety. As more people pushed and shoved, as well as one of the more dainty females constantly threatening to succumb to vapors, Eloisa let herself be led down the front stairs. The journey was incredibly slow as too many people jostled and pushed one another. Everyone seemed to feed off others' panic, illustrating, to Eloisa at least, that though the majority of them were products of many years of deportment classes, all of that learning went out the window when survival was at stake.

The most she could hope for was not to be tripped or trampled upon as they all reached the landing between the two floors, paused to take a breath, then continued their descent.

When she at last got to the ground floor, she ran out the open doorway. There, the assemblage had scattered like hundreds of red ants, spreading out in a hodgepodge maze of pairs, trios, and quartets. She looked around for Sean, but nowhere could she make out his handsome profile.

She darted around the back, looking for the other exit. When she located it, with a small trickle of people calmly walking out the door, she looked around for Katie.

But Katie was nowhere to be found.

She tried not to panic. After all, it was more than a little understandable that Katie might not have heard Eloisa's directions. But she'd seen Quentin directing Katie to a back exit, and something didn't feel right.

A crack to her right made her jerk her head, and her mouth dropped open when she saw the sight before her. The Missouri building on the other side of the Pennsylvania building, which was right next to where they were standing, was in flames. Sparks and ash were flying. Before her eyes, she saw the trees around the Kentucky building catch fire. The sight was both awe-inspiring and completely frightening.

"Eloisa?" a voice called out.

She turned to see Quentin Gardner striding toward her, a set expression in his gaze.

"Quentin, I'm so glad to see you," she said, grasping his arms.

Gently, he enfolded her in a quick hug. "I'm glad you made it out of the building, Eloisa, but you must leave the fair this minute. Come on, I'll take you home in my rig."

"I can't leave just yet." Clasping him harder when he attempted to shake off her hands, she looked at him beseechingly. "Upstairs, you were directing a friend of mine toward the back staircase."

"I directed many people that way."

"Do you remember a young girl in a blue gown? She has brown hair and blue eyes."

He looked at her blankly. "I vaguely remember seeing someone of her description standing with you and Owen Howard at the soiree, but I certainly don't remember guiding her downstairs."

"No, no, I saw you talk to her. I saw you show her where to go."

"Eloisa, I don't remember. As soon as the policeman told me to bring people his direction, I directed everyone near me to him. And then I got out of there as fast as I could."

"I need to find her." She scanned the area, but didn't see any uniformed officers. "I'm going to go around the front and look."

This time, it was he who gripped her hard. "I really must insist that you leave with me. I'm sure that girl is well on her way home by now."

"No. No, she wouldn't be. She's Lieutenant Ryan's sister, you see."

She gazed up at him, hoping he'd understand that she needed to stay in the area until Katie was located.

A crash followed by a flash of light, sounding like an explosion had gone off, suspended their conversation. Screams littered the air as the few people in the area started running toward the streets.

Quentin's gaze turned as hard as his grip. "Let's go. Now."

Using all her force, she twisted away. "No!" she cried. And in that moment, she realized she was going to fight for herself, for what she believed in, and for what she wanted.

Quentin jumped back. "I'm sorry if I scared you, but we must—"

"No, you must go. Please do. I understand."

"I can't in good conscience do that. If something further happened to you . . ."

If something further. That said it all. And so, though she knew what he meant, and that he had her best interests at heart, she realized she could no longer simply exist as a victim.

Therefore, she lied. Pointing to a uniformed policeman in the distance, she said, "I know that man. He is a friend of Lieutenant Ryan's. He'll know where Katie is."

"Eloisa—"

"I'll be fine. I'll be in good hands, Quentin, thank you."

And with that, she walked toward the officer, at least until Quentin melted into the crowd. When he was out of sight, she circled back to the front of the New York State building and scanned the few people still there.

It was becoming hard to see anyone or anything with great certainty. Not only was it dark, but now the Kentucky building, in addition to the Missouri building, was engulfed in flames. Ash and smoke filled the air, making it difficult to breathe. Though every survival instinct inside her screamed retreat, to follow the last of the crowd out of the fairgrounds, she held firm.

But Katie was nowhere. Scared to death now, Eloisa looked for Owen or Sean, scanning the gentlemen who looked all the same in their black tuxedos, their features blurred in the smoke.

Until she saw Sean running toward her. "Eloisa!" he breathed before he roughly pulled her into his arms and hugged her tightly.

No embrace had ever felt as secure or wonderful. "Sean, I'm so glad to see you," she blurted before he kissed her quickly.

Then, just as abruptly, he pulled away and scanned her face. "Why are you still here? I had hoped someone trustworthy would have already taken you home."

"I couldn't leave. I don't have Katie."

He blinked. "No, I'm sure Katie is with Owen."

"She wasn't when I got out. Owen was still upstairs. The last time I saw Katie, Quentin Gardner was directing her toward the back exit."

He stared at her, confusion in his features. "Everyone was supposed to go toward the front stairs, where the uniformed officers were stationed. The back stairwell is narrow and I didn't think it was safe enough to risk a crowd rushing down those steps. I thought there was plenty of time for everyone to safely exit out the front entrance."

"There was a uniformed officer in the back too, Sean. He was directing people to take the back way."

"We have to find Katie."

Roughly grabbing her hand, he yanked her to walk with him. Yet again they walked around the perimeter. It was difficult to do now, and Eloisa feared it wasn't safe at all. They could both feel the heat emanating from the flames. It was as if the fire were jumping from structure to structure.

While she scanned the few people who remained for either Owen or Katie, Sean strode toward one uniformed officer.

When he saw them approach, both of his hands lifted in a universal signal for them to halt. "You folks need to leave now," he barked. "Ain't no—"

"I'm Lieutenant Ryan," Sean interrupted. Sean guided her closer. "Eloisa, was this the man?"

"No. The man I saw was shorter. Dark hair, and a bit too much of it."

"Griffin, Eloisa said a uniformed officer answering to that description was upstairs directing people down the back staircase. Who was it?"

"I don't know, sir. Detective Howard told us to stay near the front staircase to usher people out. Maybe it was a man in a suit?"

"No." Eloisa shook her head. "He had a uniform and he was friendly looking." Suddenly, she had a name—and a reason to feel afraid. "I know who it was. Sergeant Fuller. He's shaved his sideburns and was obviously wearing a wig of some sort, but I still recognized his face and physique. Why would he—"

"Fuller?"

"Yes, he came downstairs with you when I saw you at the station. I remember him because he told me you were a good man."

"Where is Fuller, Griffin?"

Officer Griffin frowned. "I'm sure I have no idea, sir. He was on duty at the precinct when we left. Giving us grief about working yet another fancy society party. Said if something happened, it would be no less than the swells deserved . . ." His voice drifted off in a horrified way.

Sean seemed to freeze.

"It was Fuller," he said. "I never seriously . . ."

"You think Sergeant Fuller set the fire, sir?"

"I'm sure he did." Sean's voice was hoarse.

"Lord have mercy. Once we get the last of the civilians out, I'll spread the word to be on the lookout for him."

Sean shook his head. "No, you don't understand. Fuller is the Society Slasher, and I think he has my little sister, Katie."

Eloisa gasped. Just as the blazes burst higher and a piercing scream filled the air.

CHAPTER 31

Gathering her courage, Katie screamed again. From the moment she realized Sergeant Fuller was intent on doing her harm, from the time she eyed the stiletto knife in his right hand, she knew she had no choice.

"Stop!" he said, roughly gripping her shoulders and shaking her hard. "I haven't even hurt you, Katie."

"Don't call me Katie."

"I've known you for years. Since you were just a tyke and your brother entered the police force." His voice softened as he pressed against her. "You were such a sweet little thing. So proud of your brother." His eyes narrowed. "But you didn't remember me at the station. You had to look at my nameplate to even know my name. And tonight, you didn't even notice that I'd shaved off my sideburns, did you?"

She didn't dare mention that he was obviously wearing a wig too. "Why are you doing this, Sergeant?"

"Call me Roy."

"Roy, why?"

Abruptly, his expression turned disdainful. "Look at you. Dressed like a trollop. Dressed like your betters."

"I'm only in a blue gown. You make no sense." She squirmed against his hold.

"You aren't going to escape, Katie. No one ever does."

"Why are you doing this?"

"I'm taking care of all the ladies who act like I'm nothing."

"I never did anything of the like."

"You did today, Katie, when you were visiting here with Howard. You were gazing up at him like he was something special."

That's because he is, she silently reflected. "Detective Howard is my brother's partner."

"Yes, but you were looking at him like he was your beau." His voice turned sinister. "And you gazed at me like I was nothing."

"Roy, you must let me go. My brother is surely frightened by now."

"He probably isn't even thinking of you now. He's so wrapped up in his infatuation with Eloisa Carstairs. But this will show him. He should have known better than to forget where he came from."

"How will he know? The fire is coming."

"Not yet. But don't worry, you won't feel a thing."

She understood what he was saying. Now she knew she had nothing to lose. First taking a deep breath, she screamed as loud as she could.

"Stop!" Sergeant Fuller screamed, dropping the knife and grabbing her neck with one hand, then covering her mouth and nose with the other.

She kicked at him.

Just as the door to the small storage room at the base of the New York building was kicked open. Both her brother and Owen raced in, with Eloisa behind them. Next thing she knew, Owen had lifted her into his arms and Sean was throwing punches into the sergeant's face.

Suddenly two uniformed police officers rushed in. A wealth of grunts and curses filled the air as they tied up Sergeant Fuller.

"We got him, Lieutenant. See to the ladies," one called out. "We'll be two minutes behind you."

Still Sean hesitated. "Sure?"

"Positive, sir."

Sean leaned over to where Owen had just set her on her feet. "Are you okay?"

Though she was shaking like a leaf, she nodded.

"All right then. Owen, you got her?"

To her surprise, Owen lifted her back into his arms and exited the building. "I do, indeed. You take care of Miss Carstairs."

"You know you're going to have to marry Katie now," Sean joked—joked!—as he took Eloisa's arm and led her to safety.

"Now I won't have to figure out how to come calling on you to ask for permission," Owen called out as they put more distance between them and the fire.

Katie stared up at Owen in shock. "What are you saying?" She feared she was living in a fog.

"We'll talk about it when you are safe. But I think you heard my intentions, Katherine Jean."

"The fire is several yards away. I can walk now."

"Just let me hold you a little while longer," Owen Howard murmured. "If I know your brother—and I certainly do—he's not going to let me get this close to you for another six months."

"A year engagement," Sean said over his shoulder. "At least."

After another fifty paces, Owen gently helped her to her feet.

Then, though their clothes were full of soot, their cloaks were missing, she had bruises on her neck, and flames were casting an eerie orange glow on the area . . . Katie Ryan felt like she was the luckiest girl in the world.

CHAPTER 32

Two weeks had passed since a fire had destroyed five buildings in the White City, the Slasher had been apprehended, the fair had closed once and for all . . . and now Owen Howard was courting nineteen-year-old Katie Ryan in earnest. Everyone expected him to propose to her sometime before Christmas.

For most of those days, the reporters from the *Chicago Tribune* had seemingly worked overtime. Every morning a new story appeared on the front page, featuring interviews with victims of the fire and in-depth analysis into the mind of the Society Slasher, the man better known as Sergeant Roy Fuller.

There was, of course, the expected backlash against the Irish police, some gleefully proclaiming once again that a police force composed of so many swarthy characters could never be taken seriously.

But far more favorable were the many people who saw both Owen Howard and Sean Ryan as true heroes—and models for how the rest of Chicago society should act. Two men from opposite circumstances and education, united in friendship and by occupation. Many were using the two men as symbols of the new Chicago.

Their photographs had graced the front page of the paper no less than three times—the last time with medals from the city on ribbons around their necks, their shiny, new ranks listed under their names. Sean was now a full captain, and Owen, the gentleman detective, was now a lieutenant.

Eloisa mused on such things as she sat with Juliet on the velvet settee in her private receiving room. Since the fire, the two of them had become even closer. It was as if the last of their barriers had been broken down.

They were true friends now, though Juliet professed she quite fancied the idea of being personal maid to a police captain's wife.

Not that Sean Ryan had proposed marriage.

No, instead he had paid a call on her every day. Sometimes merely staring at her and holding her hand, sometimes talking a mile a minute.

After the first four days, her father, when he was home, had taken to sitting in with them. Two times Maeve and Katie had joined him. And once even Sean's brother Billy had tagged along to pay his respects.

But so far, Sean had not given any indication that he was on the verge of asking for her hand.

"What do you think is taking him so long?" Juliet asked.

"Katie says he's afraid I'll say no."

"Like you would have done that after the day of the fire."

Eloisa merely smiled, but she privately agreed with Juliet. Once she'd made up her mind about Sean, she'd been on pins and needles, waiting for his proposal.

To everyone's amusement, even her father had muttered that he couldn't understand why Sean hadn't proposed.

Eloisa was just about to ask Juliet to call for a pot of tea when a light knock sounded at her door . . . followed by a beaming Worthy.

"Captain Ryan is here for you, Miss Carstairs."

"Oh?" After a token attempt at looking as cool as a cucumber, she said, "How does he look?"

"Splendid. He's in his dress uniform, his medals of valor displayed prominently."

Juliet clapped her hands. "Finally," she whispered.

Wondering if Juliet might be right, Eloisa sprang to her feet. "W-where is he now?"

Worthy's smile got wider. "In with your father."

Her mouth went dry. "I see."

"I was told to ask you to be downstairs to see him privately."

"She'll be there in five," Juliet said as she pressed two hands to Eloisa's back. "We're just going to fix her hair for a moment."

Eloisa batted her hands away. "I need more than that. I need a better dress on."

"You're wearing your yellow. He likes that one, he does."

"But—"

"He's seen you in everything beautiful, Eloisa. Let me fix your hair. Don't make him wait a moment longer."

She sat, keeping herself as stiff as a board, while Juliet rearranged her chignon.

Then, before she could do anything more than hug Juliet, she was on her way downstairs, her maid on her heels.

"He is waiting for you in the solarium," Worthy announced with a faint smile.

"Yes. Thank you." Was her voice trembling as much as she feared?

Slowly, she took the long walk through the entryway, walked through the center of the drawing room, past a hallway leading to the solarium.

Lights were blazing, and a full tea service was artfully set out on the table. But all she could see was Sean standing in the center of the room, his posture tall and proud, his good looks as handsome as ever.

And his hazel eyes staring at her like she was the only thing in the room.

"Sean," she said. Croaked, actually. "It's so pleasant to see—"

He cut her off by striding forward. When she stood there, simply staring at him, Sean pulled her into his arms. Next thing she knew, he was kissing her. Kissing her with the door open and no doubt half the servants in the hall, watching.

Even more surprising was that she had no desire to do anything but curve her arms around him and kiss him back.

When he lifted his head, finally allowing her to inhale, he ran his hand along her jaw. Just as he had the first time they'd gone to Hope House and she'd been nervous.

Just as he had when she'd admitted she'd been raped and, she believed, was therefore unworthy.

Just as he had when he'd held her in his arms after she'd been attacked at the train station and she could hear him praying aloud for her to live.

Just as he had when he'd sat next to her in Owen's carriage after he and Owen had rescued Katie.

"You know I love you, Eloisa, don't you?"

Since her voice seemed unable to function, she simply nodded.

"And you know I think you are the loveliest, most perfect woman I've ever seen or met in my life?"

She nodded, because she knew he wasn't simply talking about her looks. He was talking about the real her, the part that was inside.

"If I promise you I'll spend my every last day making sure you are happy and safe and loved . . . will you?" His voice croaked at the end.

Croaked! Sean, who always was so sure. So right.

So she spoke. At last. "Will I marry you?"

"Aye." He closed his eyes, then stepped away. "Forgive me. I meant to do this correctly." And then, to her amazement, he knelt down on one knee. Gazed up at her. "Please, Miss Carstairs, would you do me the very great honor of becoming my wife?"

Eloisa looked down at him, smiled. Then did the exact opposite of what her teachers had taught her in deportment classes. She knelt down on both of her knees in front of him and nodded.

"Yes, Mr. Ryan, I will," she replied. "Because, you see, I love you too."

He smiled again, and then kissed her again.

As all the servants cheered and burst into a round of applause.

DISCUSSION QUESTIONS

1. I used the quotation from Ralph Waldo Emerson as inspiration while I wrote the novel. *"Our greatest glory is not in never failing, but in rising up every time we fail."* Do you agree? If so, how do you think failure might become someone's greatest glory?

2. I felt the scripture verse from Amos, *'Come back to me and live!'* was particularly significant for Eloisa. How do you think coming back to the Lord enables a person to live?

3. What were your first impressions of Sean Ryan and Eloisa Carstairs?

4. I particularly enjoyed writing the scenes with Owen Howard and Sean Ryan. I felt their characters played off of each other well and could see them as real friends. They accepted each other's faults and even viewed them as strengths. Who in your life knows you so well that he or she accepts all of you, even your faults?

5. I enjoyed Katie Ryan's character because I felt she represented all of the changes that were taking place for women at the turn of the century. What changes would you have been most excited about? What do you imagine will happen to Katie in her future?

6. I truly loved Eloisa's character. She worked hard to overcome the pain she suffered in a previous book. How do you think

finally admitting her pain to her maid and accepting God's guidance helped her heal?

7. Deception was an integral theme throughout the novel, both in solving the mystery and for the characters to learn to accept each other. Do you think deception still plays a part in society today? Can you think of an example?

8. *Deception on Sable Hill* takes place at the end of the Gilded Age. The turn of the century will bring the Great War, Prohibition, the women's right to vote, and the rise of the middle class. How do you think the characters in the novel will handle the many changes?

ACKNOWLEDGMENTS

Deception on Sable Hill truly became a group project, and it wouldn't have become the novel it is without the support and wisdom of a great many people. Thank you to my friend, author Julie Stone, who has now met me in Chicago twice on research trips. Only a friend like you would spend a whole day on a 'Devil in the White City' tour! Thank you to critique partners Cathy Liggett and Heather Webber who helped me work out the mystery and willingly read 'just one more chapter, please'. Thank you to Lynne Stroup, my first 'reader', for catching details, writing tons of notes, and making me feel like I had actually written the book I'd dreamed about.

In addition, I am grateful for the whole team at HarperCollins Christian Publishing. Thank you to my editor Becky Philpott, for her guidance and advice and enthusiasm. Thank you to Elizabeth Hudson for being so wonderful to work with and helping to spread the word about the series! Thank you to Jean for helping me fine tune all the details in the story and helping everything I envisioned actually make sense. And, of course, I'm indebted to Ms. Daisy Hutton, my publisher at HCCP for her kindness and continued guidance.

Finally, no formal acknowledgement letter would be complete without mention of my husband Tom. His steadfast love is the reason I can be me.

The Chicago World's Fair
Mystery Series concludes with

Whispers in the
READING
ROOM

Available November 2015

AUTHOR BIO

Photo by The New Studio

Shelley Gray is a *New York Times* and *USA Today* bestselling author, a finalist for the American Christian Fiction Writers' prestigious Carol Award, and a two-time HOLT Medallion winner. She lives in southern Ohio, where she writes full-time, bakes too much, and can often be found walking her dachshunds on her town's bike trail.

She also spends a lot of time online. Please visit her website, www.shelleyshepardgray.com to find out her latest news, or find her on Facebook at Facebook.com/ShelleyShepardGray